Contents

ACKNOWLEDGEMENTS 1

CONTENT WARNING 2

1. Chapter One 3
2. Chapter Two 13
3. Chapter Three 27
4. Chapter Four 43
5. Chapter Five 55
6. Chapter Six 67
7. Chapter Seven 81
8. Chapter Eight 97
9. Chapter Nine 111
10. Chapter Ten 135
11. Chapter Eleven 145
12. Chapter Twelve 161

13.	Chapter Thirteen	173
14.	Chapter Fourteen	189
15.	Chapter Fifteen	203
16.	Chapter Sixteen	219
17.	Chapter Seventeen	235
18.	Chapter Eighteen	249
19.	Chapter Nineteen	261
20.	Chapter Twenty	273
21.	Chapter Twenty One	285
22.	Epilogue	295
ABOUT THE AUTHOR		299
THANK YOU FOR READING		300
ALSO BY GRAEME REYNOLDS - HIGH MOOR		301
ALSO BY GRAEME REYNOLDS - HIGH MOOR 2		302
ALSO BY GRAEME REYNOLDS - HIGH MOOR 3		303
ALSO BY GRAEME REYNOLDS - DARK AND LONELY WATER		304
ALSO FROM HORRIFIC TALES PUBLISHING		305

ACKNOWLEDGEMENTS

It's been a while since I released a new book. I want to thank Dion Winton-Polak for the brilliant editing job, as usual, Amanda Raybould for turning the proofreading job around in record time, my wife Charlotte for the pointers in the early part of the book to help me write it like a real crime novel, and my beta readers, Vix and Kerri, for wielding the pointy stick with brutal efficiency.

Thank you for taking the chance on this book. I know that there are many amazing books out there by some incredibly talented authors, so it means a lot that you've chosen to spend your time with this one.

I hope you enjoy it.

This book, however, is dedicated to Chris Barnes. Chris has been doing my audiobooks since day one and is the antithesis of his namesake character in this book. I named the character that way and made him act the way he does because it's so unlike the real-life Chris and the idea of him having to read those words aloud amused the hell out of me. Thanks for being one of my most trusted colleagues and friends.

CONTENT WARNING

This is a horror novel, and while there are plenty of nasty supernatural goings on, I thought I should give you a heads up on some of the other things that happen in here, that are potentially far more upsetting. There are some graphic depictions of people taking their own lives in this book. Characters think about doing it, and other characters go through with it. This, understandably, is likely to be extremely traumatic to anyone whose life has been affected by suicide.

In addition, there are some rather unsavoury characters in this novel. One, in particular, drinks to excess, takes illegal drugs and routinely engages in casual sexism and homophobia. This is a fictional character and his views do not represent that of the author or publisher, but if this sort of thing upsets you, then you may be better off reading a different story.

I should also warn you that this is a British novel, set in England and written by an English author. So, for some of you, there might not be enough "z's" in the text. This is entirely normal. Try not to worry.

Resist the urge to have a nice cup of tea and scone. It will pass.

There is also rather a lot of swearing, which I know upsets many people far more than the torture, death and mutilation.

You have been fucking warned.

Chapter One

As I turned the corner, I noticed the men waiting outside my office. A small mercy. I didn't recognise any of them, but I knew their type and made a snap decision to stay the fuck out of their way. I hunkered down in a doorway and made like a beggar. Invisible to most. One of the three – a hardcase in a sheepskin jacket and cap – was peering through the glass, looking for movement inside while his two mates leaned against the car, smoking rollies. Good. There was nothing worse than being chased by a non-smoker. I patted the tobacco pouch in my jacket pocket and felt a burst of gratitude for my own addiction.

If I'd been home when my callers arrived, things would have turned awkward fast. As it was, I'd just returned from the off-licence with fresh supplies and a front row seat to this comedy of terrors. Sheepskin cupped his hands around his eyes to reduce reflection, then shrugged and strolled back to his companions, shaking his head. The three of them squeezed into a Ford Focus that groaned at their combined weight. As the car slowly pulled away, one of the men, whose head looked like a boiled egg, wound down his window and flicked his cigarette into the street.

I breathed a sigh of relief and rolled my own cigarette, hands shaking. Some instinct warned me to stay put for a while, but my arse was getting sore. I nipped up the street to a shadowed alleyway instead, my neck hairs bristling. Luck never lasted long for me. I lit up and waved the cigarette about to take the edge off the garbage stink. Nothing much I could do about the piss and vomit. I took a few sweet puffs, then hid it behind my back. Sure enough, there was the same bloody Focus pulling up again, having circled the block a couple of times. Sheepskin got out and peered through the window one last time. Sneaky fucker. It takes one to know one, I'll freely confess. Finally satisfied my absence was genuine, he got back into the car and they vanished once more into the London traffic.

I wondered who sent these particular jokers after me. The list of people I owed money to or had upset in some way was a long and illustrious one. Came with the day job, and my winning personality. The landlord would have let any bailiffs in himself, and I could rule out legitimate businesses. British Gas were hardly likely to send East End knuckleheads round to collect their debts, even after Brexit. Not yet, anyway.

I stayed in the alley long enough to finish my cigarette to be on the safe side, then scurried across the road and hastily unlocked the door to my office.

I say office. It's actually a two-bedroom flat above a Chinese takeaway. One of the less salubrious parts of town. The living room was dominated by a desk and a couple of chairs. I had a sofa, an elderly flatscreen TV and a second-hand Xbox console in the larger bedroom for downtime. I slept in what was laughingly called the second bedroom by the landlord. Single bed, of course. Barely room to swing a cat, and God knows I've tried it. Ozzy, my Bengal cross, had a habit of jumping on my head at three in the morning because his food bowl was only half full.

On cue, the little shit sauntered over to me as I hurried up the stairs, and I almost tripped over him in my urgency. I locked the interior door behind me and put the chain on for comfort. They'd be back, I was sure of it. Maybe not tonight. Ozzy seemed nonplussed by my startled curses, headbutted my leg and tried to steer me toward the kitchen.

I reached down to scratch his ears. "Alright, Oz. Miss me?" He rose on his hind legs to meet my outstretched hand, making a happy 'prrp!' noise, then turned toward the kitchen and his presumably empty food bowl. *Yeah, yeah.*

I stepped over the pile of junk mail and final demands, crossed my office space, and entered the little kitchen.

Ozzy jumped up, knocking a cup from the worktop into the sink. I took a box of cheap cat food from a cupboard and poured some into his empty bowl. The cat sniffed the food, looked at me like I was playing some sick joke on him, then flicked his tail and fucked off, leaving the biscuits untouched. I made a mental note to check my slippers later for any further expressions of dissatisfaction.

The kitchen looked as if a small bomb had gone off in there. There were unwashed cups and plates across every work surface, as well as those clogging the sink. Seeing it depressed me even further, and I contemplated taking the drastic step of washing up and cleaning the flat. Someone, possibly my ex-wife, once told me that the act of cleaning can improve your mood and general demeanour. She found it impossible to relax and unwind in what she charitably called The Bombsite. I'd long since become immune to it and given my general circumstances, I decided that I'd rather wallow in my misery. The mess was a pretty accurate reflection of the state of my life right now, and

I had neither the energy nor any kind of notion how I'd even start dealing with either.

I rinsed out a cup that didn't appear to have anything growing in it. Yet. The slogan on the side soured my mood even more. I pulled the second purchase from my off-licence expedition out of my jacket pocket and gave it a cautious sniff. It was cheap brandy in a plastic bottle, but it'd do the trick. I poured out a decent helping for the 'World's Best Dad' then decided that if I was going to wallow in my misery, I may as well go all the way. I picked up the pile of unopened letters and headed into my tiny living room.

As expected, most of the letters were demands for payment, growing increasingly terse. Electricity bills, water rates, and council tax were all present and sadly correct. I crumpled them up one by one and launched them towards the bin. Work had been slow of late, and I had no way to pay them. One letter caught my eye, though. It had the logo of the local family court on the envelope. My hands shook as I tore it open, hardly daring to hope.

'Dear Mr Carlton, we have reviewed your appeal for visitation rights and the supporting documentation provided by the Children and Family Court Advisory and Support Service. Unfortunately, your former spouse feels that your mental state and current domestic situation are not stable enough to warrant access to Stephanie at this time and, upon review, this court agrees with her. Your appeal has therefore been rejected.'

The letter went on for another half a page, but I didn't read it. My ex seemed determined to keep piling misery on me, and all I could do was take it if I ever wanted to see my daughter again. I took a hefty swig of brandy, coughing on the burn.

I screwed up the letter and tossed it at the wastepaper basket along with the overdue bills. In the space of three years, I'd gone from having a beautiful wife and a kooky daughter, each of whom adored me, to a burned-out shell of a man with nothing to look forward to but a savage beating from some hired thugs, and cirrhosis of the liver.

I'd not been entirely blameless for the scandal that unravelled my life, but there had been plenty of blame to go around. Stuart Hartington for one. He was the lawyer working on the Baker case and, when things turned sour, he'd weaselled out of the spotlight to leave me blinking in its beam. I took another swig and wondered how I would end my life, in a purely academic manner, of course. Slitting my wrists was a non-starter. I'd seen enough of those in my time with the Met to give me nightmares for the rest of my life. Pale corpses in bathtubs; bleached white flesh stark against the dark red water. I shuddered at the thought. Hanging was out for sure. It's all about the drop. Hard to get right so the neck breaks; most people fuck it up, thrashing and clawing at their improvised noose as they choke to death. No, thanks. Pills and alcohol seemed like a far easier method. More dignified, less traumatic. But if I were seriously considering that route, I'd need a lot more of both. That would cost, and it wasn't like clients were beating my door down right now. I mean, who'd hire a private investigator whose massive fuckup had made the front page of most national newspapers? They'd have to be pretty damned desperate.

I finished the brandy from my mug and sat there staring at the wall. The rest of the bottle was out there in the kitchen, calling to me, but I didn't have the energy. Instead, I lay back on the sofa and tried to ride out the crashing waves of emotions that threatened to drown me.

I don't know how long I lay there, but I must have fallen asleep. When I opened my eyes again, the daylight filtering through the window bore the distinct orange tinge of pre-twilight. My head was thumping, my lips were cracked, and a sandpaper tongue was stuck to the roof of my mouth. Cheap fucking brandy. It won't kill you; it'll just make you wish that it had.

Then the banging came again, and I realised it was coming from the front door. I sighed. Sheepskin and the Chuckle Brothers back again, probably.

My levels of self-loathing were such that I half felt that getting the crap beaten out of me would be a good thing. Penance. I might even get a few good punches in myself. A grin flickered across my lips. One way or the other, someone was getting hurt.

I stood on shaking legs and, before I could talk myself out of it, stormed down the stairs and threw open the front door, ready to rumble.

But instead of the bully boys, I found a well-dressed, middle-aged woman standing in the street. She gave me a hard look for keeping her waiting, but if my appearance bothered her, she managed to hide it well. She offered me her hand and said, "Mr Carlton? My name is Margaret Wells. I need your help. May I come in?"

It took me a moment to understand what she'd said. Fortunately, some dormant sense of professionalism kicked in. I shook her hand, apologised for the delay, and ushered the woman upstairs to my office.

I offered her a seat and asked her if she'd like tea or coffee, pushing aside the mental image of the mouldy arboretum growing in my sink. Fortunately, she shook her head, having presumably taken in her surroundings enough to gauge the quality of my refreshments. "Thank you but no. I'm fine. My apologies for simply turning up out of the blue and not giving you the opportunity to tidy your office."

I felt a flush of embarrassment, tinged with irritation at that comment, but decided to let it go. The customer is always right – until their cheque clears, at least. Now that we were sitting, I could get a better sense of the woman. Her clothes were top quality, and she wore a diamond wedding ring with a stone big enough to choke a pelican. How she'd made it through the streets around here without getting mugged was a mystery in and of itself. Her hair had been professionally styled, probably that day. I could still smell a little of the salon's products over the top of her Chanel perfume. She was obviously a woman of considerable means, which made me wonder what the hell she was doing in this part of town. I moved to the far side of the desk and took my seat, trying to force myself into what I hoped was a professional demeanour.

"So, Mrs Wells, what exactly can I do for you?"

She let out a small sigh and crossed her legs, placing her hands on her lap, fingers laced. "I don't know if you're familiar with the King's College case...?"

Of course I was. Everyone had heard about it. It was the sort of massacre you would generally associate with American high schools rather than some private academy in Hertfordshire. Details had been sparse, with images kept out of the press, but the place had become a slaughterhouse over the Christmas break last year. From memory, only four people had actually died, but it was the way they had died which set tongues wagging. At least one of the attending police officers had retired on traumatic grounds after what they'd found. The posh-school angle made it about as high profile as it got. The haves felt threatened, stirred into action, while the have-nots fetched popcorn and concocted ever more elaborate theories. I gave Mrs Wells a tight smile and nodded. "I know what was printed in the papers, but not much beyond that."

She cast her eyes down to her knees. "Well, my daughter attends... attended the school, I should say. She was present when it happened."

"I'm so sorry for your loss, Mrs Wells. There's nothing worse than losing a child. But forgive me, I understand the police investigation is still underway. How do you think I can be of any help?"

"You misunderstand me, Mr Carlton. My daughter wasn't killed. She was the sole survivor, and the police are saying that she is responsible. I need you to help us prove her innocence."

More fragments of information wormed their way up from the depths of my subconscious. There *had* been a survivor, yes. A teenage girl they'd found in a catatonic state, covered in blood beside one of the victims. She would have vital information if she ever woke up, but this was the first time I'd heard about her being a suspect rather than a victim.

"Listen, I don't know how much help I could actually be to you. The police won't give me access to any of the evidence in the case, let alone discuss it with me. I'd be starting from scratch and looking for something the police haven't found. Now, how likely do you think it is that they'll have missed something critical?"

"Not very, I suppose, but some hope is better than none. Please understand, I can pay, Mr Carlton, and pay well."

"Good for you, but the problem stands. If the Met are convinced she's guilty, they'll have evidence to back them up. Without something solid to the contrary, you'll have a hard time proving otherwise. Has your daughter—"

"Alice," she said sharply. "Her name is Alice."

"Has Alice managed to speak about what happened yet? Give her side of the story at all?"

Mrs Wells dabbed her eyes with a tissue. "No," she said quietly. "Alice is still too traumatised to speak. She's been in care since it happened, but she hasn't responded to treatment. Don't you see? This is why I need your help. I need you to find out what really happened, to tell the story that she can't."

Every instinct I had screamed at me to decline politely. Times were hard, and God knew I needed the money, but if the papers found out I was involved, it would be splashed across every front page in the country. My career had barely survived one high-profile clusterfuck. A second could finish it off, and me along with it.

"I'm sorry, Mrs Wells, but I really don't think—"

She pushed an envelope across the table to me. A large envelope, quite full. "There's ten thousand pounds in there, Mr Carlton, regardless of the outcome. I have twenty thousand more for you if your investigation is successful."

"And by successful you mean...?"

"That the case against my daughter is dropped, or that she is found innocent."

Innocence was always a hard thing to prove, but getting cases dropped? I had a lot of history there. Reasonable doubt, that's all you need. Reasonable doubt.

"Plus expenses, of course," she added. "Please, Mr Carlton. I'm begging you."

I leaned back in my chair and said, "There's one more thing that's bothering me. You are obviously a lady of considerable means, so I have to ask – why are you here? In this dump? There must be dozens of other investigators who have a better reputation than mine. Far better. So, why me?"

For the first time, Mrs Well's composure cracked, and she seemed decidedly uncomfortable. She looked down to the table and took a second to compose herself before she straightened her back and looked me in the eyes. "I would be lying if I said you were my first choice, Mr Carlton. Or even my tenth. The fact is that, given the high-profile nature of the case, most of the, shall we say, more reputable firms have expressed reluctance to be involved. And as I understand it, you have a certain moral and ethical flexibility that may be necessary to conclude our business. Does that answer your question?"

Unfortunately, it answered it only too well. Her directness was chilling. If things went to hell, I'd be a convenient scapegoat. Not that there was anything new there. I scratched my chin, performing the ever popular 'man struggles with conscience' bit, but who was I kidding? I was sold there and then. Or bought, I suppose.

"It does," I said. "Thank you for your candour. I can't promise anything, but I'll do my best."

Satisfied, she stood up and passed a business card to me. "Thank you, Mr Carlton. That is most gratifying to hear. I'd like you to come to my offices tomorrow to meet with my solicitor and discuss the case. Would that be alright?"

I took the card and nodded, doing calculations in my head. Even if the case went nowhere, I'd be able to clear my gambling debts and pay those final demands. I wouldn't be rich, but square one was better than a kick in the bollocks. And if I *could* clear the kid? A high-profile case like this would go a long way to repairing my professional reputation, and that fat bonus wouldn't hurt either. It may even be enough to convince the family court to let me see my daughter.

I barely remembered escorting Mrs Wells to the door. Once she'd gone, I retired to my sofa with a more celebratory splash of brandy. World's Best Dad, I mused. That could be me. Things were looking up, I thought.

What a mug.

Chapter Two

When presented with a large, unexpected sum of money that could swiftly lift a person from the shit, a sensible individual would deposit that cash straight into their bank account. Then they would go through their outstanding debts in order of priority and get them cleared.

I don't think I've ever been called a sensible individual, but back then I was a fucking moron. Straight down the line.

The first thing I did was head straight to the shop and buy myself a litre of top shelf brandy. One that had VSOP under its brand name. Letters you could lick! I also picked up a few tins of branded cat meat for Ozzy. This, despite knowing that once I'd gotten him hooked on the good stuff, he would refuse to touch the old cheap shit forever more. What can I say? I was feeling generous.

Then, once my supply run had been accomplished and safely tucked away, I did the worst thing I could possibly have done.

I decided to go down the pub.

I wish I could say that I'd just decided to treat myself to a half-decent meal for a change and things went south from there, but even I'm not that good at self-deception. I had money for the first time in months, and I'd be fucked if I wasn't going to celebrate.

The Dolphin would be referred to as a 'traditional pub' in a tourist guide. In reality, The Dolphin was a rough shithole of a place that had last been refurbished in the seventies, with a regular clientele of thugs, dealers, recreational drug users, far-right nationalists, prostitutes, career alcoholics and the occasional perfectly lovely couple that had wandered in by mistake and were now too scared to leave. The carpet sucked at your feet as you walked across it, and the ceiling bore the stains of several decades' worth of cigarette smoke. Twenty years of the smoking ban and they still hadn't redecorated. The ambience, if it had such a thing, was one of stale beer and the wholesale embrace of despair. I loved the place, though I tried to avoid conversation with some of its more colourful denizens. There had been one or two incidents over the last year or so when disagreements over Brexit or asylum seekers had descended into more 'heated' discussions, often resulting in a trip to the local A&E department for both participants.

Tonight, the pub seemed mercifully empty of the nutters. A group of twenty-somethings with greasy hair and leather jackets were setting up their instruments at the far end of the bar for a gig, which promised to be a raucous affair. 'Explosive Dysentery' was an interesting name, unlikely to be topping the charts any time soon. I was already looking forward to it. I'd been a proper metalhead in my youth, though I'd had to temper my musical tastes during my marriage. Thrash metal tended to keep the baby up for some reason. One of the few positives from the divorce was that I'd been revisiting my musical roots, even if I was too old for the dancefloor these days. There are few things sadder than seeing a middle-aged man leaping around a mosh pit with the kids.

I spotted a few people I recognised and nodded in acknowledgement as I made my way to the bar.

"Evening, Jean," I said as I caught her eye. "Pint of the usual, please, and a brandy chaser."

Jean owned The Dolphin and may well have been here since the place was built in the late eighteen hundreds. She was as much of a permanent fixture as the horse brasses that adorned the bar. Piercing blue eyes shone from her weathered, lined and overly tanned face and they narrowed as she recognised me. She pushed her glasses up from the bridge of her nose to take in my full glory. "Fuck off, Jack," she said. "You're barred."

"Still?" I replied, a little hurt. "That was a month ago. Come on... I hardly touched the guy."

Jean Smart was not a large woman. She had a thin, wiry frame that could have been mistaken for fragile if you hadn't witnessed her dragging seventeen-stone bruisers out of the pub with alarming regularity.

She folded her arms and glared at me. "You hit him in the face with a cast iron chair. I hear he's going to need reconstructive surgery."

"He's playing it up and you know it. Besides, he was—"

"Don't you dare tell me he was asking for it. It's never your fault, is it? Yet you're always there when trouble's going on. I've had enough of it! I'm trying to run a respectable establishment here."

My eyes briefly flicked to the teenager trying to buy weed in one of the alcoves, then back to Jean. She wasn't biting, so I tried another tack. "Look, I'm not going to tell you he was asking for it, but that little prick pulled a knife on Dave and told him to fuck off back to his own country. He was fucking *born* here, Jean. And even if he hadn't been, what should I have done? Let the skinhead shank him in front of the fruit machine?"

Jean's eyebrow arched even further. "But did you have to smack him with a chair? I thought you coppers were taught special ways to restrain people. You know, without using the furniture."

"Ex-copper. And yeah, we are, but I'd had a skin-full at that point. I didn't have the fine motor skills to do it properly. Look, I admit I could have handled it better, but it's not like there was much time to decide. I saved his life; how can you hold that against me?"

Jean let out an exaggerated sigh, but her bullshit detector was satisfied. "Fair enough. I'd have hated to see anything happen to Dave. But consider this your last warning. I've had enough of your shit."

I smiled at her, relieved but conscious that this was probably 'last warning' number six. "Thank you for being so understanding. Can I have my drinks now?"

"No." Jean grinned at me. "Your tab currently stands at..." She retrieved a small notebook from behind the bar and flicked through the pages, "two hundred and forty-three pounds and seven pence. You're out of credit, love."

I was a little surprised at the amount, truth be told. I knew I owed a lot, but that much? Really? I wasn't sure if that said more about the sorry state I'd allowed myself to sink into or the tolerance and pity of The Dolphin's owner. Probably more than a little of both. I smiled broadly at her and got a little expansive. "Ah, milady, I'm happy to announce that I've come into a little money, so please... allow me to settle my tab in full. With a little extra for your patience." I peeled off several twenty-pound notes from a roll I'd brought with me. Jean took them from me with an air of suspicion and checked each one under the ultraviolet light before eventually popping them in the till. When she turned back to me, her demeanour had improved considerably.

"Thank you, kind sir. A pint with a double brandy chaser, was it?"

"Two pints, if this tight arse is buying," came a distinctive Edinburgh burr from behind my right shoulder. I should have known this would happen. Chris Barnes had an almost superhuman ability to appear if there was a chance of a drink in it. And funnily enough, he had a similar ability to disappear without a trace for three or four days after his benefit cheque arrived, to avoid returning the favour. He was as predictable as the tides, but I was glad to see him. I nodded to Jean, and she began pouring Chris a pint alongside mine.

Chris and I had bonded over drinks a couple of years earlier. We were both men who had realised that life was not quite playing out how we'd hoped. Cut adrift from our respective careers, we took solace in the bottom of our pints and reassured each other that it was just bad luck. That we weren't bad or stupid people, and we didn't deserve life's shitty turns. We were peas from the same dysfunctional pod, watching middle age approach with a sense of fatalism numbed through the frequent application of alcohol and the occasional illicit substance. He was the closest thing I had left to a friend. Him and Billie, I suppose.

"Where the fuck have you been, ya cunt? I've not seen ye for ages."

I shrugged. "Jean barred me."

"Over that skinhead? Ye hardly touched him."

"He's going to need reconstructive surgery, apparently."

Chris picked up his pint and drained half of it in a single gulp. "Ah, well. Ye probably did the fucker a favour. It's not like the wee shite was much in the looks department in the first place."

I knocked back my brandy, savouring the spreading warmth. "Yeah. Shame they can't do anything about his personality."

"Who knows? Gettin' smacked in the face with a cast iron chair might have adjusted his attitude a tad. Reset to factory settings."

I grinned at this. "I doubt it, but you never know. So, what about you? Been up to much?"

Chris finished his pint in another gargantuan gulp and signalled to Jean for more. "Na, not a lot, man. Bit of this and that, ye know. Spent most of the month tryin' te avoid the ex. She's been crawling up my arse over ma alimony payments again, and she can get te fuck, I tell ye.

She's livin' the life of Riley with that dickhead, Jeff, while I'm stuck in bedsit city without a pot te piss in."

I finished my pint and paid Jean for the next round with another fresh twenty. "You think she'll drag you back to court?"

Chris laughed. "She can do whatever she fuckin likes. Ah've got a plan, like. I figure if I drink every penny ah get, there'll be nothin' left for her te get her claws on. Speaking of, what's with you being flush all of a sudden? You win on a scratch card or something?"

I beckoned Chris to join me in an alcove and whispered my answer. "Actually, I've had a job land in my lap. You remember that shit at the boarding school a few months back?"

"What? The King's College Massacre? How could ah forget? Billie knows all about it. She reckons they had to get a fire ladder in te retrieve one of the corpses. She says it was splayed open and draped over one of the statues in the main hall. What the fuck are you gettin' involved in that mess for?"

"The survivor's parents want to prove their daughter isn't a murderous psycho. And I'd take anything Billie says with a whole truckload of salt. She told you her uncle got eaten by werewolves, remember?"

Chris shook his head. "I dunno, man. That's still some bad shit there. Ah wouldn't touch that case with someone else's, if ye get ma meanin'."

"Well, job offers aren't exactly coming at me thick and fast. Who knows, this could be good for me."

Chris took another swig of his pint. "Aye. If ye don't fuck it up."

My laugh was short and hollow. I tried to ignore the tight knot of anxiety in my stomach. "Yeah, if I don't fuck it up."

Things got messy after that, as they sometimes can when you don't have to watch every penny. By the time the lights dimmed, and Explosive Dysentery began their set, I was already pissed as a fart. By contrast, Chris seemed to be hitting his stride. In fact, he appeared to be sobering up. It took my drunken brain's detective skills a few minutes to piece together the evidence: his frequent visits to the toilet, the small dusting of white powder beneath his nose and the fact that, if anything, he was talking louder and faster than usual, if such a thing were possible. His charm tended to evaporate when he was on the coke. Fights usually followed, and I wasn't about to push my luck with Jean. I slipped away the next time he went to powder his nose and headed to a dark seating area at the back of the pub to roll a cigarette and try to get my head together.

That was where I saw her.

She was stunning. There was no other word for her.

Long dark hair cascaded across her shoulders, framing large brown eyes, full lips and a button nose that could have made her seem cute if not for the sensuality she exuded. She was tall – maybe five feet ten – and wore a leather one-piece with a tattered denim jacket over her shoulder. And better, she was making a beeline for me. I checked over my shoulder to see if someone else was lurking in the dark nook, but no, I was alone.

She reached my table, leaned across to me, and said something I couldn't make out. I'd been distracted by her perfume and proximity. Cherries and vanilla. Sweet and intoxicating.

"Sorry, what?" I said louder than I intended. "I can't hear a thing over the music."

She leaned in closer, breath warming my cheek, her lips brushing against my ear, and she yelled, "I hate to be cheeky, but can I get a cigarette from you? I left mine at home and I'm gasping."

I nodded. "Sure, no problem," and I pushed my tobacco pouch across to her. I tried to ignore the brush of her fingertips against my hand as she took it, but she felt the flinch. It was electric. She quickly rolled herself a cigarette and pushed the tobacco back to me. As I reached to take it, she placed her hand on mine.

"Keep me company while I smoke it, yeah? I forgot my lighter, and if I take yours, I might wander off with it."

I gave her what I hoped was a winning smile but was, in all likelihood, a drunken grimace and said, "Of course. After you."

The beer garden of The Dolphin was in keeping with the rest of the establishment in that it was dismal, poorly maintained and seemingly designed to drive the patrons to drink. The 'garden' was a concrete paved area around forty feet square, with a few rotting picnic benches positioned randomly for those who wanted to enjoy an alfresco drink with added wasps in the summer months. The entire area was surrounded by solid brick walls, topped with barbed wire and broken glass. The overall effect was that of a prison exercise yard. The one concession to comfort was a ramshackle metal roof in one corner to accommodate smokers when it rained, which, of course, it seemed to be doing all the time. The place was depressing in a way that only an Ed Sheeran double album could be, even at the height of summer. Now, on a cold, rainy night in early March, it was positively grim. My companion took refuge beneath the scant shelter of the corrugated iron sheet and held her roll-up between ruby-red lips. I offered her a light, then lit my own cigarette while desperately trying to get my drunken brain to think of some witty, interesting topic of conversation that would engage her rather than send this spectacular woman running with a look of disgust on her perfect face.

"So," I slurred, "don't think I've seen you here before. Do you come here often?"

As soon as the corny line left my mouth, I prayed for the ground to swallow me up or for that sheet of iron to come loose and slice my stupid head from my stupid shoulders.

Instead of recoiling in horror, she smiled and said, "No. This is my first time. I'm a Dolphin virgin, I suppose." She unconsciously bit her lower lip after she said this, which made my heart race. She held out her hand and said, "I'm Robyn. Nice to meet you."

I took her hand and managed to mumble, "I'm Jack."

She took a drag, blew a series of little smoke rings, then sighed. "God, I needed that. You have no idea. You are a lifesaver, Jack. Thank you."

"No worries. So, what brought you here tonight? You with the band?"

She let out a chuckle. "God, no. Explosive Dysentery doesn't exactly sound like a good time, does it? Nah. I've not long moved into the area, and I just got bored of staring at the same four walls each night. And Netflix doesn't really do it, you know? Mindlessly scrolling for something to watch. Sometimes you need a little... human contact. So, I thought I'd go out, meet some neighbours and see how it goes."

If I had a superpower, it was the uncanny ability to misread, misinterpret or just flat-out miss any signs of interest from the opposite sex. I have been largely oblivious to women flirting with me since my teenage years, probably due to my generally low self-esteem. However, I had also spectacularly over-interpreted the intentions of a few female friends over the years, leading to horribly awkward situations, damaged relationships and a real reticence to make any first moves. Drink could always shift that needle, of course. Even through the alcoholic haze, Robyn's signals were pretty unmistakable. At least, it seemed that way. I couldn't for the life of me understand why, but I decided to take a chance. I gave her a half-smile and said, "What kind of human contact were you hoping for?" Part of me was just waiting for the inevitable slap to the face, knee to the groin and furious storming off, but she surprised me with a wink.

"Why, what kind of contact are you offering?"

It took a full second for me to reset my brain from 'expecting a face full of pepper spray' to attempting to be flirtatious. I grinned and said, "Whatever kind you want. I've got no plans."

"Do you live nearby?"

"Just round the corner."

"Got any booze at your place?"

"A bottle of brandy. Couple of beers."

She took a last drag of her cigarette, flicked it into the water-filled bucket that served as an ashtray, then took my hand. "Shall we fuck off, then?" she whispered.

I didn't need to be asked twice. She led me back through the pub, across the dance floor and out onto the road, still holding my hand as we walked the short distance to my flat.

I had the good sense to avoid further attempts at conversation, but my brain was spinning in self-sabotage mode.

Why the hell would a woman like this be interested in me? Is this a windup? How long has it been since I've been with a woman? A year? Two? Jesus! What if I blow my load as soon as she touches me? What if I've had too much to drink and can't get it up? Oh God, the flat's a bombsite. Do I even have any clean glasses? Oh shit, oh shit, oh shit.

We reached my place, and she examined the plaque by the front door while I struggled with the key. "Jack Carlton: Independent Observation and Situation Analysis," she read out loud. "Sounds impressive. What does it mean?"

"I'm a private investigator," I said, trying to sound nonchalant as the door creaked open. "The title was an attempt to make it seem a bit more professional."

"Well, it's certainly made an impression on me. Shall we?"

She followed me upstairs, and I had a flash reminder of how disgusting my lounge area was right now. I was pretty sure there was a pile of unwashed clothes on the sofa. I made a snap decision to use the office area for socialising instead.

"Have a seat," I said, motioning at the comfortable chair I reserved for clients. "I'll sort our drinks out. I don't have any mixers, I'm afraid."

Robyn sat in the chair and spun around in it with delightful abandon. "Neat is fine, thanks."

I darted into the kitchen and dug through the washing up until I found two glasses. I cleaned them up then poured a liberal measure of brandy into each and returned to my guest.

She smiled as she took the glass, smelled the liquor, and took a sip. "Oh, nice. Courvoisier, right?"

"I'm impressed. You have a good nose."

She grinned again. "You should see the rest of me."

I almost spat my brandy out. The small talk continued for a minute or two, but we both knew where this was headed. My brain spun on and hit another moment of panic. "Won't be a moment," I said. "Just need to pop to the loo." I almost ran from the room to straighten things up.

The living room and my bedroom were just as bad as I'd feared, if not worse. I closed the living room door, ejected Ozzy from my bed and stuffed all the crap on my floor into my wardrobe. Then I went into the bathroom and splashed water on my face, hoping to sober myself up a little. When I returned to my office, Robyn was sitting cross-legged on the swivel chair. I tried not to notice. She smiled and handed me my brandy glass.

"Cheers," she said, clinking our glasses and downing the amber liquor in a single gulp. I followed suit.

"Bit of a waste to neck nice brandy like that, but it does the job."

She frowned. "You know what, you're right. Let's have one more as a nightcap – something to savour…"

I'd had all the nightcap I wanted, but I couldn't refuse her a thing. I retrieved the bottle from the kitchen, slapped my face a couple of times to sharpen myself up, and headed back out there.

I poured her another liberal glass but made a point to have just a splash myself, feigning my first sip.

"So," she said, saluting me with her glass, "a private investigator? That's very cool. What sort of thing do you do?"

"Mostly, I catch people cheating on their spouses. Sitting in car parks with a camera, taking photos and stuff. A lot of it is done through social media these days as well, to be honest. It's amazing how much you can get from a Facebook account."

Robyn looked slightly disappointed. "Not quite so glamorous, then. You're basically stalking someone for money."

I was aghast. She wasn't wrong, but why did I start at the low-rate stuff when I had a full-blooded massacre on the books? I tried to shrug it off, play it cool. "A job's a job. It's not all cheating spouses or insurance claims. I get the juicy stuff, too."

She brightened at this. "Ooh! Do tell."

Professionalism be damned, I probably would have done, but the room began spinning. My mouth had gone dry – parched. I put the glass down clumsily and tried to stand, but my legs had no strength in them. My office chair skidded from under me, slamming into the desk as I crumpled to the floor.

"Are you all right, Jack?" she asked. "Jack?" Her foot moved my head from left to right. As the room darkened around me, she tutted. "Took you long enough."

Chapter Three

I awoke to the sound of a dog barking outside in the street. I was lying face down on something much harder than my bed and I struggled to roll over. When I opened my eyes, the weak grey sunlight filtering through the blinds felt like a thousand-watt lamp an inch from my face. But I'd glimpsed enough to understand that I was on the floor of my office. I tried to peel myself from the carpet and felt a wave of nausea wash over me. Sweat burst out across my skin, and my stomach gave a lurch. I forced myself into motion, sensing what was about to happen, and scrambled over to my bathroom. I made it just in time, but someone had put the toilet lid down.

The splashback was as sudden and severe as you'd expect, covering my face and shirt. When my stomach finally finished cramping, I collapsed into a shivering heap on the lino, a pool of vomit spreading around me. It was gross, but there was nothing I could do about it. I just lay there panting for what felt like hours.

Eventually, I felt able to peel myself from the floor, remove my stinking, sodden clothes, and crawl into the shower. As the tepid water washed away the puke and sweat, I tried to piece together the previous evening because, whilst I had been unwell after a heavy night plenty of times before, I'd not been this ill since my teens. I remembered the pub, getting my ban rescinded, drinking with Chris, of course, until the band began playing and then...

Right. Robyn. Shit.

I carefully stepped out of the bathtub, trying to avoid the large puddle of stale alcohol and bile, dried myself off, then went in search of clothes.

The first thing I noticed was that someone had cleaned the place, top to bottom. The ashtrays in the living room had been emptied and cleaned. The empty takeaway containers were gone, and the books, magazines and DVDs scattered across the floor had been neatly put away. The carpet had been vacuumed, and the whole flat smelled strongly of shake-and-vac. Similarly, all the dirty clothes in my bedroom had found their way into the laundry basket. My bedding had been changed, and it looked reasonably nice. I mean... what the fuck?

As I stumbled about the flat, dazed and confused, I saw the kitchen had also been cleaned. The washing up had been done and put away – including, I noticed, the two glasses I'd used for our drinks. They were spotless in the cupboard, with not so much as a fingerprint on them. And all of the expensive cat food I'd bought had been piled up in Ozzy's bowl, although the little prick had vomited much of it back up on the living room carpet since then.

It made no sense. Why the hell would Robyn drug me unconscious and then clean the flat as if it were an end-of-tenancy inspection?

It took a second for me to catch on. Removal of physical evidence seemed a more likely reason than her being some sort of vigilante cleaning lady. But even that made no sort of sense. I still had all of my vital organs, and nothing worth stealing.

Oh, God. Nothing but that fat brown envelope stuffed full of cash. The wave of nausea that hit me then had nothing to do with the drugs.

I raced into the office and checked the desk drawer.

Predictably, it was nowhere to be found. Even the remains of the five hundred pounds I'd gone out with had been taken. She'd even stolen the bottle of expensive brandy we'd been sharing, for fuck's sake. Talk about kicking a man when he's down.

At least it seemed she'd left me my tobacco pouch. I rolled myself a cigarette and flopped down on my annoyingly floral-smelling sofa while I tried to work out what had happened.

I'd been targeted, that much was certain, but how? There were better targets than me for an opportunist – I didn't exactly radiate a look of financial stability – so she knew about the money. She must have overheard my conversation with Chris in the pub. It was the simplest solution, and Occam knows best. I could picture the scene easy enough: she'd earwigged then gone home, dolled herself up and come after me once the band started.

The alarm on my phone went off, derailing my thoughts as I recalled my appointment. I needed to be on the other side of London in an hour and a half to meet with my client and her solicitor.

The thief had neglected to iron my suit or shirts, so I hurried to the tube station looking like I'd spent the previous night crumpled up in the bottom of a wardrobe. Not a million miles from the truth. I grabbed a coffee and bacon sandwich from a cafe as I hurried to the tube station and was rewarded for this sliver of self-care with a blob of tomato ketchup on my shirt. Perfect. As I crammed my way onto the packed train, someone bumped into me, slopping black coffee down my trousers and, honestly, at that point I gave up trying. All I wanted to do was get there without adding vomit to the list. The jolting, lurching movement of the train, combined with the cramped confines of the carriage and the body odour and halitosis of my fellow passengers would challenge even the hardiest stomach on a good day. By the time I reached Kensington and popped out of the carriage like a cork, I was holding myself together by force of will alone. Even the stale, slightly cabbage-smelling air on the platform seemed as fresh as a mountain breeze.

I grabbed another over-priced coffee as I left the station and made my way to my client's offices.

Chemosh Property Management Services were located in a quaint cobblestoned mews about ten minutes from Kensington High Street. The offices were in a three-storey terraced property, with wisteria vines snaking around the doorway. I imagined it would look spectacular in the height of summer, but for now, the vines were bare, skeletal things that seemed to enhance the bleakness of the cold, grey morning. I walked through the front door and found myself in an ultra-modern reception area. White marble tiles covered most of the floor and walls, with lighting discreetly inset. The receptionist's desk was a dark marble. The receptionist forced a smile as I approached and, whilst she didn't overtly look me over, she exuded disapproval at my general dishevelment.

"May I help you?" she said through the single most forced smile I'd ever seen. I couldn't help but wonder if her porcelain skin would crack if she tried to form another expression.

"I'm here to see Margaret Wells. I have an appointment."

A single, razor-thin eyebrow arched at this, and she turned her attention to the computer. "What's your name... sir?"

"Jack Carlton. Ten o'clock."

The receptionist returned her attention to her screen. She seemed to be entering a vast amount of information onto her computer, making me wonder if she was updating her social media feed rather than checking her boss's diary. Eventually, she looked up with a smile that could curdle milk and said, "Take a seat, Mr Carlton; Mrs Wells will be here presently."

I shuffled over to sit in one of the leather and chrome seats to the side and leafed through the magazines with little interest. Country Life, The Spectator, Tatler – the usual guff for this kind of place. I'd had quite enough of seeing how the other half lived. Best to get my head in the game.

I'd hardly had time to start mulling over what I knew about the case when Mrs Wells emerged from an elevator to greet me.

She was wearing a white fabric suit, perfectly tailored and probably handmade. I adjusted my estimate of her net worth accordingly. It was both a comfort and a warning; payment would be no problem, but she'd be merciless when it came to failure. You don't amass that kind of wealth treating proles like people. She glided over to me and offered her hand. "Mr Carlton, thank you for coming."

I got to my feet and shook her hand. "No problem, Mrs Wells. Nice to see you again."

"Can I get you anything? Tea?"

Ordinarily, I'd decline an offer like that out of politeness. However, the after-effects of last night's drugging were still clouding my thoughts, plus the idea of the snotty receptionist having to perform the menial task appealed to me.

"Sure," I said, "why not? Coffee, please. Strong, black, no sugar."

"Of course." She turned to the receptionist once more. "Take care of that, would you, Justine? We'll be in the conference room. I'll have my usual green tea."

I saw Justine bristle as Wells turned away. It was the highlight of my morning so far. She disappeared into a back room without complaint, and I followed Mrs Wells.

Rather than return to the elevator, she led me to a flight of chrome and glass stairs that spiralled up to the mezzanine floor above the reception area and through a set of double doors that she unlocked with a key card. I was a little surprised that an elevator was needed at all, given that there were only three floors, but perhaps they had staff with mobility issues.

The conference room was huge. The space was dominated by a glass table that could easily seat twenty people. Each chair was upholstered in black leather and probably cost more individually than the entire contents of my apartment.

There were viewscreens on two walls and a digital whiteboard on a third. A tinted window graced the exterior, looking out over a tastefully designed garden to the rear of the building. I took a seat facing that window and relished the sensation of sinking into soft leather.

Mrs Wells sat on the opposite corner to mine, presumably to avoid the stench of my cheap aftershave. After a few minutes, Justine arrived holding a silver tray on which our drinks were balanced. I thanked her insincerely as she handed mine over, earning an acid smile for my trouble.

"We won't be a moment," said Mrs Wells. "We're just waiting for—ah, there you are, Stuart. Mr Carlton, I believe you two know each other?"

I blew on my coffee and looked up with a smile. It was just as well I hadn't taken a sip yet because the next moment would have seen me spray it all over the table. Standing in the doorway was Stuart fucking Hartington, the piece of dog shit who had ruined my career.

"Is this some kind of joke? What the hell is he doing here?" I snarled, biting down on the string of expletives that had leapt to my lips.

Mrs Wells finished her sip and said, "Mr Hartington is our family solicitor. It was his recommendation that led me to your door."

"Was it, indeed?" I glared daggers at the man. "Feeling guilty, were you, Stu?"

Her cup clinked against the saucer a little harder than necessary. "Mr Carlton—"

I cut her off. "Did Mr Hartington tell you about the last time we worked together? About how he left me carrying the can for his mistakes?"

Stuart Hartington opened his mouth to speak, but Mrs Wells raised a hand to silence him. "Yes, Mr Carlton. I'm aware of your history and relationship. I don't engage anybody without first researching them and I have weighed my decision carefully. I believe the benefits of your experience within and beyond the Metropolitan Police, along with your previously effective working relationship with Stuart are worth the minor friction of discomfort you're feeling at this moment. I expect you to behave professionally while you are in my employ and to set aside your gripes." She turned her piercing gaze to the solicitor. "Both of you."

I stood up. "I'm sorry, Mrs Wells, but I cannot work with that man. Trust is essential and he lost mine a long time ago."

Mrs Wells took another sip of her tea. "That is disappointing, Mr Carlton, but I quite understand. I shan't take up any more of your valuable time. If you could just return the ten thousand pounds retainer on your way out, I'll start looking for another investigator. Cash or transfer will be fine."

Fuck. Fucking bastard fucking fucker.

Lightbulbs came on and the tumblers whirled in my head. Hartington. Robyn. The disappearing envelope. It was a set up. That's how she knew about it! They had me over a barrel, and from the sly little grin on the solicitor's face, they knew it.

Fuck.

Mrs Wells seemed content to wait for a while as I reviewed my options and realised they were slim to buggery. Much as I'd love to tell them to go fuck themselves, I knew Hartington had planned for this contingency. I'd seen him do it before. The first thing he'd do would be to buy up my debt. My rent arrears would be paid off, and he'd handle my contract with my landlord, making me homeless. Bastard probably had a team of bailiffs standing by that made Sheepskin's crew look like rank amateurs. They'd empty my flat and impound my belongings before I could get back there. It was illegal but pushing the matter through the courts would take months and I couldn't afford to get representation anyway. Then he'd drive a stake through the heart of my reputation. What was left of it. I'd be lucky to get a job as a security guard after that. I didn't have much in the way of self-respect left, but one thing I had always taken pride in was getting the job done. No matter what. I finished what I started.

I swallowed the bile in my throat and fought the urge to smash his smug fucking face into the glass table. "You misunderstand me. I didn't turn down the case, but I do have two conditions. Number one is that this prick is kept far, far away from me. I don't want to see him; I don't want to speak to him unless it is absolutely necessary. Number two," I said, turning to Hartington, "I want to see my fucking daughter. I want to see Stephanie."

Hartington's grin spread. "Now, Jack, you know that's not up to me. Given your current circumstances, Sarah doesn't think that contact with you is healthy right now, and the court agrees."

"Stuart, I honestly couldn't give a single, solitary fuck. I've not seen my daughter in three years. Sarah works for you. You're old college buddies. Make it happen, or else I walk – consequences be damned."

He took a moment to consider this, then gave me a wink. "I'm sure I can arrange something, Jack. I'll get one of my associates from the office to be your liaison if that would make you more comfortable. I'll even speak to Sarah on your behalf. See if I can smooth those ruffled feathers for you."

Mrs Wells cleared her throat and said, "Very well. If you are both quite finished with the pleasantries, I'd like to get down to business."

I grunted my assent and sat back down. I was on the hook and I knew it, but at least I hadn't lost my dignity. I sipped my coffee and covered the ketchup stain with my jacket. It took me another minute to focus my mind on the case, and start looking for an in. "Okay," I said at last. "Have the Crown Prosecution Service charged your daughter with anything yet?"

Mrs Wells nodded. "Yes, the charge was brought last week. It seems that the police have concluded their initial investigation, and the Crown Prosecution Service feels there is enough evidence to proceed."

"What are the charges, precisely?"

"Multiple murder."

"Let's start with that, then. If the charge was brought last week, they won't have disclosed the prosecution evidence yet. Have they at least provided some narrative for what they think happened?"

"Nothing particularly imaginative," said Hartington, setting my teeth on edge with the mere sound of his voice. "The usual teenage party, with drugs triggering a psychotic break in one or more of those attending."

"Why is he still here?" I asked Mrs Wells.

"Don't be childish, Mr Carlton. Mr Hartington has far more information than I in this matter. Needs must."

I sighed and turned to the solicitor. *Fine.* "So, what kind of drugs are we talking about?"

The smarmy grin had disappeared, but he still had a sparkle in his eye. "Nothing serious. Some cannabis and alcohol. No hallucinogens or stimulants, according to the toxicology reports."

"Wait, you're saying they *have* disclosed the evidence?"

Hartington's grin returned with a vengeance. "Well, just because the Crown Prosecution Service haven't provided the disclosure pack yet, it doesn't mean that we haven't managed to obtain... let's call it an early draft."

I rolled my eyes. Due process mattered not one shit to that man and if things went south, well, there was always some mug he could pin the blame on. I'd been almost impressed at this ability when we worked together, right up until the moment he used it on me.

"Okay, this is starting to sound like lazy police work, which is surprising considering the profile of the case. They just... what? Jumped on the first semi-plausible theory then bent the facts to fit the narrative? Jesus. The tox report alone should be enough to blow that story out of the water in court. I'm surprised the CPS are going with it unless they have something else."

Hartington picked up a remote control from beneath one of the vast view screens. As the screen flickered on, automatic blinds dropped to cover the windows.

"Obviously, none of this information is to leave this room. And Jack, I suggest you prepare yourself. Some of these images are quite disturbing."

"I'm a former police officer," I sneered. "There's nothing you can show me that I haven't seen a hundred times before."

How wrong can you be?

The first image flashed onto the screen, and it took me a moment to work out precisely what I was looking at. There was a lot of red, with glistening wet coiled things amid the shredded mass. I recognised a human hand in the carnage, and a breast jutting out. The scattered remains of a teenage girl. I kept myself from vomiting across the conference table, but it was a close-run thing; the after-effects of last night's brandy and Rohypnol cocktail for sure. Sweat beaded on my forehead. I must have looked just as ill as I felt because Mrs Wells pushed a glass of water across the table to me. Hartington's grin widened, if such a thing were possible.

"These are the remains of Anastasia Grier-Snelling. She was discovered in the college cafeteria."

Jesus, I thought as I took a sip of water. *What the hell could do that to a person?* I'd seen my share of bodies but nothing so visceral outside of a traffic pileup on the M25.

"Are you alright to proceed, Jack?"

"Yeah… I just— Of course. Yeah, sorry. Dodgy kebab last night. Do the police have any idea what the murder weapon was?"

"It's unclear. The coroner said there was no evidence of a bladed weapon in the injuries. It appeared she was torn apart, but the results were inconclusive."

I shook my head and tried to wrap my mind around what I'd just been told, because the implication was that those injuries had been done by hand. That didn't seem possible.

Hartington flipped to the next image, which was, if anything, worse than the last. A teenage boy was impaled on a marble statue of an angel. The hands of the statue punctured the boy's triceps so that his posture mirrored that of the angel. He was naked and split open from throat to crotch; his ribcage cracked open, internal organs glistening in the light. His lower body had been tied to the statue with his intestines. Oh, and the boy had been castrated. I noticed afterwards that his missing genitals were stuffed into his mouth as a gag. And as bad as all of this was, it was far from the most disturbing thing about the grotesque tableau. The statue was twenty feet in the air, with no visible means of access. Hartington seemed to sense where my mind was heading and flicked to another image, this from a wider angle, further back.

"That's got to have been staged," I managed to croak out from a throat gone suddenly dry. "Did they find any evidence of... I don't know... climbing gear? A platform?"

Hartington shook his head. "Not that forensics have been able to discover. No climbing cleats in the ceiling. No drag marks or indentations on the floor to indicate a scaffold. And the pathologist thinks that the boy, Aldous Jerome, was alive through almost all of it. Whoever did this took great care to avoid inflicting any fatal injuries. The ultimate cause of death was blood loss."

I felt my grip on reality slipping away from me. While it was difficult to be sure, given the scale of the pictures and the damage done to him, Aldous Jerome looked to be a tall, powerfully built young man. He probably weighed at least thirteen stone. Even discounting the impossible picture presented here, it would have been difficult, if not impossible, for a fully grown man to carry him as a dead weight. But still conscious? Struggling? Fighting for his life?

"I'm sorry," I stammered, shaking my head to wipe the images from it, "but this makes no sense. This had to have been the work of three, maybe four big men, with detailed anatomical knowledge, a load of surgical implements and a scaffolding tower. I really can't see any other way that this could have been pulled off. And the CPS think this was the work of a seventeen-year-old girl? I don't know why you think you need me. Even you should be able to tear this apart in court. There's no way it's physically possible for one lone girl to have done all this."

The grin had vanished from Hartington's face. "I'll get to that in good time," he said. "But first, you'd best prepare yourself for these next images. They're probably the worst."

Hartington moved to the next slide, and I couldn't help the small cry that escaped my lips. A young woman was spread across a wooden table, her body pinned to it like a butterfly by several large knives. Her beautiful face had been left mostly untouched, apart from her eyeballs, poked out with wooden skewers, bloodied jelly congealed across her cheeks. There was no doubt in my mind that she'd died screaming. Below her neckline was where the nightmare truly began. Every inch of her skin had been removed, and not just the outer layer. The girl looked like an anatomical model. The flensed skin lay beside her like crumpled clothing.

"You are now looking at the remains of Cassandra Eulalia Foss," said the solicitor. "Most of the work was done with a filleting knife, from what the coroner said. She was Alice's best friend."

"The two of them were inseparable from the age of five," Wells added. "Poor lamb."

I took a minute to compose myself, then spoke. "Everything that happened to these kids took time. A lot of time. And physical effort – more than a girl could manage on her own. There had to be other perpetrators there, keeping them trapped. Right? I mean, why didn't the others escape? Or gang up on the killer? Or call for help at least? It doesn't make any sense."

"Valid questions," said Hartington. "We'll rely on you to seek out the answers."

The screen flickered again, and now I saw a teenage boy. Victim. Corpse. Compared to the extended, sadistic levels of violence committed against the other children, this death at least seemed to have been quick. A machete had been driven through the top of his skull with enough force to reach his neck. The expression on both halves of his face seemed to be one of surprise more than anything. I tried to ignore the bloody grey brain matter that leaked round the blade and closed my eyes. This was all too much, hangover aside. I wouldn't get much sleep that night.

"Finally, we have Jarod Virgil Darby, the long-term boyfriend of Alice. According to the pathologist, this wound was inflicted in a single powerful blow, and when the police arrived, the weapon was still gripped in Alice's hand as she stood there. She was in shock, completely unresponsive to the emergency services."

I looked away from the screen and took a deep breath to steady myself. If I'd felt unwell when I arrived, I was absolutely bilious now. I'd had no idea that it had been this bad. The media must have been just as much in the dark, or had super-injunctions shoved so far down their throats they could barely breathe, let alone report on anything but the broadest outline of the situation. Seeing it on a hundred-inch screen, in high definition, really did bring the horror home. And none of it made sense.

"Is that why the police are pinning this on Alice?" I asked when I'd regained my composure. "Because she had hold of the murder weapon on the last victim? Because, I've got to tell you, it looks like she was just defending herself from Darby. The attack was fast and brutal but really didn't have much in common with the others. I mean, those other three were beyond sadistic."

"No," said Hartington. "They are charging Alice because her DNA is all over the bodies. One of her fingernails was found in what remained of Miss Grier-Snelling, and her fingerprints are all over the knives used on Miss Foss. And that, Jack, is why we need you."

I sat there, battling with numerous emotions as I tried to take it all in. I was sickened at what had been done to those young people, bewildered as to how the case for the prosecution could hope to prove that a single seventeen-year-old girl had committed such atrocities, and

I was still furious about having to work with Stuart fucking Hartington. But mostly, I was scared. More scared than I'd ever been in my life.

Chapter Four

I left Kensington in something of a daze. The tube station was considerably quieter than it had been when I arrived, for which I was grateful. Just a couple of teenagers and a pensioner holding a small, angry looking dog populated my carriage, and I found a quiet seat at the far end of the train where I wouldn't be bothered.

Hartington had thoughtfully provided me with an encrypted pen drive containing all of his illicitly obtained evidence. I'd need to go through it all over the next day or so, make notes, work out my angles of investigation. Nauseating as it was, I'd have to immerse myself in every last detail of the case until it consumed my every waking moment. Not something I relished for a second. Not something I could handle today. I needed to process the big picture first. Oh, who was I kidding? I needed a drink.

None of it made sense. Alice Wells was five feet tall and weighed about eight stone. She wouldn't have been physically capable of carrying out those acts even if she was out of her skull on PCP. The timeline bothered me as well. Apart from the machete embedded in Jarod Darby's skull, the murders would have taken a long, long time to carry out. With a lot of preparation, maybe a single person could have carried out one of them over the course of a single night, but not four of them. This meant that there was at least one more killer out there. More than one, probably. That thought didn't exactly give me a warm, fuzzy feeling.

I got off the tube a little before lunchtime and headed straight to The Dolphin. A quiet pint might help my crippling headache and the fluttering anxiety I'd been struggling with since seeing those photographs. And maybe, just maybe, Jean or one of the other regulars would be able to tell me where Robyn lived or when she might be back, assuming she'd been truthful about living locally. Assuming anything about that night had been real. My best guess was that she was a sex worker who'd been paid off by Hartington. If so, there'd be other customers locally who might recognise a description. Pimps I could talk to with discretion. Christ, it was a mess. Professional pride be damned, all I really wanted to do right now was return that ten grand and get the fuck away from this case, but to do that, I needed to find Robyn and the money.

I pushed open the door and entered the pub, steeling my stomach against the nasal assault. Chris was sitting at the bar, nursing a pint and looking the worse for wear. He was unshaven, wearing the same clothes he'd been in the night before, and sporting a large, lurid black eye. Jean had given him some ice wrapped in a bar towel to help reduce the swelling, but beyond that showed little sympathy. It seemed my predictions for how his night would end up were pretty accurate. He broke into a wide grin when he saw me, then winced at the pain this caused. One of his front teeth had been chipped by the looks of it and he held himself awkwardly on the stool. Bruised ribs, probably. Lucky fucker still had a better night than me, though.

"There you are, you sly dog," he crowed from his perch. "I heard you left with a tasty bit last night. I want details. Juicy ones."

"Jesus, let me get a pint down first," I said. "It's nothing to brag about."

"Why? Did she have a bigger dick than you?"

I shook my head in disgust. "Chris, you're a fucking pig. But honestly, I wouldn't know. Bitch slipped me a mickey, then robbed me."

"She fuckin' what?" His eyes were practically popping. "Jean, give us another pint each and a couple of whiskeys, yeah?" He turned his attention back to me. "C'mon then, tell your Uncle Chris what the bad lady did."

I sat down beside him and spewed up the whole sordid story, give or take. I described Robyn to Chris, but he didn't recognise her. Neither did Jean, Dave or the other regulars when I asked them later. It was a thin sliver of hope, but I couldn't let it go. Getting that money back was the quickest way out.

"Jesus, pal. So not only did ye get turned over by Robbin Cunt, but you've also got to work with the Shart?"

This was a private joke based on the solicitor's business card. S. Hartington had become Shartington, then cut down for full comedic effect.

I nodded ruefully.

"And ah thought *my* night went tits up. Poor bastard." He took another swig from his pint and then changed the subject with all his trademark tact and subtlety. "You sure you can't spill some o' the gory details about the case?"

I shook my head and gulped the rest of my whiskey, willing the liquor to dissolve the ball of anxiety in my stomach. "I wish I could, mate, but they'd know it came from me if any of it got out. And then I'd be proper fucked."

"Ah, balls. It's not like I'm gonna tell anyone. And even if I did, what's the Shart gonna do?"

"Plenty. I've seen the way that prick operates up close and personal. Remember, I worked cases with him for nearly three years before he screwed me over. He's a nasty, devious, vindictive piece of shit."

Chris pondered this for a moment, then asked, "Ya think he's setting you up again?"

"Without a shadow of a doubt, mate. The only way he's coming to me for anything is because he needs someone to throw under a bus, and I've proven to be particularly suited to the job."

"And the only reason ye've not told him to stick his job up his arse is cos Robbin Cunt nicked the retainer. You think that maybe those two facts are related?"

I took a long drink from my pint, then wiped my mouth with the back of my hand. "Does the pope shit in the woods?"

Chris pressed the bar towel against his black eye again. "So, my friend, the ten-thousand-pound question is this… what are ye gonna do about it?"

I thought about this for as long as it took to finish my pint. "Well, first I'm going to have to work out what he's stitching me up with, then how he's going to do it, and then I'm gonna have to outsmart him."

"Fuck," said Chris. "Things are worse than ah thought. You're proper screwed."

Unfortunately, I couldn't disagree with his assessment.

Despite that, I was starting to feel better; the alcohol wrapped me in a warm, familiar hug, but I couldn't let myself get carried away. Too many 'quick' drinks with Chris had devolved into all-day and night sessions in the past. I had too much to do and needed to keep a relatively clear head. I sipped my second pint and tried to change the subject before he could pump me for more information on the case. Chris knew exactly what buttons to push when he'd plied me with alcohol.

"So," I asked, "what the hell happened to you last night?"

"Ah, this, ye mean?" he asked, pointing to his black eye.

"And the broken tooth."

"What tooth?" he said. He retrieved his phone from his pocket and angled the selfie camera to get a better look. "Ah, bollocks. The fucker's spoiled mah good looks."

"So, what happened?"

"Just a wee misunderstanding. There ah was, having a perfectly innocent conversation with some lassie, and her meathead boyfriend took offence for some reason."

I rolled my eyes. This was a situation I'd seen play out many times before. "Innocent conversation?"

"Aye, I wasnae tryin' ta pull. Ah just paid her a compliment, like. Ah told her how nice her tits looked in her lycra top. She slapped me across the face and then this fucking gorilla in a biker jacket swung round and sparked me out. Jean dragged me into the back room until ah woke up again, which was about an hour ago. Dead comfy, that pool table."

"Mate, you never learn. You need to pack this shit in."

"Ach, it's nothin but a wee bit of harmless fun."

"It doesn't seem too harmless from the look of your face."

Chris winced and pressed the icy bar towel against his swollen eye again. "Ah may have to concede your point this time. I've nae seen so many stars since I moved to the big smoke." He drained the remains of his pint. "Another?"

"No, mate. I've got stuff to do. One thing I did want to ask you, though. Do you still have that old laptop?"

***

It was around five in the afternoon by the time I arrived back at my flat. The city sulked beneath a dark blanket of cloud. The sun was up there somewhere, hazy and insubstantial, but it did little to warm the hearts of the miserable masses. A haze of drizzle hung in the air and seeped into everything, including the allegedly waterproof jacket that I was wearing. The streets were clogged with traffic, headlights making angry fireflies of the rain while the drivers inched forward, blaring their horns in futile howls of frustration.

The drinks had taken the edge off my anxiety, and better than that, the beginnings of a plan were beginning to form as to how I might approach the investigation. Because, despite being forced to work on this case by Hartington, having my retainer stolen – not to mention the horrific nature of the case – it really was good to be working again. To have a purpose rather than drifting from bottle to bottle. It lifted my black mood, to a muted grey. I'd take that over a brandy and paracetamol cocktail. After a cursory check of the street for anyone lying in wait, I slipped between the stationary vehicles with Chris's ancient laptop tucked inside my jacket, gratefully unlocked the door to my flat and stepped inside.

The only illumination came from the streetlights outside, but I could see enough to notice the unnatural neatness of the place and recall who perpetrated the crime. This triggered a swell of rage, and I almost emptied the dustbin out on the floor out of spite. Almost. Instead, I ensured my blackout curtains were securely drawn before turning on any lights. Because, knowing my luck, Sheepskin and the Chuckle Brothers would be back any time now.

I poured myself a cup of nasty instant coffee, filled the cat bowl with cheap cat biscuits, and got to work.

The first thing I did was fire up the elderly laptop. As it rattled into life, I dug out some antiseptic wipes and carefully cleaned the screen, the keyboard, and anywhere else that bore suspicious splash marks. It was grim. Then, I threw the wipes into the toilet and washed my hands. Twice.

The machine eventually flickered into life, displaying an old Windows XP start-up screen I hadn't seen for at least a decade. Next, I was greeted by a dazzling array of popup windows. The device was riddled with more viruses than its owner.

Satisfied, I retrieved another USB drive from my office desk and booted the machine from that, bypassing the hard drive completely, creating a new partition and chucking in a lightweight Linux distribution. My brief time in the cybercrime unit hadn't been a complete waste. The upshot was that I could now work on the machine without touching the infested systems. Sure, I could have done a full factory reset, but it wasn't my machine. There was, after all, an outside chance that Chris's laptop held more valuable contents than porn and malware. Besides, I had the beginnings of an idea forming. This computerised cock-rot might come in handy.

While the antique laptop took the traditional century to install the software packages, I flopped down on the sofa and dug out my phone.

It took me less than a minute to locate the social media account of Alice Wells. It took considerably longer to scroll down through the posts from other users left after the massacre. Most of the comments were variations on the "thoughts and prayers" theme. Hundreds of them. Some of these people would have known Alice either personally or were trying to leap onto the bandwagon, hoping that someone famous or important might see their outpouring of public empathy and give them a Like. They'd be able to dine out on a little blue tick for months. Among the platitudes, however, one comment stood out. It simply read, "Burn in Hell, you Evil Fucking Bitch." That post had gotten a whole lot of attention. Over three hundred angry face emojis and one hundred and fifty-six comments so far, all of them outraged. The poster – a teenage girl called Chloë Davidson – seemed unperturbed by this negative attention and had, in fact, doubled down with a single response: "The whole bunch of bastards had it coming. I'm glad they're dead. I hope she's next!" If anything, this had provoked more anger than the original post.

I clicked on Chloë's profile because the chances were high that she was just a random internet troll, but no. Pupil at King's College, it said. One hundred mutual friends with Alice Wells, although she was not actually friends with Alice or any of the victims herself. I noted her profile details in an old spiral-bound notebook that I kept on my desk, as a bleep informed me that the installation on Chris's dinosaur of a laptop had completed.

It took me another hour of swearing while watching glacial progress bars before the machine was in a state I could use. It didn't help that Ozzy came to complain about the contents of his bowl. I had to physically prevent him from cancelling the installation by walking across the keyboard several times before finally kicking him out. Once the laptop was ready, I dug out the USB drive that Hartington had given me, stuck it into the computer and opened up the files. There were hundreds of them: witness statements, statements from the first responders, photographs of the crime scenes from every conceivable angle, video walkthroughs, coroners' reports – everything a curious private investigator could ever hope for.

I took a long swig of my cheap, nasty coffee and got to work.

***

I stood on a hard tarmac courtyard peering into the mist. Things moved out there in the swirling shadows, dancing in the periphery of the white blanket, masking the dark shapes hidden in its depths. Fear threatened to root me to the spot. I could feel it weighing down my legs but, nevertheless, I found myself drawn into the chill, hazy embrace, powerless to resist.

A tall, imposing building with ivy spidering across a red-brick clock tower emerged from the mist. Though I'd never been there before, I recognised it at once: King's College, site of the massacre. As I drew near the building, I saw faces pressed against the decaying window frames – dozens of them – pushing against the glass in a futile attempt to escape, their screams deadened. I turned, unable to look, but wherever I looked, the sight remained the same. The window. The screaming faces.

My footsteps echoed around the courtyard but were strangely muted, as if even the echoes were hesitant at giving themselves away. I could understand that. I wanted nothing more than to find a warm, dark hole to curl up and hide in. However, my legs continued to operate without volition, and soon, the building was swallowed up by the fog once more.

I left the courtyard and stepped onto spongy, colourless grass as more shadows emerged from the billowing mist. People this time. They stood motionless with their arms by their sides neither fearful nor aggressive. I knew them. Every single one. They were people that I'd known throughout the course of my life, frozen in time like some grotesque tableau. My parents were both long dead, yet here they stood. My brother, whom I'd not seen or spoken to since my father's funeral. Former lovers and friends I'd not thought about for years.

Old playmates immortalised as the children they were rather than the adults they became. Colleagues from the police service. Chris and Billie, Dave and Jean from The Dolphin. And Sarah, of course, my ex-wife. And standing beside her, our daughter Stephanie, whom I'd not been allowed to see or speak to for the past three years. I grabbed her hand and held the cold flesh tight.

"Steph, love. Please wake up." But my daughter didn't move. Showed no sign of recognition or life. I let go of her hand and moved to her mother, speaking softly, begging for some kind of response. There was nothing. Nothing but the sweet stench of decay. I watched in horror as their flesh tightened on their frames, their milky eyes receded into sockets, and I wept freely.

I reached the centre of the human forest, and I noticed something strange – or stranger. Someone I had never met before, though I knew her face: Alice Wells. Her presence here seemed like a violation of some kind. Every other person here had been close to me at some point. I'd loved all of them one way or another, but not Alice. She wasn't really even a client, just someone whom I was investigating as part of a case. She didn't belong here. Nevertheless, I repeated my actions, trying to make a connection, to shake her out of this strange catatonia. I took her cold hands in mine and said, "Please! You have to wake up."

And she did.

Her head snapped around to look at me, and something shone in the dark orbits where her eyes should have been. A silver pinprick of malice and hunger. It glinted, then spread out from Alice like a wave, washing over the bodies of my friends, my family. And, as one, they turned their heads to face me.

I screamed.

And woke.

I was lying face down on my desk. The skanky laptop was still open, fan whirring away, and my "World's Best Dad" mug lay in pieces on the floor beside me. My clothes were soaked in sweat, clinging to my body like a second skin. I tried to push myself into a sitting position and cried out as my cramped muscles objected.

It didn't take a genius to work out what had happened or understand the source of my nightmare, but that didn't make it any less affecting.

I forced myself to my feet and swept the blackout curtain aside, wincing at the bright sunlight. I let the curtain fall back with a grunt and checked my watch. It was almost nine a.m.

I stripped out of my stinking clothes and stayed in the shower until I'd used up all the hot water. I felt stained, as if the images my brain had conjured had corrupted me on some fundamental level. I stood there shivering for some minutes before I was able to shake off the feeling and get myself ready. I needed to look my best today. It was time to go visit an old friend.

Chapter Five

I found myself crammed once more into a packed tube carriage, for the second time in two days. I didn't own a car, so the underground was my only option for getting around the city. Despite this I avoided using it when possible, and I only ever did it outside of the rush hour. Being squashed in around so many other people did little for my general stress levels. Someone nearby began coughing, and my post-pandemic anxiety went up another notch. I held my breath. The rest of the carriage seemed to do the same thing. There was a palpable tension in the confined space. We'd been bombarded with enough images showing those germ-laden particles hanging in the air, waiting to be breathed in and spread their infection, to traumatise several generations. Some people hurriedly fished facemasks out of their pockets, elbowing the person beside them in the ribs, while the coughing fit went on and on. Not a slight dry cough, either. It was thick, wet, and laden with phlegm. A heavy, germ-ridden rattle that he seemed determined to share with the rest of us. When the tube arrived at Green Park, I could not have been more relieved to spill out of the carriage and be carried away from that man and his illness in the general wave of humanity.

As I stood on the crowded platform, waiting for my connecting train, I pondered how best to approach this interview. As an old friend or strictly professional? Each angle had its benefits and drawbacks. Marcus and I had been friends while we were at the police college at Hendon, along with Zoe, the WPC who would become his wife a few years later.

Marcus and I had been thick as thieves back in the day. Our shenanigans had landed us in hot water with our instructors more times than I could count, but we held true to each other. Marcus was a big, amiable guy. He was a keen rugby player who liked to play elaborate practical jokes on his friends, sometimes taking weeks of preparation. After graduation, we found ourselves assigned to different parts of the city and, inevitably, we drifted apart over time. I think the last time I saw him was at his wedding, probably ten years ago.

So, I was surprised to find Marcus listed in the evidence as being the first responder at the King's College massacre. Then, as I thought it through, the old thrill of the chase began to build. This could be the break I needed. He'd have arrived at the scene of the crime with fresh eyes, unspoiled by rumour or preconceptions.

I'd dropped him a casual text message this morning, 'just catching up' to bait the hook, only to have Zoe call me back. She wanted me to come over to their flat in Wembley. There was an edge of panic in her voice that I'd never heard before. Marcus was on medical leave, she said, and she was worried about him. Could I come over today? This morning? Now, if possible? Of course, I told her. Right away.

I decided to play the situation by ear. There was something about Zoe's tone that worried me. To my relief, the next tube was considerably less congested than the last one in every way, with most of the commuters shuffling off at Baker Street. The rest of the journey only took another fifteen minutes, which, while it was still busy, at least allowed me to stand without having someone's armpit in my face. Once out of the station, it was a shortish walk to the tower block where Marcus and Zoe had set up home.

The building was depressing to look at: a grey, concrete slab of social housing dumped out in the capital's suburbs. Twenty-seven floors of prefabricated hell, with paper-thin walls and dodgy cladding. God help them if it ever caught fire. The elderly elevator stank of urine and, once again, I held my breath as the doors shuddered closed. Someone had tried to pry off the buttons, which was a real kick in the teeth for anyone living on floors fifteen to seventeen. I pushed the button for floor twenty-seven, and the elevator lurched into motion. No one else got in during my journey to the top of the tower block, for which I was deeply grateful. I hated these death boxes at the best of times. Company, I could do without. It was still too early in the morning for the local druggies to be out of their beds, and the kids would be in school already, which gave the building an oddly deserted feel. One hundred and twenty apartments, and not a single soul in sight. Felt kind of post-apocalyptic. The elevator randomly stopped at the fifteenth floor, and the doors shuddered open to an empty walkway. Thank fuck. When no one appeared to enter the elevator, the doors closed, and the stinking metal coffin carried on to the top floor without further incident.

I stepped out of the elevator quickly and breathed a sigh of relief. I'd become increasingly convinced by the strange groans and squeals that it was going to plummet down the shaft again any second. I breathed the relatively clean air nice and deep, steadying my nerves. In for four, out for eight, repeat as necessary. Then I made the mistake of peering down over the balcony and felt my legs turn to rubber. I wanted to turn around, crawl to the stairs and get back to the ground level. Where sane people stayed. But my friend needed help, and things must have been pretty fucking desperate if I was the only person Zoe could call. Besides, I had a case to solve.

I stepped deliberately back from the guardrail and focused on the row of wooden front doors. Some were freshly painted in strong primary colours, others were faded and washed out, their paint peeling. The shabbier ones sported patches of rot on the frames or panels. Beyond the odd paint jobs, there were few attempts at personalisation. No plant pots by the front doors or exterior ornaments at all. Bird feeders would have been banned to avoid attracting vermin, or perhaps the local feral teenagers had dropped them over the balcony for sport, seeing how close they could get to unsuspecting pedestrians. It was that kind of place. The whole building exuded an atmosphere of desperation, underlined by the stench of piss that permeated the air. There was no one around. The only sign of life at all was a black crow sitting on the rooftop opposite. Big bastard. It regarded me with a tilt of its head, then took to the air and flew out of sight.

I arrived at Marcus and Zoe's front door, pressed the bell, and stepped backwards. I didn't have long to wait. A shadow passed behind the meshed frosted window, and Zoe opened the door. It was disconcerting how much she had changed in the ten years since I'd last seen her. She'd always taken such pride in her appearance, turning second-hand garments into ensembles that would be acclaimed in the more expensive parts of the city. Not anymore, though. Torn, stained, grey sweatpants and a pink t-shirt with what looked very much like red wine stains across the front.

It wasn't so much her looks as her demeanour that left me aghast. She'd always been such a bright spark, her grin infectious, eyes gleaming with joy. She was someone who seemed to dance through life. Now she sagged against the doorframe, helpless and miserable as the greasy mop that hung across her forehead in lank, dirty strands, and those bright blue eyes were sunk in dark hollows that spoke of unrelenting misery.

"Jack," she said. "Thank you so much for coming. I... I honestly was at my wit's end. I didn't know what to do, so when your text came through, I thought..."

"It's okay, Zoe. Why don't we have a sit-down? You can tell me all about it?"

Zoe nodded and led me through the hallway into their flat.

Whilst Zoe seemed to have stopped taking care of herself, she still kept the house spotless. I'd seen this behaviour before: people taking obsessive control over their environment when every other aspect of their life was in chaos. It was a sliver of sanity, a way to hold on. The curtains were drawn, despite it being the middle of the morning, but the cushions were plumped and the carpets clean. A close inspection would show the books and Blu-rays to be in tight alphabetical order, I was sure. I sat at one end of the sofa, shifting the cushions to make room. I never understood the point of the damned things.

I refused the offered refreshments and patted the sofa, encouraging her to settle down.

Zoe did so, then leant in, voice lowered. "I don't know what to do with him, Jack. He was first on-site at King's College, and he's not been right since."

"What are we talking here? PTSD?"

"That's what the counsellor says, but I've seen veterans coming back from Iraq and Afghanistan – people shattered by conflict – and even the worst of them were nothing like this."

My eyes flicked towards what I assumed was the bedroom. "What do you mean?"

She seemed to deflate. "He's haunted, Jack. Terrified. He doesn't sleep, barely eats. He stopped going to see the therapist. I've been sleeping on the sofa for the last month because he won't let me into the bedroom. He says he doesn't want to hurt me. He won't talk about what happened at all. I don't dare leave the house in case... in case he does something stupid."

I struggled to imagine Marcus being anything other than the big, belligerent force of nature that I'd known all those years ago. Nothing had scared him. We'd been out on a routine call just after we graduated, and he'd faced down a guy waving a machete around. The man was clearly out of his skull on drugs. Marcus had just told him in a calm, even voice that he would get hurt if he didn't stop waving that thing around. And by hurt, he'd explained, he meant he'd break his arm so badly he'd never be able to wipe his arse again. No fear. Not so much as a tremor in his voice. But this broken man Zoe described... I couldn't make the mental images mesh.

"Have you thought about getting some respite care? Let the hospital look after him for a bit. Or speak to one of the mental health charities? I can see what this is doing to you, Zo. You need help."

Zoe wiped her eyes. "I can't just palm him off on somebody else. He needs me. But you're right, I'm exhausted. It's a lot to carry. I haven't seen him for weeks; I just hear him in there, talking to himself or crying, screaming in his sleep. It's killing me. But I don't know how he'd react if I tried to force the matter. I'm scared, Jack."

"*For* him, or *of* him?"

"Both," she mouthed, eyes filled with tears and shame. "I came close a few times, but when I saw your text come through, I thought maybe you'd be able to get through to him. As a friend. I'm sorry to drag you into this, but I didn't know what else to do."

"I can't make any promises, but I'm happy to try."

I rapped twice on the wood gently and said, "Marcus? Mate, it's Jack. Jack Carlton. Can I come in?"

There was no response for a moment, then I heard the creak of the bed, and furtive, shuffling footsteps made their way towards the door.

"Jack?"

Marcus's voice sounded different, and I felt the dissonance once again. It just didn't sound like him. It had the gravelly hoarseness of throat cancer.

"Yeah, mate. It's me. Been a while, I know."

"A while? Years, more like."

"Yeah. Sorry. You know how it is." He snorted but didn't bother to reply. I probed a little further. "I thought you'd moved away. You had all these plans."

"Plans, yeah. They turned to shit; didn't you hear? It all did."

I leaned against the door. "I'm sorry, man. I didn't know."

"Why would you? You had your own shit going on – climbing up the greasy pole, getting your fuck on with the birds…" His laughter was a dry cough. "Came crashing down though, didn't you, eh? Back into the shit with the rest of us."

"Right up to my neck. But I'm here now, Marcus. Here for you if you need me. Let me in, eh? Please. We can talk properly."

Heavy furniture was dragged back from the door, and it opened a crack.

I glanced back to Zoe, who was wringing a tea towel in her hands, and gave her what I hoped was a reassuring nod. Then, I pushed the door open and squeezed through the gap, closing it behind me.

There was an animal stink in there that was more reminiscent of a zoo cage than a person's bedroom. It was the smell of stress, fear and neglect, trapped behind sealed glass and magnified in the heat. It made my stomach do somersaults.

As I passed him, Marcus pushed the dresser back against the door then retreated to a nest of bedding and clothes in the far corner of the room. I'd never seen anyone in a state like this, even in all my years on the job.

"She told me you were coming, you know," Marcus croaked.

"She's worried about you. Thought I might be able to help."

"Not her. The other one. Alice. She told me you'd be here, playing nice. Why don't you tell me what you really want?"

"Alice? Do you mean Alice Wells?" He nodded wearily. "She's been catatonic since you found her, Marcus. She hasn't spoken to anyone."

Marcus stabbed his finger against his temple, over and over, denting his skin with little red crescents. "She talks to me in here, Jack. All the time. She keeps whispering things. Terrible things. I can feel her fingers in my brain, trying to make me do..." He left the unspoken words hanging in the air between us.

"What things, Marcus? What does she want you to do?"

I stepped towards him, but he recoiled, pulling the bedding over him. I sat myself up on top of the dresser and tried a different tack. "Tell me what you saw at King's then. The stuff you kept out of the reports."

There's always something. Gut feelings, micro-expressions, instincts or whatever; things that guide a copper but can't be quantified. The kind of shit that'd get laughed out of court, that don't fit the strictures of evidence but make all the difference to how we handle the case. Truths we can see but struggle to prove. It can lead impatient cops down some dark paths, falsifying evidence and all sorts.

"You know what I mean. You and I have been through some shit before, and I've never seen you this upset."

He slapped himself across the face suddenly, savagely. "I can't!" he cried. "She won't let me."

A dark rivulet of blood snaked slowly down from his right nostril.

"There's no one else here, Marcus. Just you and me. It's okay. I won't let anyone hurt you." I shifted tack once again, clicking into shorter, sharper questions. "You responded to the emergency call at King's College and found the bodies. What did you see?"

"You know what happened. I know you know. She saw you looking."

I let the babble pass.

"I need your insights."

"You must have seen the CCTV footage. It's all on there."

I shook my head. "There *was* no CCTV. Nothing but photos and testimonies. I need to know what you saw."

"Bastards have covered it up, then," he growled. "You find that footage, and you'll see. You'll see it all. It won't make any difference, though. She told me about you weeks ago. She's coming for you, Jack, and there's nothing you can do about it."

"You're confused, mate. I only got involved a couple of days ago." Curiosity got the better of me and I asked the fatal question. "What... what did she tell you about me?"

Marcus let out a laugh that chilled my bones. It was a dark, miserable sound, devoid of humour. "She told me that you'd come to see me, pretending to still be my friend. Using me for your poxy job. And she told me I'd die for it." He laughed again, an edge of hysteria creeping in. "You're killing me, Jack, but that's okay. I've had enough of it all."

I wasn't getting through to him, that much was obvious, but this was a dark turn. Suicidal ideation was one thing, but this was a man running towards death. It took me a moment to process this, reassess the situation. I'd talked a few people back from the edge over the years, but best not to take any chances. I spoke to Zoe through the door, told her to make the call, get him some professional help. In the meantime, I'd do the best I could.

I turned back to Marcus and held his gaze. "You're not going to die, mate. We're going to get someone out to—"

A bottle crashed against the wall beside me, and Marcus let out a strangled screech. "She's going to get you, Jack. I can already smell her on you. You stink of her. Rotten meat and old blood."

Another bottle smashed into the wall, showering me with stale urine. I scrambled to the door as Marcus rose from his nest and rushed toward me. I tipped the dresser over and barely made it out before Marcus's six-foot-four frame crashed into the wood. "She's coming! She's coming!" he howled at me through the plywood.

Zoe stood unmoving by the kitchen door, one hand over her mouth, the other behind her back. I had a feeling I knew what she held, and I didn't like it. We could hear Marcus dragging the dresser back into place, and I breathed a sigh of relief. I didn't want to have to fight him.

"I'm sorry, Zo. I tried."

"I know. Thank you. But... I think you should go now."

I glanced back at the door, then held her gaze again. "I don't think that's a good idea."

"There's nothing else to be done. It's okay. I'll be all right."

"I should wait with you until the unit comes at least. You did make the call, yeah?" I clicked my fingers, but her eyes had glazed. "Zoe. I'm staying with you, okay?"

Her mouth twisted into a snarl. "You've done enough damage, Jack. GET OUT OF MY FUCKING HOUSE!" Spit flew from her mouth as she screamed, and she revealed the knife in her hand at last. She'd grabbed it from the kitchen when Marcus kicked off, though

I doubted even she knew whether she had protection or murder in mind. Fear fucks you up.

Still, never let it be said that I can't take a hint.

I picked myself up from the floor and backed towards the front door. If she followed me, I'd have to disarm her, but chances were she'd just lock me out. It didn't have to get violent, and I sure as shit didn't want to provoke her.

The door slammed behind me, and the chain was put in place, just as I'd predicted.

Something told me that Zoe hadn't called anyone, and if that were the case... Zoe hadn't moved from the door. Her hazy outline was visible through the reinforced glass and the knife clacked against it like a metronome. *Shit!* I fished my phone out and called 999 myself. As much as I wanted to stay close, I was only making things worse, agitating the situation and so, reluctantly, I took the stairs back to the ground level and waited for the police and ambulance to arrive.

Once I made it to the ground, I looked up to the top of the tower block. I had no idea what was about to happen, it was just an impulse to look back up at my former friend, sad that I couldn't do more. The last thing I expected to see was Marcus and Zoe, wrapped in a tight embrace and plummeting headfirst towards me. Zoe was screaming, but Marcus... *Fuck!* Marcus was grinning all the way.

Somehow, I managed to urge my leaden legs into motion, diving to the side as my two friends hit the concrete, right where I'd been a fraction of a second before.

They exploded as they hit the paving slabs. There was no other word for it. Their heads hit first, rupturing like watermelons. The shock of the impact must have shattered their bones, and their liquid contents spattered over me in a hot, sticky spray.

Ten minutes later, I was still sitting there, among what was left of my friends, when I heard the first sirens.

Chapter Six

I sat in an interview room in Wembley Police Station, wearing borrowed grey jogging bottoms with a blanket draped over my shoulders. I held a hot cup of coffee in my hands, but I had yet to take a sip. All I could do was look down at the steaming cup. It was so strange, I thought. My hands should have been shaking but they just lay there, quite relaxed. What was wrong with me?

My clothes had been taken for forensic examination by a very polite WPC. I thought about asking to use the showers, but that would involve moving and speaking. The paramedics at the scene had given me some wet wipes, I remembered, but there weren't enough in the world to clean the blood, brains and tissue from my body. I'd never feel clean again.

God knows why I decided to accompany the officers to the station and give my statement straight away. I should have pushed back, arranged to speak to them in a day or two when I'd had a chance to process what happened. It was just easier to go along with them. Safer somehow.

Looking back, none of it made any sense. Marcus had lost it, that much was clear. The things he'd been saying were insane, but there had to be something behind them, however twisted the logic. Why did he say that Alice Wells had been talking to him? Why did he kill himself and Zoe when, minutes before, he'd been scared for both of their lives? And what had happened to the CCTV footage that he mentioned? Would the CPS really exclude something like that from the evidence pack, and if so, why? Either the police investigation was tainted, the evidence pack was incomplete, or Stuart fucking Hartington was keeping it from me for some reason. And if that was the case, I had to wonder what else he was hiding.

I closed my eyes and was rewarded with the slow-motion playback of skulls hitting slabs. That particular scene would be a staple of my nightmares for many years to come. Therapy was becoming more and more certain in my future, though with the state of the NHS, I could be waiting five or six years to get my first appointment. Until then, I'd have to rely on my old, unhealthy coping mechanisms to get me through: blot it out with brandy.

The door to the interview room opened, and I raised my head at last. Unfortunately, I recognised the officer who had just entered. What was this, Candid Camera? They were all coming out of the woodwork today. Julie Adams was a tall, slim woman. Almost six feet without heels, with dark voluminous hair that was currently tied up in a severe bun at the back of her head. I'd not seen her since Marcus and Zoe's wedding, and we were no longer on speaking terms by then. I'd been stood with Sarah and our little girl, near the back of the gathered guests. Julie had glanced in our direction once, then made a point of avoiding us for the entire time that we'd been there. I couldn't blame her, considering our history. Less than six months after Julie and I had moved in together, I'd left her for Sarah. Not my proudest moment.

As she sat down, she gave me a look that would have made birds fall from the sky, stone dead. She set a manila folder and notebook out before her, drew a pen from her pocket and clicked the end on it. "Before we start, Mr Carlton, I need to formally ask if you are ready to provide your statement?"

The coldness in her voice stung more than I'd expected.

"I'm not in the best state, Jules, but I'm here and I'm ready. I have to ask, though, are you really the best person to conduct this interview? It seems wildly inappropriate to me."

She pushed her glasses up the bridge of her nose and regarded me with cold, green eyes. The combination of pity and disgust there made me feel like a man caught masturbating.

"You will refer to me as Detective Inspector in this room. What you call me in public is your own affair." The last word was calculated to sting, but she didn't leave it hanging. "Believe me, Mr Carlton, I'd rather not be conducting this interview, but I have a job to do and can act with professional disinterest. You may or may not be aware that Marcus Jacobs worked for me directly. I want to hear what happened, straight from the horse's mouth. Now, this is just a witness statement at this stage. Nothing to worry about; it's not as though you're under caution." She left the 'Yet' unsaid, but I felt it, nevertheless. "So, shall we get this over and done with so I can start investigating the death of my employee and you can get back to... whatever it is that you do?"

I agreed readily, eager to escape her barely concealed contempt. She started the interview room Digital Interview Management System, and we spent the next thirty minutes reviewing my statement until satisfied that we'd covered all the pertinent facts. I signed the statement, thanked her awkwardly and got up to leave.

"Sit down, Jack," she snarled, slamming her hand on the table. "We aren't done yet."

I retook my seat and sighed. "Look, if this is about us, I'm sorry. I really am. But things just happen sometimes..."

She let out a sharp, sardonic laugh. "Us? Do me a favour! I've barely given you a thought in fifteen years. No, I want to know the *real* reason why you turned up at Marcus and Zoe's flat this morning."

"It's all in my statement, Jules. Want me to read it back to you?"

"The recorder's off, Jack. No need to play games. You've not seen him for a whole decade, and just happened to choose today for a catch-up? Pull the other one!"

"That's exactly what happened."

She leaned across the table and scorched my soul. "Let me tell you what I think happened, Jack. I think you're up to your old tricks. Working with that weasel-fuck Hartington, trying to discredit a material witness in a high-profile case. I think you went over there under false pretences when Marcus was vulnerable, struggling with deep fucking trauma, and you pressurised him. You may not have killed him literally, but you pushed him over the edge emotionally. Tell me I'm wrong!"

My throat was tight, eyes wide, but I kept my mouth shut.

"We've already spoken to the neighbours, and they all heard raised voices while you were there, just prior to their deaths. Tell me they're all lying."

"Look, I don't know where you got that idea that..."

"Save your fucking bullshit, Jack. We had a message from Hartington's office yesterday, telling us you would be working the King's College case on their behalf and asking us to extend every professional courtesy to you. As if you're worth more than spit. Honestly, the only thing that surprises me is that you're stupid enough to work with that man again."

"It's not like I've been given much choice," I muttered.

"There's *always* a choice." Julie gathered her papers and walked to the interview room door. "What the hell happened to you, Jack?"

The door closed behind her, and I was left alone with my guilt.

***

There are moments in a person's life when they have to take stock of where they are, what decisions led them to that place, and what kind of person they have become. Mine came while standing in a porcelain bathtub with my shower on full blast as I watched the water turn from reddish-brown to pink and finally clear. I soaped and scrubbed myself long after the hot water had turned to medium-pressure streams of burning ice.

Julie Adams had looked at me, not with disappointment or distaste, but with utter revulsion. That is a difficult emotional response to reconcile with someone you once loved and who, in turn, had once loved you. And to make it worse, if I was candid with myself, I knew I deserved every ounce of it.

I found myself tracing every bad decision that had brought me to this place – scrubbing the remains of my friends from my body in a fleapit flat above a Chinese takeaway, back to one drunken night fifteen years ago.

Julie and I had been living together for a few months, and things had been going well. The only problem was that, as two newly qualified coppers, we often found ourselves stuck on opposite shifts. We shared a bed and a flat, but we hadn't really seen each other for weeks. I'd gone out with some friends one Friday night while she was on shift, and things got messy drinks-wise. Next thing I knew, I was waking up with a stinking headache in somebody else's bed. I could have ended it there, should have done, but she woke up as I was slipping away and dragged me back to bed. I didn't fight her; it was a thrill to be wanted. We both had partners, both felt something was missing. Things kind of escalated from there. Within three months, I'd left Julie to be with her. Sarah and I were married within the year, with Stephanie on the way, and that was that. Life changed.

If I'd been faithful to Julie, I'd have still been in the Met instead of slumming it as a PI working for the likes of Hartington. And that ultimately led to my downfall. Would Marcus still have taken his death dive? Who knows, but it wouldn't have been on my account. Julie had been spot-on with her accusations. I'd dug up dirt on the witnesses for the prosecution for all of Hartington's high-profile cases. He paid pretty well, on time, and he didn't give me shit. I have to admit, I hadn't given a single thought to the morality of this line of work until I turned my attention to Claire Baker.

Claire was the fifteen-year-old stepchild of an extremely wealthy financier. She was also the victim in a rape case against him. I'd done my job. Nothing illegal, nothing that constituted a professional breach. The courts decided what they decided on the basis of the evidence before them, and that's where I'd come in, digging up the dirt. It didn't matter how much of it was circumstantial, how Hartington twisted words and prejudice to his advantage, how society was predisposed to sacrifice any woman for the sake of a man's career and reputation. I'd completed my task, and the weight of prosecution evidence was found wanting. Claire had been humiliated on the witness stand and ran from the courtroom in floods of tears. Three days later, her body was found in the woods near her home. Foul play was discounted. She'd overdosed on her mother's prescription painkillers and red wine. The press had a field day.

Over time, I managed to convince myself that my fall from grace was entirely due to Stuart Hartington's superhuman ability to cover his own arse, but the truth of the matter was that I hadn't even considered the child at the heart of the case until it killed her. The guilt of it broke me. Every time I closed my eyes, I saw Claire's face in that courtroom, eyes rimmed red with torment as her most private thoughts and interactions were placed on public display for condemnation. I started drinking to block it out, and that was the second step on my road to damnation. No kid should have to see their dad passed out in his own puke, let alone on a regular basis. Divorce proceedings became an inevitability.

And now I had two more deaths on my conscience. Because no matter how much I tried to tell myself that I'd gone to see Marcus to help him, both he and Julie had seen through my pretence. Somehow, over the course of a decade and a half, I'd gone from an idealistic young police officer to a bitter, burned-out piece of shit. It should have been me taking that dive. What did I have to offer the world except pain and misery?

Nothing.

I stood under the cold spray and wept, my tears vanishing down the drain, invisible and insignificant in the grand scheme of things. Eventually, I emerged from the water, shivering as I drip-dried on the lino. Then I got dressed and left the flat.

Because what I really needed right now was a drink.

***

I stepped out of the flat to discover that the temperature had fallen considerably since that morning. The almost constant rain had become a grey, driving sleet that stung my face and froze my fingers. I shoved my hands deeper into the pockets of my jacket and bunched my shoulders as I hurried through the dismal streets of London towards The Dolphin.

Where else was I going to go? I pushed through the double doors, almost falling into the pub's warmth. The familiar scent of stale beer and ancient cigarette smoke was a welcoming hug to the senses. After everything I'd gone through that morning, I was going to need something considerably more robust than a pint, so I ordered two doubles and downed them both in quick succession.

"Bit early for that, isn't it, ya pisshead?" boomed Chris's familiar voice from a booth near the fruit machine.

I waved and ordered another double before joining him. An attractive woman with oversized glasses and mousy brown hair sat across from him, nursing a half of lager. The default reaction to seeing anyone of the opposite sex spending time with Chris (who was not being paid to do so) would be one of shock or pity, but this was Billie. She was alright, that one. Fucking nuts, but nobody's perfect.

There are many different flavours of conspiracy theorist in this world, ranging from the relatively harmless flat-earthers to the frothing, right-wing QAnon psychopaths. New ones had even sprung up over the pandemic, preying on people who were terrified for their lives and looking for answers on the internet. Billie's particular brand of bonkers fell somewhere between those two extremes and I found it endearing rather than offensive most of the time. With all her heart, Billie believed that monsters were real, and that some nefarious government agency was covering up their existence. She'd been stuck on this subject for as long as Chris and I had known her, which, looking back, was almost as long as we'd known each other. She was smart, kind, and a little intense, but she could be fun, too. A good drinking companion. We just rolled our eyes and took the mick out of her when she got onto the subject of werewolves.

I took another swig from my brandy, wincing at the harsh taste that was not improving though it did its best to burn my tastebuds off. I was fairly sure that the bottle it had originated in was very different to the classy bottle behind the bar, but fuck it; it was doing the job, and I doubted Trading Standards would be doing spot checks in The Dolphin any time soon.

"Pisshead? Hah! Guilty, I guess. But if you'd been through my morning, you'd be doing the same, believe me."

Billie put her hand on my arm, looking concerned. "You do look pretty pale. What's happened?"

I felt emotions welling up within me on a toxic tide, but I drowned them in brandy before they could break. I sucked a deep breath in through my nose, let it out, then smacked the glass on the table. "Oh, nothing much, you know. Just narrowly avoided death."

"Fuck! Yeah? Really?" said Chris. "Who'd ya piss off this time?"

Billie kicked his shin under the table, earning a bark of pain. "Don't be a twat, Chris." Then she turned to face me, her mask of irritation replaced with one of concern.

"I... I went to see my old mate and his missus. He was the first responder on a case I'm working on, and I wanted to get his thoughts. But he was in a right mess. Lost his shit— I mean, *really* lost it. I didn't get anywhere with him, just some garbled psychic shit and a bottle of piss chucked at my head. It was... sad really. Then, after I left, he grabbed his wife and jumped off the top floor. Twenty-seven storeys, straight down. They hit the pavement just a few feet from where I was standing."

"Fuuuuuuck!" said Chris. "Although, to be fair, I've felt that way once or twice after you've visited. OW! What the fuck was that for?" he yelled, reaching down to rub his shin.

"That was for being a bellend, Chris. Last warning," Billie said in a low, even voice. "Next time I'm stamping bollocks."

"Alright, alright. No need te be like that, I was just havin' a laugh. Makin' light of the situation, like."

"You should try empathy once in a while. Eight out of ten cats say it's less painful. Now shush. The grown-ups are talking." She turned her attention back to me. "I can't even imagine what you must be going through right now. Do you want to talk about it?"

I recounted the whole sordid tale, starting with Mrs Wells's unexpected visit and ending with Julia's thinly veiled threats. Chris sheepishly bought another round of drinks while I spoke and then sat in silence, rubbing his sore shin.

When I'd finished talking, Billie sat back and shook her head. "You want my opinion? I think you need to get the hell away from this. Tell them to do one."

"I wish it were that easy, but they've got me by the ten grand nut-sack."

"No, they only think they've got you trapped, but what have you got to lose? Really?"

I grabbed a handful of dry-roasted peanuts from an open bag that Chris had left on the table. "Oh, I don't know. My home, my reputation, my career, the small amount of self-respect I still have?"

Billie gave me a wry smile. "Jackie-boy, your flat is a shithole. No loss. Your career and your reputation went down the toilet years ago, and as for self-respect…? If you had any of that left, you wouldn't be seen with the likes of us, would you? Look, worst comes to the worst you can sofa surf until you sort yourself out. I could put you up for a bit, so long as you behave yourself."

I didn't know what to make of that perspective. On the one hand, she'd given me a sense that options existed – however slender – but on the other, I felt about ten times worse now about the depths I'd sunk to. "Thanks, Billie. I really don't know what to say. But I also don't want to impose on anyone. I'm hard work at the best of times, and if Hartington puts the boot in, then I don't know if my head will be in a good place. I wouldn't want to inflict that on anyone."

I was sincere, but that wasn't the whole story. I didn't want her or Chris to find themselves in the firing line if Hartington started playing rough, much less if my debtors turned up at the door.

Her expression changed then, and the mask slipped for a fraction of a second, showing what looked like genuine fear. "Listen, Jack, I didn't want to bring this into it... God knows you have enough reason to walk away from the whole mess, but— Shit..." She drained her drink. "Jack, I've been hearing things about this case on the down-low for a while now. And I'm not just talking about the murders. Your employer – Mrs Wells. What's the name of her business again?"

An odd word itched at the back of my mind, but I fished out my notepad to double check. "Chemosh Property Management Services."

"That's the badger. Do yourself a favour and Google the first word. If I'm right, Mrs Wells is into some dark, dark shit."

"Oh, for fuck's sake, Billie. Why do you have to do this? Just when I think you're levelling out, you start going down the rabbit hole again. Let me guess: it's a front for a bunch of vampires, draining their tenants of blood as well as money?"

Billie flinched like I'd slapped her, and my regret was instant. She didn't deserve that. Batty she may be, but Billie had a good heart, and everything she was saying came from a place of genuine concern.

"No," she said, her voice cracking and barely above a whisper. "Not vampires. But your employer isn't just a glorified estate agent. She makes her bank elsewhere. Rumours are the whole family is involved in arms dealing." She reached across and grabbed my hand, eyes widening. "And I've seen things on the Dark Web that suggest an occult angle to the whole King's College thing. There's not much. It gets taken down as quickly as it gets posted, but it looks fucked up…"

I snatched my hand away. "Jesus, Billie, will you listen to yourself?"

She picked up her coat and stood up. "I have to. Nobody else will. Do what you want, Jack. You usually do. The couch is free if you change your mind, but I've got to go." She said goodbye to Chris then turned and walked out into the rain.

"I see ye haven't lost yer touch with the birds," Chris said, grabbing a handful of nuts and winking.

Twat.

I finished my drink and ordered another when my phone rang. The caller display flagged up "The Shart", and I realised that Chris must have fiddled with my phone at some point. I'd have to set aside a bit of time to see what else he'd done with it in my absence, the cheeky fucker. I really wasn't in the mood to deal with Hartington, so I let the phone ring out. It started ringing again shortly after.

Billie's words were still rattling around in my head when I pressed pick up and I snapped, "Fuck off."

"And good evening to you, too, sunshine."

I could imagine the smug expression on the Shart's face and suppressed the urge to stamp on the phone.

"Listen," I said. "I've thought about it and decided you can shove the job up your arse. It's entirely personal. You want the ten grand back, feel free to take me to small claims court. You can claw it out of my benefits. Ten quid a month – how does that suit you?"

Hartington gave an exaggerated sigh. "Oh dear, Jack. Just when I thought you were getting yourself straightened up again. Stephanie will be so disappointed."

A wave of anxiety broke over me, leaving sweat in its wake, prickling my skin.

"I did as you asked and put in a word for you with Sarah. She had agreed you could see Stephanie tomorrow afternoon after she finishes school. But... well, if you're not interested anymore..."

The fucking shitweasel! The jaws of the trap had closed around me. I had nothing to lose, sure, but everything to gain if I could just fix things with my daughter. I stood there, choking on this for a while until Hartington spoke again.

"It's not too late, Jack, but this is your last chance. Will you play ball?"

"Fine," I snarled, "you've got me. I'll carry on with your fucking case, but I want to see Stephanie tomorrow. Tell her to meet me at the Starbucks on Whitechapel Road, 4.30."

"Of course. No problem. Now that's out of the way, I have some good news for you. Remember that little stipulation of yours? You wanted to liaise with someone other than me in the office. Well, I have just the person for you. I'll tell you what, let's make things easy. She'll be there to meet you in the same coffee shop tomorrow at six. That'll give you and Steph a bit of time to catch up first."

"Is that all?"

"I'd say so. Try not to turn up drunk, eh?"

"Go fuck yourself, Hartington. Tell Sarah I'll be there. Then go fuck yourself again." I hung up.

"Kissed and made up, then?" asked Chris.

"I dunno. I mean, yes, I'm getting to see Steph again. Tomorrow afternoon. But I'm going to have to carry on working for the prick."

"Ah, bollocks to him, mate. See Steph, then tell the cunt te shove it where the sun don't shine after. It's a win-win. Shall ah get another round in te celebrate?"

I pushed my latest brandy across the table to him. "No, mate. I think I'd better call it a day, go home and get my shit together."

I grabbed my coat and made my way across the pub without swaying or stumbling too much. I wasn't sure how many drinks I'd had, but it was definitely more than a couple. I'd need a good night's sleep and a ton of black coffee tomorrow, but I hoped I'd be in something approaching a fit state by the time I met with Steph tomorrow afternoon.

The temperature had dropped again, and the sleet had turned into thin, watery snow that was driven into my face by the cold northerly wind. It was melting as it hit the wet pavement now, but with the wind chill, I felt certain there'd be a layer of the stuff the next day, and the city would grind to a halt as it always did.

I'd been lost in these thoughts as I hurried across the street and put the key in the front door of my flat. More fool me. I only realised my mistake when heavy hands grabbed me from behind. They turned me round so my back was to the door, and I found myself face-to-face with the debt collectors. *Stupid, stupid, stupid!*

Sheepskin took a drag of his cigarette and blew the foul-smelling smoke into my face. "Ah, Mr Carlton. I was hoping I'd run into you. Shall we go inside and discuss our business in private?"

Chapter Seven

I was bundled unceremoniously through the front door and up the stairs to my flat. It occurred to me that if I were going to attempt anything, now would be the time. Only one of Sheepskin's pet gorillas could squeeze through the narrow stairwell at a time, so only one could hold my arms. Sheepskin took the lead, and the other slabs of steroid-enhanced muscle brought up the rear. I waited until we were almost at the top step, then slammed my head back into what I hoped was Egghead's nose. As it cracked, I bunched my legs and kicked myself backwards, with all the enthusiasm and idiocy a bottle of cheap brandy can produce.

I expected my assault on Egghead to at least loosen his grip, while my backwards leap would throw us all down the stairs in a ruined heap, with me landing gracefully on top of them. Imagine my dismay when Egghead merely grunted and failed to budge a bloody inch. He might have been welded in place. All I got for my trouble was a blow to the back of my neck that rattled my teeth and a laugh from the meathead below.

"Oh, mate, you shouldn't have done that."

So much for that bright idea.

Egghead almost lifted me off my feet and shoved me up the remaining stairs like an angry mother might manhandle a three-year-old who was having a temper tantrum in Asda. He all but dragged me into my office, while Sheepskin pulled out the office chair. Egghead dumped me into it with rather more force than was strictly necessary and glared down at me. A drop of blood hung on the end of his nose, but he was otherwise unharmed.

A sensible, sober person might have tried to talk their way out of the situation – perhaps attempt to calm their assailants down, promise them anything they want and then get the hell out of town at the first opportunity. Sensible? Nope. Sober? About that...

"Come on in, gentlemen. Please, make yourselves at home. Can I get you anything? Coffee? Tea? Big bag of steroids?"

Sheepskin laughed at that. "Did you hear that, boys?" he said in a strong cockney accent. "We've got a funny one here. You like it when we get comedians, don'tcha Herbert?"

Herbert smiled at me through bloodied teeth. "That I do, Arthur. I like nothing more than seeing how long it takes them to stop thinking they're funny." He cracked his knuckles when he said that, and my guts tightened.

The other Chuckle Brother, a hulking beast of a man with a bleached blond flat-top haircut, made his way to stand behind me and then pinned me in the chair. He had astonishingly big hands. Sheepskin leaned in close with false bonhomie and said, "Now then, Mr Comedian, we are here at the request of our employer, a gentleman you know by the name of 'Big Eddie'. It seems you have a rather large gambling debt outstanding. We're here to collect. With interest."

"Oh, God," I gasped. "I feel sick! Please, God, I'll do anything."

Arthur smiled at me through yellow and brown teeth and patted the pockets of his sheepskin. Then let me have a full blast of his horrific halitosis. I'd honestly never smelled anything like it: a rank mixture of old cigarettes, sour coffee and parmesan cheese, with an undertone of a last-day festival toilet. "See, boys? Violence is useful, but sometimes all you need is a polite reminder. Chicken shits are surprisingly cooperative." He unwrapped a boiled sweet and popped it in his mouth.

"Jesus, please!" I gagged. "Seriously, mate. There's some Listerine in the bathroom. You can have it all. But I'd get a doctor to check that breath out next time you're in. That can't be normal."

Arthur's face registered surprise, shock, and absolute fury within moments, and I heard a snigger from behind me.

"See," I said, throwing all sense of self-preservation to the wind. "Vanilla Ice here knows what I'm talking about. Poor sod has to sit in the car with you all day. I'm amazed he can keep his protein shakes down."

Arthur punched me hard in the stomach. I'd been expecting the blow. Hell, I'd been counting on it because, frankly, a beating from Sheepskin seemed more survivable than at the hands of his gorillas. What I failed to consider was that Arthur had a great deal more experience in the business and was pretty handy in the art of pain himself. I folded over, desperately trying to suck some air into my suddenly empty lungs and slid to the floor.

Arthur, however, wasn't finished. He lashed out with a boot that, from the feel of it, had steel toecaps and I felt a sharp, agonising pain flare up in my left side. Then he leaned in close and spat his sweet in my face.

"Mr Carlton," he breathed softly through another cloud of toxic fumes, "you've hurt my feelings. Not a good idea." This time, the punch came straight for my nose. I managed to throw myself back just enough to avoid a bone breaking blow, but my lip exploded, and blood filled my mouth. Concussion was a distinct possibility. I couldn't focus, couldn't even hold my head up.

"Wait," I coughed through bubbles of blood. "I'm on a job. Got a big payday coming. I swear, I'll have Eddie's money by next week."

Arthur leered at me, but his words were aimed at the Chuckle Brothers. "He'll have the money next week, boys. I'm not sure I've heard that one before. What do you think?"

"I think he'll tell us any old shit. Especially if he thinks he'll keep some of his fingers."

'Some' of my fingers? *Fucking hell*.

My eyes came back into focus just long enough to see Arthur reach into his sheepskin coat and remove a small set of bolt cutters. Just the job for cutting through a padlock, for example. I clenched my fists tight in terror.

"Wait, I'm serious," I stammered, barely able to stem my rising panic. "I started work on it yesterday. It's surefire. I'll be able to pay Eddie off in full. With interest."

"Oh, rest assured, Big Eddie's been keeping count of the interest. Your current balance is just shy of four thousand pounds."

"Four grand!" I stammered. "I only owed him three hundred quid."

"Yes, Mr Carlton. Unfortunately, you've been rather slow in settling up. Our services bring their own costs and tracking you down has taken up more time than any of us would have liked. Then there's fuel, equipment and other such expenses. You get the idea."

I felt sick, and it was only partly due to the beating I'd taken and the after-effects of the drink. Four thousand pounds was more money than I usually saw in four months. It would put a significant dent in the money I'd get from the case, assuming I could even wrap it up in time. "Listen, I can cover that, but if you fuck me up so badly I can't work, then you won't see any of it. Think about it for a second."

Arthur grinned at Herbert and Nicholas, then turned his smile to me. I could see a gold tooth sitting proudly where one of his canines should have been. "Okay, Mr Carlton. You have four days. Your interest will go up by another thousand a day until then. If you don't have the cash to settle the balance in full when we return, we'll take what's owed out of your dead body. You'd be surprised how much organs go for on the black market. Are these new terms agreeable to you? Or should we take our pound of flesh now?"

I spat blood onto the carpet. "I'll have your money."

Arthur doffed his cap and left. I looked up to see Herbert smiling down at me.

"This is for the headbutt," he said.

I barely even saw his fist as it hammered into the side of my head. And after it connected, all I saw for quite some time was darkness.

***

I slowly crawled back into consciousness. The first thing I was aware of was the sticky-sweet taste of blood in my mouth. Then, as my body slowly rebooted itself, the torment made itself known. A sharp, stabbing pain lanced through my left side in time to my laboured breathing. My lips throbbed and had scabbed together, then I felt the swollen ache across my cheek and jaw. No part of my face felt like it fit anymore. I was broken. I did my best to ignore the pain as I opened my eyes, a sudden urgency overwhelming me, and I had to scramble into the bathroom to chuck my guts up. Red blood mixed in the bowl with clotted lumps of older, black ichor. Something plinked against the gore-stained porcelain, and I realised with dismay that one of my teeth was missing.

I sat there staring at swirling clouds of red for what might have been five minutes or a couple of hours. I knew I should probably go to hospital and get myself checked for concussion at least. My lips probably needed stitching, while my ribs could be either bruised, cracked or outright broken. The daylight streaming through the blinds was making little explosions go off behind my eyes, but I had to make do with just closing my eyes and resting them against my forearm. I was strangely calm in the aftermath. The porcelain felt cool against my chin, and for a moment, I savoured its touch. Then my phone chirped its reminder.

Steph.

Fuck.

I forced myself to stand and held onto the side of the bath as I fished my phone out of my pocket. Miraculously, it still had a fifteen per cent charge remaining. It was a little after one in the afternoon; I'd been unconscious for almost twelve hours, which really didn't bode well concussion-wise. Somehow, I needed to get my shit together and make it halfway across London in time to meet Steph. I considered cancelling because I really didn't want my daughter to see me in this state, but the cold truth sat in the pit of my stomach: if I bailed on her now, I might never get another chance.

I crawled into the bath and got the shower going. The streams of hot water stung my battered lips and made my face throb even more, but I stuck it out and even felt a little better by the end, though that was a relative term. The wooziness had faded at least.

I clambered out of the tub and stood before the sink, dreading the mirror. What would Steph see when she came to meet me? Her beloved old man, much missed, or a useless, washed-up has-been who destroyed everything he touched? I wiped the condensation from the mirror and began to sob in great heartfelt heaves of grief and self-pity.

The left side of my face was swollen, with a dark bruise already forming. There were four distinct knuckle marks across my cheek where Herbert's massive ham of a fist had connected. My lips were worse; the lower one had split completely open, mashed against my teeth. There was a visible gap between the two halves. The shower had cleared the clots from the wound, and it bled freely once more. *What a mess. What a fucking, fucked-up mess...* I didn't have any antiseptic cream to apply, but the Listerine mouthwash was right there, daring me to try it on the wound. I carefully cleaned my teeth to get the taste of blood out of my mouth, then I poured close to half of the bottle of antiseptic mouthwash across the gaping wound. That was special. The damned mouthwash burned like acid at the best of times, but it nearly threw my entire nervous system into shock when applied to the open wound. Eventually, the sting receded, and I considered my options. There was no time to get it stitched at the hospital, and my hands were too shaky to attempt anything like it here and now. Only one thing for it. I retrieved a tube of superglue from under the kitchen sink and tried to glue the wound together. The first attempt left me with my fingertips stuck to my lips, and I ripped the wound open again in panic. I was more successful on my second attempt, but I'd never be pretty again.

Then, it was just a matter of getting dressed without aggravating my damaged ribs too much. It hurt to breathe and move, but despite the purple boot-print on my side, I was cautiously hopeful that my ribs weren't actually broken. I'd had a broken rib before, and I was bedridden for weeks. Though absolute agony, this didn't seem as bad, but maybe all my other injuries were spreading the load on my pain receptors.

Eventually, I managed to stagger down the staircase into the street and limped my way towards the tube station. Fortunately, my carriage was mostly empty, and I could sit down well away from the other passengers, most of whom took one look and made deliberate moves to avoid me. I made it to the Whitechapel Road Starbucks with scant minutes to spare, my body screaming the whole way. I pushed my way through the doorway and came face to face with my ex-wife for the first time in three years.

Shit.

She didn't say anything at first, just pushed her glasses up her nose then looked me up and down slowly, her face a mask of disgust.

"Hi, Sarah," I said, attempting upbeat but only managing to wheeze. "How are things?"

She shook her head and said, "I knew this was a mistake. I don't know what Stuart was thinking when he suggested it. How DARE you turn up to see your daughter looking like that? Do you have any idea what this will do to her?"

I had to concede that I'd seen better days, but I wasn't going to admit that to her. Instead, I growled, "Yeah, I had a disagreement with some large gentlemen last night on a case I'm working on. I'd have gone to the hospital this morning if I thought there was any chance I'd still make it here on time. It was a flat choice, and I picked her."

Sarah gave me a look that she usually reserved for people on benefits. "You never change, do you, Jack? You're always ready to blame someone else for your situation, always ready with an excuse. Well, you've blown your chance. There's no way I'm leaving my daughter with a—"

A hand reached up from the booth and rested on Sarah's arm. "That's enough, Mum. It's okay. I want to see him."

Sarah's face reddened, and she sputtered, "Stephanie, I don't think that's a very good idea."

"I don't care what you think," Steph snapped with real venom. "It's not your decision. I'm fourteen years old, not four."

Sarah pursed her lips, and her eyes widened. She looked as if she were about to go into full meltdown, and my flight-or-fight reflex kicked in. I'd been on the receiving end of that look more times than I could count, and what followed was never pleasant. But Steph wasn't fazed at all. She waved her hand towards the door dismissively instead. "Goodbye, Mother. I'll see you in an hour."

And, wonder of wonders, Sarah grabbed her bag from the seat and stormed off as quickly as her expensive high heels would allow. I slid into the cubicle and looked at my daughter for the first time since her mother had thrown me out.

She was hardly recognisable from the sweet-natured girl I'd last seen. Her hair, usually a natural mousy brown with flashes of auburn, had been dyed flat black with fluorescent pink extensions. The colour scheme carried over into her makeup, which was heavily applied but rather striking. A silver stud shone in the side of her nose. She regarded me with a mixture of bemusement and pity.

"Hey, Dad," she said. "Still alive, then? You look like shit."

My mouth was suddenly dry, and I found myself floundering. I'd blame the concussion, but in all honesty, I had no idea what to say. The little girl of my memory was gone. The gothed-up teen in front of me was a stranger. But I had to say something.

"Just work stuff," I croaked. "Nothing to worry about. So... How have you been?" My inner voice railed at this. *Cack-handed idiot.*

"Oh, I've been fine," she said sweetly. "Peachy really, except for, you know... everything. Where were you, Dad? I can't believe you left me alone with that fucking woman – for three years! And not bothering to so much as text. Did you know she took me out of school? I lost all my friends and got stuck in some poncy academy for posh kids."

"Steph, I'm so sorry—"

She held up a finger, silencing my protestations.

"We don't even live at home anymore. She's stuck us in some neon nightmare penthouse in Canary Wharf with paper-thin walls. Paper-bloody-thin. It's a nightmare. Apart from that, Dad, I've been fucking fantastic. How about you?"

I felt my cheeks flush. I'd been so caught up in my own self-pity that I hadn't considered what all this might have done to her. "Listen, Steph. It wasn't my choice – not seeing you. I've been trying to get access, going through the courts like I said—"

"Yeah, Dad," she said, her tone acidic, "but you left. You left me alone with her."

My heart was aching, my throat clogged with pain. There was so much I wanted to say, so many things I wanted to explain, but it would have been hollow. There were reasons, sure, but she'd hear them as excuses. She wasn't wrong, she just didn't have the tools to see the situation from our perspective.

"Look, Steph, I'm not saying I didn't screw up, because I did. Massively. But after everything that happened, I kinda fell apart. I couldn't look after myself, let alone you and your mum. She made a decision to protect you – to protect you both – from the fallout. And maybe... I don't know. Maybe she wasn't wrong to get shot of me."

Steph's expression blazed with fury, a mirror of Sarah's earlier rage. "Will you stop making excuses for her? I remember what it was like, Dad. I remember it all. We should have gotten through it together, like a family. But she never wanted a family – I was always an inconvenience to her. You know why she threw you out? It wasn't for me; it was for her! Do you know how long it took for them to start shagging after you left, Dad?"

I winced. My battered brain wasn't dealing with this very well. "No..." I muttered. I wasn't very quick on the uptake that day, and I couldn't wrap my head around who she was talking about. *Shagging? Shagging who?*

"Three days. Three. Fucking. Days. And that's just when I found out about it. For all I know it had been going on for years. How's that for news?"

My mind reeled at this choice nugget of information as the penny finally dropped. Sarah and Hartington had been college sweethearts, and he'd been a bone of contention in our relationship from the start. I still remember the arguments when Sarah passed the bar exam and went to work at Hartington's law firm. Even when he and I worked together, he'd made no secret of his feelings about my wife, although it was always done in a 'joke but not quite' manner that made me want to punch his teeth in. It made sense that they'd rekindle their relationship once I was out of the picture. I'd just not wanted to think about it.

I was in no fit state to open that particular can of worms right now, though. I had one chance here to salvage my relationship with my daughter, and it seemed I was blowing it.

"Steph, I'm so sorry. I had no idea anything like that was happening."

She took a long slurp from the green, sugary drink in front of her, then said, "Pretty shit detective, then."

I laughed at that, and my ribs immediately made me wish that I hadn't. "I suppose so. We all have our blind spots, but what can I do? Your mum moved on without me. I'm really sorry you got caught in the middle of all this, but if your mother was shagging the Shart behind my back all this time, then screw them. They deserve each other."

Steph spat her Frappuccino across the table. "The Shart?" she said, wiping her mouth on her sleeve.

"Huh? Oh. My mate Chris came up with it. Stuart Hartington. Shartington, the Shart." She giggled at this, which only encouraged me. "Of course, it varies from time to time: Shartmeister, Shart-to-Shart... You know, if him and your mum split up, we could ask him What Becomes of the Broken Sharted?"

Steph full-on laughed at that, and I saw my little girl beneath the neo-goth exterior for the first time. "Oh, I'm keeping that one!" she said.

"Chris has a talent for stuff like that. But don't tell your mother you got it from me, or she'll keep me away till you're thirty."

Steph's eyes hardened. "Screw that bitch. She doesn't get to decide that."

"She's done a pretty thorough job of it so far. I think she must know the family court judge or something. I've not been able to get anywhere with visitation rights."

"Give me your phone," she said, holding her hand across the table.

I fished my battered mobile from my pocket. Steph looked at the cracked screen and pulled a face. "Eww! A Samsung? Does this thing even work?"

I felt quite upset by this for some reason. "It might not be the latest model, but it does everything I need."

"Latest model? It must be, what? Five years old?"

"Six, I think."

She frowned and handed the device back to me. "It belongs in a museum, but you have my number now. Send me a text so I have yours."

I felt a flutter of anxiety. "I don't know if that's such a good idea, love. The family court said..."

"Stop being such a pussy, Dad," she said, the grin back on her face. "I don't seem to remember that 'doing as you are told' was one of your strong suits."

I had to concede that point as I sent her a text message. A few seconds later, she waved her brand-new iPhone in my face. "There you are. I've put your contact down as Karen. Mother will never know."

"Your mother knows everything. She's omnipotent."

"She's a suspicious cow, but she's not omnipotent. Believe me, I've been getting stuff past her for years."

The rest of the hour passed in what felt like moments. Steph talked to me about the bands she liked, the arseholes she was at school with, and she positively delighted in telling me about all the ways she'd bent or broken her mother's rules. I was content to sit back and just enjoy her company. I had no idea how much I'd missed her until right at this moment. I mean, I'd missed her, but just being here, listening to her ramble on about everything and nothing felt like the best thing in the world. I never stopped aching but at some point, my injuries sank into the background. When her mother arrived with Hartington in tow, Steph got up, kissed me on my bruised cheek, and breezed past her mother without a word. Hartington just winked at me, then hurried after Sarah before I could put my Grandé Americano mug through his face.

I wondered how long it would take Steph to find a way to utilise Hartington's new nickname. Not long if I was any judge of character. I'd be amazed if she didn't find some excuse before they'd even made it home.

I took a mouthful of my cold coffee and enjoyed the moment – which was much shorter-lived than I would have liked.

A shadow passed over me, and someone slid into the seat opposite me that Steph had occupied mere moments before.

"Jesus, you look like shit. What happened to you?" said a familiar female voice. My warm, fuzzy feelings evaporated in a second, replaced by a cold fury as I looked up.

"*You* happened to me. Where's my fucking money, Robyn?"

She put her hands up and had the decency to look at least a little guilty. "Look, Jack, I'm not proud of what I did, But I wasn't given much choice. My boss needed some insurance to help keep you on track."

"Your boss?"

"Mr Hartington. He said you were headstrong, likely to make rash decisions unless properly… motivated."

The suspicion had been niggling at the back of my mind, but it was good to hear it confirmed. The Shart was turning out to be a real puppet-master. *Motherfucker.*

"I'm guessing you're my liaison for the case, then?"

"Correct. Though again, not my choice."

"I'll bet," I snarled. "He'll have been laughing his cock off at that one. But you didn't answer my question. Where. Is. My. Fucking. Money?"

"In the company bank account, of course. You don't think he'd let me keep it, do you? Don't worry, you'll get it back once the job's done, along with your bonus if all goes to plan."

I shook my head. "I can't wait until then, Robyn. Look at my face. This is what happens to a man when he can't pay his debts – and do you know why this happened? Take a guess."

Robyn paled and mumbled something. I bellowed over the top of it: "Because some fucking bitch drugged me and stole my money!" I took a breath, centred myself again. "So, here's the score – I've got until

Sunday night to pay them off or I'll be floating down the Thames in five or six pieces. No joke. So, if you want me to get the job done for that piece-of-shit boss of yours, you need to get me that money back, pronto!"

"Yeah, I can see that. Shit. I'll see what I can do. Honestly, Jack, I really am sorry. I didn't want to do it. Any of it, but you know Stuart. You know what he's like."

"I thought I did. Turns out he's even worse. Do you know that cunt stole my wife, too? Wrecked my career. Stopped me seeing my fucking daughter..."

I sat there, fuming. The Shart was at the centre of it all. God, did it all happen just to get me out of the way, or was that just a convenient bonus? Tumblers continued to click in my mind.

"I know it won't make up for any of it, but I did bring you this," she said, producing a rather expensive bottle of brandy from her bag.

"To replace the bottle you stole? Gee, thanks."

Robyn's face flushed. "Yeah. I don't even know why I did that. Just a spur-of-the-moment thing. This is a better bottle, though. It's the best one I could find. Sort of a peace offering."

I snorted. "It'll take a lot more than a bottle of booze to make peace between us."

"I get that. And I get that you don't trust me. But we should be able to work together, I hope."

I drained the last dregs of my coffee and glared at her. "If you want that, you can start by telling me what happened to the rest of the evidence. Where's the CCTV footage?"

A look of confusion washed over her face, but Robyn had already demonstrated her ability as an actor. "There wasn't any as far as I know."

"My friend Marcus was the first responder and he said the whole thing was caught on camera. He wouldn't be wrong about an important detail like that, and he had no reason to lie. Not to me."

She shook her head. "I honestly don't know. Mr Hartington told me that everything had been handed over to you. I'll look into it for sure. Have you turned up anything else?"

"Not much yet. I've been too busy getting my head kicked in. I'm going to track down one of the victim's classmates. Chloë Davidson. She didn't seem to think much of Alice or the dead kids. I'm hoping to persuade her to dish the dirt on what was going on behind the scenes in that creepy college. I'll let you know if I get anywhere. And after that, I want to see Alice in person."

She frowned. "I really don't see how that's pertinent to the case. As I understand it, she's catatonic. Completely unresponsive. What do you expect to gain from it?"

"When you've been doing this for as long as I have, you get a sense of people. Even those who aren't very talkative. I need to know who I'm dealing with. Sort it, yeah? By tomorrow."

Robyn shook her head. "Even if I were able to convince Mr Hartington, he'd need to get clearance from the client. There's no way..."

"I'm not interested in excuses. Make it happen. I can't work with one fucking hand tied behind my back."

I stood up to leave, but Robyn gently took my arm. "You really do look like shit, Jack. Can I drive you to the hospital or something?"

I pulled my arm away. "I'll be fine," I snarled. "Just get me my money, soon as you can. Every day counts, but Sunday's the deadline. Literally. Don't leave me hanging."

Chapter Eight

The buzzing of my phone awoke me from a fitful sleep. I'd been awake, on and off, for most of the night, getting no more than ninety-minute snatches of sleep at a time before I rolled over onto my injured ribs or unconsciously bit my split lip and was shocked once again into wakefulness. I'd finally found a solution, wedging myself into position with some spare pillows, and peacefully dropped off around six in the morning, only to be rudely awakened just over an hour later by the buzzing of my phone. I didn't recognise the number and felt the fury building. If this was a telemarketer, they were going to have a really unpleasant start to their day.

"This better be good," I growled into the handset.

A female voice said, "Meet me outside in thirty minutes. And try to make yourself presentable."

"Huh?" I responded. I hadn't had the two coffees it generally took for my brain to engage yet.

"It's Robyn, Jack. You told me to organise a visit with Alice Wells yesterday. I'm on my way to take you there."

"Wait... you're what?"

I heard an exasperated sigh, and she said, "I was on the phone with Mr Hartington and Mrs Wells for over an hour last night, trying to convince them to honour your request. Which wasn't easy, just so you know. Their one stipulation was that I accompany you. Have you got a car, Jack?" I didn't need to reply. It was clear she knew that I didn't. "Because the clinic is in the middle of the countryside, and there's no train station nearby. So, guess what, you've got a chauffeur for the day. Isn't that nice?"

I dug around for a reason to say no, my every instinct warning against this. The way I'd been played, just the thought of Robyn set my teeth on edge; being stuck in a car with her for hours sounded like a special kind of hell. I needed to see Alice, though. It felt imperative, central to the investigation. I lacked the cognitive ability to find a third way, so I sighed and said, "Fine, but give me an hour. It's going to take me longer than usual to get ready thanks to that kicking you caused me."

I put the phone down without giving her a chance to respond, then, wincing at the renewed pain from my battered body, I shuffled to the bathroom for a shower.

Despite expectations, I managed to get myself cleaned up, fed and caffeinated in a little over thirty minutes. What can I say? My beauty regime isn't exactly extensive. Frustratingly, that left me rattling around my flat, scrolling on my phone until the full hour was up. There are few things that bug me more than dead time when I'm ready to do something – I struggle to give anything else my attention, knowing I've got this other thing hanging over my head. But I'd be damned if I set foot outside of my flat one second before that hour had elapsed.

Because fuck her.

Eventually, I made my way downstairs to find the city shrouded in a white blanket of watery snow. Not quite enough to bring the city to a standstill, but enough to make the footpath treacherous. It soaked through my shoes almost immediately, chilling my toes and leaving me profoundly uncomfortable. Robyn waved to me from behind the wheel of a top-of-the-line white Range Rover. I half staggered across the street and got in the passenger side.

"Nice wheels," I said. "How many people did you need to drug and rob to pay for this?"

She shook her head and said, "Fuck off, Jack. It's too early for this shit. Neither one of us likes what we have to do for this job, but we're stuck with it. So just... give it a rest. Please."

We set off smoothly, wheels shushing through the snow. There wasn't much traffic around yet, but we still got caught by traffic lights from time to time. At the second set, I decided to prod her.

"Got my money yet?" I asked.

Robyn turned her head and glared at me. "Yeah. I spent the evening walking round different cash points, taking two hundred quid out at a time. What do you think? The banks aren't even open yet! I've explained the situation to Mr Hartington and it's going to be sorted. Jesus, Jack. I've apologised for what I did, I'm putting it right and I'm playing fucking taxi driver to you all day instead of doing my actual job. I don't know what else I could possibly do to get us past this."

I felt a momentary surge of guilt, because I was being an utter bastard on purpose and part of me recognised that, really, she was just another victim of Hartington's machinations. However, my ego wasn't quite prepared to let it go just yet.

"Seriously, though," I said, "how do you afford this on a junior solicitor's salary? It can't be a company car."

Robyn glanced at me warily and said, "It's not, and my wages are shit. But my family have money. This was a graduation present from my mother."

How the other half live. A full spec vehicle like this must have cost over sixty grand.

"And here was me thinking you had a lucrative sideline as a high-price call girl," I said. "You can hardly blame me after The Dolphin."

What looked like genuine hurt flashed across her face, but she gritted her teeth and let it pass. She turned her head to the front and tersely said, "I picked you up a coffee."

"As if!" I snorted and threw the steaming hot liquid out of the window. Apparently, I wasn't done being a prick yet. The rest of the journey was undertaken in a stony, uncomfortable silence, which suited me just fine.

It took us over two hours to make our way to the secure mental health unit that Alice was being held in. We drove up to a pair of heavy iron gates, and Robyn gave our details over the intercom. Moments later, the gates swung open, and we drove along the picturesque tree-lined driveway until we reached the car park.

The building was an impressive Victorian affair, with several modern outbuildings clinging to the original house like some sort of obscene growth. I got out of the car and Robyn followed suit. "No need for you to accompany me," I said to her. If I was expecting an argument, I was disappointed. She simply shrugged, popped a cigarette out of a pack, then leaned against her car and lit it. I'd not had time for a smoke this morning, and the sight of her lighting up made the back of my throat constrict. My fingertips tingled with the craving. I wasn't going to lower myself to asking her for one, though, so I turned my back and walked into the secure unit.

I'll admit, I had certain preconceptions as to what the place would be like. I'd been expecting muscular guards with white smocks and riot batons to lead me through a series of security doors, down white tiled corridors, past straight-jacketed inmates screaming in their own private torment. My first impression was that the reality was nothing like that. I guess some Hollywood images are quite deeply ingrained.

Instead, I found a building that looked more like a residential nursing home than an insane asylum. The receptionist was a young man who greeted me with a smile, got me to put my details in the visitor's book and asked me to take a seat while my escort came to collect me.

After a few minutes, the inner door swung open and a middle-aged man with greying hair, round glasses and a kindly face strode toward me.

"Mr Carlton? I'm Joseph York, Alice's primary physician."

I shook his hand. "Thank you, doctor. I appreciate you arranging this at such short notice."

"That's not a problem, although I'm not sure exactly what you are expecting. Alice hasn't said a word since she was brought in."

I returned his smile. "I'm trying not to come in with any preconceptions at all," I lied. "I suppose I just want to get a sense of her. Try to reconcile the girl with the things she's supposed to have done."

He nodded. "I understand, but I think your journey might have been in vain. Her body is here, but the girl within is elsewhere. We've barely caught glimpses of consciousness."

I followed Doctor York through the facility. It seemed to have been recently renovated, with new carpets in the common areas, and lots of open plan spaces where the patients sat, either lost in their thoughts all alone or engaged with some activity such as jigsaw puzzles, reading, or drawing. Some sat around in groups, with a staff member leading the session. It all looked very normal at first glance until you realised that all the furniture was quite securely bolted to the floor, the windows reinforced with wire mesh, and that there were no ornaments on any of the tables. No vases that could be thrown, or picture frames that could be torn from the walls. Nothing, in fact, that could be utilised as a weapon. On the surface, the facility was all pastel colours and group therapy, but beneath that it remained a prison of sorts for disturbed and possibly dangerous people. More luxurious than Broadmoor, but no less secure. I spotted the discreetly placed cameras that covered each room, and understood that the white-smocked, muscular attendants with riot batons were most likely playing cards in a room somewhere out of sight, ready to spring into action in the event of an incident.

Doctor York arrived at a heavy wooden door, with a small, reinforced glass window in it at head height. He pushed a button on the wall, then opened the door.

"Alice," he said, "this is Mr Carlton. He'd like to ask you a few questions, if that's okay?"

Alice Wells was sitting behind a table that, like the rest of the furniture, was securely fastened to the floor. A pair of handcuffs were around her wrists and a chain ran between the two bracelets, branching out into another, longer chain that ran through an eyelet inset in the desk, then down to a pair of manacles around her ankles. In turn, these were fastened to a metal plate on the floor. She had a slight frame and negligible muscle definition on her arms. I doubted that she'd have been able to lift even one of the dead girls off the floor for more than a second, let alone six-footers like Darby and Jerome. The contrast between her physicality and their precautions was chilling. What did they think she was capable of? I found it impossible to credit her with the full-scale slaughter at King's College, but they were clearly taking no chances. It gave me pause for thought and, as I recalled the crime scene photos, a little shudder ran through me.

"Thank you, doctor," I said and took a seat opposite the girl.

"I'll be outside if you need anything," Doctor York said. His professional smile was still in place, but his eyes told another story. The good doctor was scared shitless. If I'm honest, I felt more than a flutter in my stomach as he locked the door behind him.

Alice Wells didn't respond to my presence in any way that I could see. She stared right through me, as if examining the wall. Her brown hair had been washed, combed and styled, and she was wearing subtle but expertly applied makeup. Her clothes – a loose Union Jack t-shirt and jogging bottoms – were clean. I could smell the fresh scent of the fabric conditioner from where I sat. All of which was clearly done for my benefit, demonstrating a level of care despite her bonds. Alice wouldn't give two shits in her current state, and none of the other patients I'd seen had the benefit of a morning beauty treatment. No. The hospital wanted to give her mother's employee a good impression, just in case word happened to get back to her. Given that it was only just after ten, I could imagine the panicked grooming session this morning when the visitation request came through.

"Hi, Alice," I said. "My name's Jack. I work for your mother."

Alice carried on gazing right through me, her head canted slightly. A rivulet of saliva ran from her mouth and pooled on her t-shirt.

"She wants me to try to help you. Maybe get you out of here. I know that you've been through a lot, but it would really help me if you could tell me what happened that night. To you and to your friends."

No response, but then I hadn't been expecting one. Not at first, anyway. I decided to push a little harder.

"Were they your friends, Alice? It got a bit... messy. Tell me, do you remember what happened on the night of December fourteenth? At King's College?"

Nothing. A fresh tendril of drool began snaking its way down her chin, but there wasn't even a flicker of recognition. Of remorse or fear.

"Do you remember how your friends were killed, Alice? Do you remember how Anastasia, Cassandra and Aldous died?"

The clock on the wall ticked away. My insides burned with acid indigestion. I should have had that coffee. Alice's face remained an impassive mask. I decided to try a different tactic.

"Can you remember why you killed your boyfriend, Jarod Darby, with a machete?"

Her eyes remained unfocused, and her mouth hung slightly open. I'd hoped for some kind of response when I mentioned Darby by name, but I wasn't really surprised. It was a long shot, but one worth taking.

I tapped on the window and Doctor York let me out, quickly closing the door behind me.

"As I said, Alice hasn't responded to anyone or anything since she got here. I'm sorry you wasted your journey but really, I could have told you this over the phone."

"That's okay, doctor," I said, as he walked me back to reception. "This was actually really useful for me. I got everything I wanted out of the session."

And that was true. Firstly, what was painfully obvious was that Doctor York was terrified of Alice Wells. The second thing I learned was that Alice wasn't just catatonic, she'd been drugged. Sedated out of her fucking mind.

***

There was an accident on the M4 motorway on the way back into London, which meant I was stuck in the car with Robyn for far longer than I'd planned. After the second hour sitting in stationary traffic, she wound down the driver's window and lit up a cigarette, then offered the pack to me. I considered asking her if that was drugged as well but decided against it. I didn't trust her as far as I could throw her, but given her visible levels of discomfort, I was prepared to believe Hartington was screwing her over almost as much as me. Perhaps she'd bruised the tosser's ego in some way, and this was her penance? Who knew. Anyway, instead of being a prick again, I accepted it with gratitude and savoured the nicotine rush I'd been craving since I woke up.

"So," I said at last as I flicked the cigarette butt out of the window. "What did you do to piss him off?"

"Piss who off?"

"Hartington."

She thought about my question for a while, as if deliberating whether to say anything. Then she said, "Okay, fine. There was something a couple of months ago. Stuart had been acting... inappropriately in the office. Lewd jokes. Unwanted physical contact. Subtle, you know. Brief enough that he could pass it off as accidental. Textbook stuff."

"That sounds like Hartington. What did you— oh shit."

"Yeah, shit is right. I lodged a formal complaint against him with HR and—"

"And you didn't realise that his mum was Head of HR."

"No, although I bloody well found out soon enough."

"I'm surprised you didn't leave. Or sue the shit out of the whole company."

Robyn's cheeks flushed. "At the end of the day, it was his word against mine, and it's not like I've got tons of commercial experience yet. If I made a fuss, tried to escalate things and it got worse, I'd lose my job, maybe even get blacklisted from the other firms in town. The whole industry is very much old boys' country club crap. She sent him on a course, and I got light duties for a while. Seemed easier to just suck it up, keep my mouth shut and do as I was told. At least for now. I thought he'd forgotten about it until this week."

I understood, or at least I thought I did. "I'm sorry that happened to you," I said, and with uncharacteristic good sense, I managed to keep my big mouth shut until we got back to London.

With the ongoing snowfall, and the rush hour chaos that caused, it was close to six when Robyn dropped me off at my flat. And this presented a problem.

"Robyn," I said. "I wasn't joking about the people I owe money to. If I don't pay them off by Sunday, I really am a dead man. And the banks are closed now. What are you going to do?"

"I called the office and asked Stuart to arrange it while you were in with Alice. I'm going there now, so hopefully it's all been dealt with. Try not to worry, okay? I'll get it sorted out, even if I really do have to go from cashpoint to cashpoint."

I nodded and said, "Thank you. And I'm sorry for being such a prick. I know none of this was your idea. I'll try to be a bit more professional from here on in."

She gave a small smile and nodded. "That's all I could hope for, given the circumstances. Try to enjoy your evening. I'll be in touch about the money."

I got out of the Range Rover and hurried across the street to my flat. I didn't particularly expect Arthur and his gang of would-be children's entertainers to be lurking nearby since I still had a couple of days left, but I checked the street anyway to be on the safe side. I did not intend to be caught out the same way again. Once I was satisfied the coast was clear, I let myself through the front door and limped up the stairs. Ozzy was waiting impatiently for me and made sure that my first stop was the kitchen, where I noticed that his bowl was still overflowing with this morning's cat biscuits. Damn. I'd really messed up by letting him get a taste of the good stuff. I picked up a handful of the biscuits and dropped them back into the bowl in the hope he'd believe they were fresh ones, but he gave me a look bordering on contempt and stalked away. I hadn't heard the last of this...

I had a nutritious meal of leftover pizza that had probably been in my fridge for less than a week, and I manfully resisted the urge to crack open the expensive bottle of booze Robyn had guiltily given me. Things hadn't gone half as bad as they might. Still, after a few days on this case, I had more questions than answers. It was time to take control of things, and I needed a clear head for that.

What did I really have? A primary suspect that was being kept sedated. A bunch of evidence that had been misplaced or hidden from me. And not one person that was prepared to tell me the truth.

I couldn't do much about Alice's mental state, but I could try to make some headway with the other two.

A quick internet search told me that the head of security at King's College was one Stanley Armitage, an ex-army man who lived in Ealing and had been divorced for almost a decade. If anyone could tell me what was on that CCTV footage, it would be Stanley. I called the college and was told he would be working tomorrow morning if I needed to speak to him. Fine and dandy.

Chloë Davidson was next on my list. However, speaking to her wasn't quite as easy as I'd hoped. A carefully worded but unsolicited message on social media got me a response of "Fuck off, pedo" and I was immediately blocked. Hm.

As I lay back on my sofa, freshly irritated by the residual smell of shake-and-vac and pondering how to proceed, my phone buzzed. It was a text message.

Hey dad u okay? (It's Steph btw) xxx

My mood lightened immediately, and I felt a smile crease my face.

Yeah, love. All good (my face notwithstanding). How are you? All good with your mum and Satan?

They had a massive row when they got back home. Mum was NOT happy

Oh shit... You okay?

You kidding? It was fckin glorious. The Shart didn't know where to put himself. I thought he was gonna shart for real

What was it about?

Duh! You, of course. Mum was pissed that he'd pressured her into the meeting. Especially cos you turned up looking like you'd gone ten rounds with Jake Paul

Who's that?

Youtuber. Knobhead. You wouldn't understand

No, I think you're probably right

Have been calling the Shart by his true name btw

I chuckled. *Thought you might have. How long did it take you?*

In the car on the way home. Don't worry, I was subtle about it

That I very much doubted. Something told me that subtle was not among my daughter's life skills. She did, after all, have me as a role model. I asked her what she'd been up to lately.

Just school. Boring. Got a detention for calling Amber an NPC.

A whatnow?

NPC. Non Player Character. Like in games... FFS, doesn't matter. CBA to explain to a boomer.

Hey, I'm not a boomer! I'm Gen X

Same thing. Old and Tragic. xxxx Anyway, wot u been up 2?

Just work stuff. Spent all day chasing leads and getting nowhere. Usual.

U neeed me to help?

I was about to decline, and then an idea popped into my head. A terrible idea, obviously. Sarah would have a fit if she found out, but what the hell...

Actually, maybe. I'm trying to speak to someone – a 17 year old girl – about the case, and she won't talk to me.

Eww! Not surprised. Talk about sus! Send me her deets and I'll snapchat her.

I sent Steph the details of Chloë's Facebook and Instagram accounts with something like hope.

There was no activity on the phone for a while, so I made myself a cuppa, and flicked the TV on. After about half an hour my phone buzzed again.

Okay, have facetimed her and told her you're not a pedo. She's unblocked you and will meet tomorrow. But take money – it's gonna cost you

Thanks, love xxxx

Okay, mum and the Shart are home. Gotta go! Byeeee! Xxxx

I messaged Chloë again and made arrangements for the following day. I dicked around on the Xbox for half an hour, then decided to get an early night. Maybe it was the stress of the past few days, or all the early mornings and late nights, but my eyes started to go. I was exhausted. I clambered off the sofa with a great deal of effort, ejected the cat from my bed and was practically asleep before my head hit the pillows.

Chapter Nine

I found myself standing in the courtyard of King's College once more, but this time I knew I was dreaming. The mist swirled around me, and I thought I could hear things: whispered words and guttural growls coming from the shadowy shapes within. Some of them were roughly human in size and shape, others paced like large dogs, but they moved oddly. Beyond, rising in the distance were vast figures, bigger than buildings and moving with ponderous power. I was thankful that the fog obscured them. I felt that my sanity might not survive a closer look, although I also suspected that if I drew their attention, my sanity would be the least of my concerns.

I felt a crushing dread envelop me as I was drawn forwards. Part of me wanted to run screaming into the fog – better to be torn apart by the monsters in its depths than to face a repeat of last time – but my dream body moved through the landscape automatically, each step bringing me closer to the source of my fear.

The clock tower appeared from the fog, but this time it was ruined. Half the roof was gone, and the tower bricks were blackened from fire damage. Where the windows of the college had been filled before with silent, screaming faces, they were now empty, the glass broken, revealing nothing but a chill darkness within. In some ways, that was even more unnerving. I passed the main college building and stepped onto the playing field. The ground squelched and sucked at my feet and, when I looked down, I saw that the earth was saturated with blood. It bubbled up with every footstep and pooled in the footprints behind me.

It didn't take long for me to arrive at the forest of people. This time, their faces were directed upward, and their mouths were wide open, locked in a frozen scream, tears glistening on their cheeks.

I didn't waste time trying to wake them. Instead, I pushed on, past the petrified bodies of former friends and lovers, until I reached the centre. Steph was standing there – looking more like the young woman I met in the café now than the child of memory – with Billie and Chris flanking her, the trio set apart as if for special display. Their faces were locked in the same eternal scream. I followed their gazes upward but could see nothing but shadows through the shifting white shroud of fog.

A voice whispered in my ear, quite clearly: "You can't save them."

I spun around to find Alice Wells standing next to the frozen body of one of my favourite teachers. She looked just like she had yesterday at the hospital, right down to the clothes, but her eyes were bright and alert. Chestnut brown hair cascaded across the shoulders of her baggy Union Jack t-shirt. Her hands were shoved deep into the pockets of her ripped jeans, and designer trainers squelched in the bloody mud.

"What do you mean?" I murmured nervously. This might be 'just a dream' but the fear was real. I didn't dare make a sound in this place in case it alerted something to my presence.

A hand touched my shoulder from behind, and I leapt away with a little shriek, only to find another Alice Wells standing there, smiling. "You can't save any of them, Jack. They're all going to die," she said.

"No. I'll find a way to protect them. I have to."

A third Alice stepped out from behind my father, her face twisted into a manic grin, radiating malice. "And how are you going to do that?"

She was playing with me. I felt anger surge, pushing the fear down. "You tell me. I'm supposed to be helping you, after all. Tell me what happens so I can stop it."

Yet another Alice joined the circle around me, and they took each other's hands. She smiled sweetly and said, "Stop it? You can't stop it. You're going to kill them all for us. We're very grateful."

I yelled in defiance and tried to grab one of the girls, but she skipped out of reach, giggling. "Bang up job you're doing, Jack," a fifth Alice said, her voice dripping venom. "You must be proud."

Huge black ravens flew through the mist, cawing loudly and circling my loved ones. They landed in a flurry of black feathers, screeching at each other and fighting for purchase on the living statues, pecking and tearing at the cold skin. I watched in horror as the faces of Billie and Chris were reduced to bloody ribbons, skulls visible beneath the shredded flesh. One raven pecked at Steph's lips, tearing the lower one off, while another plucked an eye out, gulping its prize with glee. And I just stood there, shrieking and shrieking in the dead white haze of madness.

***

I awoke far too early on Saturday morning, if you can call anything morning before 6 a.m. I spent an age trying to get comfortable, but eventually gave up and went for a shower. I had an awful lot to get done today. My bruises were coming along nicely, with some interesting hues of purple and yellow breaking out across my face and ribcage. Still, at least the swelling was going down. I was looking less like the Elephant Man at any rate.

I washed two paracetamol and two ibuprofens down with a swirl of instant coffee and tried to gather my thoughts as I waited for the pain medication to kick in.

When I'd messaged Chloë Davidson last night, after Steph had vouched for me, she'd been reticent, but eventually agreed to meet and discuss her former classmates. The only stipulation was that the conversation took place in person, in a public location, and that I paid her a hundred pounds for her time. I'd agreed because I didn't have many other leads in the case and, frankly, I planned to claim it back on expenses. The only problem I could see was that Ms Davidson was unlikely to write me a receipt for the payment, and with the cost of travel, my bank account was looking pretty sparse. It was slim consolation to know my problems would all be over by Monday if Robyn failed to come up with the cash. Given what little I'd learned and, barring physical evidence dropping into my lap, the most likely route for success seemed to be painting Alice as the victim. If I could dig up enough dirt on the two boys, Darby in particular, it could firm up the self-defence argument. Yeah, I wasn't happy about it. Trying to assassinate the characters of dead children wouldn't exactly be a classy move, and it was a little too close to what I'd done to Claire Baker for comfort. But at least they were already dead. Oh, God. This was probably what Mrs Wells was alluding to when she mentioned my 'moral flexibility'. As if my levels of self-loathing weren't high enough.

Even though I was quite pushed for time, I went as far as ironing a shirt, so I didn't entirely come across like a vagrant. By the time I shuffled out of my flat towards the tube station, I could have almost passed for a normal human being – so long as nobody looked at my face.

The trains were quieter on Saturday than during the week, thanks to the drop off in commuters, and the persistent snowfall had put off many of the capital's visiting tourists. Despite this, the underground services were operating at around fifty per cent capacity, and the journey to Waterloo station, which should have taken me about thirty minutes, ended up taking almost three times that. Fortunately, the connecting train out to the affluent areas to the west of the city was running on time, and I was able to board an empty carriage.

Despite the motion of the train jarring my ribs, I felt almost relaxed as I watched the yellow-brick buildings of the city turn into glass and steel corporate towers and then into open snow-covered parks, infested with excitable children.

I fucking hate snow, though. It's nice enough to look at from, say, a nice warm pub window, but once you're out in it, it's a nightmare. Hard to keep your footing in; cold wetness seeping in through your shoes, soaking your socks. And when it turns into slush, it's even worse, turning the most innocent patch of pavement into a slippery roulette wheel of injury. It was rare to get a covering this time of the year, but the nasty white shite had been falling unabated for more than forty-eight hours now with no signs of stopping. The weatherman on the BBC had said the magic word, 'unprecedented' and every miserable bastard like me laughed bitterly.

The journey began to lull me half to sleep, and I had a panicked scramble to get off at my stop. The station was little more than a pair of concrete platforms linked by a narrow, grey metal bridge over the tracks. The exit was on the other side, so I had to be careful on the steps, thankful for the orange rock salt crunching beneath my shoes.

The wind was gusting as I made my way through a snow-covered park beside the train station, and I was reminded of the fact that my jacket was rather old. The insulation was bunched in some places and conspicuous by its absence in others. I trudged along the road toward King's College, loathing every second that the slush seeped through to my socks and the frigid wind chilled my bones. The journey to reception only took me about half an hour, but the walk felt much longer.

The entrance to the college was surprisingly low-key. A gap between a row of terraced Georgian houses, with a simple blue sign adorning the walls, white text directing me to the school reception. Other, less friendly signs reminded passersby that King's College was strictly private property and that trespassers would be prosecuted.

This was not the gothic locale of my nightmares. I stamped the last vestiges of snow from my shoes and opened the door to the reception area, enjoying the rush of warmth as I stepped inside.

If the exterior was relatively modest, the same could not be said of the interior. The floors were hardwood, polished to a high sheen and surprisingly free from damage considering the average daily footfall. Oil paintings adorned the wall, along with imposing statues and busts of former headmasters. I looked up to the twin angels guarding the huge staircase and couldn't help but shudder as unbidden bloody images came swimming back to my mind.

"Yes?" came a woman's voice, somehow managing to express a query and accusation at the same time.

I turned to face the woman and put on what I hoped was a winning smile. Given the state of my face, that might not have been one of my better ideas, but if my injuries bothered her any more than the simple fact of my presence, she hid it well.

"Hello," I said. "I'm here to see Stanley Armitage. I was told he would be available today?"

The woman peered at me from over the top of her glasses and pursed her lips. "And you are?"

"My name's Jack Carlton."

She leaned back on her chair, and I noticed her eyes flicking to the telephone. She could, of course, be about to call Mr Armitage, but the police seemed an equally likely proposition. "And will Mr Armitage know to what this pertains?"

"I hope so, yes," I said, irritation seeping through the cracks of politesse. "I'm a private investigator employed by Mrs Margaret Wells, and I'm here to speak to him about the… incident in December last year. She is a significant donor for the school, I believe."

This latter detail was an educated guess, but a good one. It brought about a rapid change in the receptionist's attitude. She tried to smile at me, but the frozen expression she landed on made the hairs on the back of my neck stand up. Not a big smiler, this one, then.

"Please take a seat, Mr Carlton," she said in honeyed tones. "I'll let Mr Armitage know that you're here."

I thanked her and settled into a large, extremely comfortable leather chair. There were CCTV cameras covering almost every square inch of the entrance hall, confirming what Marcus had said. A place this exclusive would want to make absolutely certain that the rich kids were well looked after, even if that meant living under constant surveillance.

Despite the fact that it was a Saturday morning, there were still plenty of youngsters coming up and down the stairs in full school uniform, bags slung over their shoulders and books under their arms. What was missing was the general hubbub and noise that I remembered from my own school days. No one ran. There was no yelling, nor did there seem to be any fights breaking out, let alone smaller children being bullied by the larger kids. It was like a fucking Stepford school – so far removed from my frame of reference that I may as well have been on another planet.

Within ten minutes, a thin, wiry man with thick grey hair and a pencil moustache walked over to me and said, "Mr Carlson?"

"Carlton," I corrected, and shook his hand. "Jack Carlton."

Armitage squeezed hard enough for me to feel the bones crunch. One of those guys, I thought. *Prick.* I returned the grip as well as I could, but he didn't even flinch. Whatever else he was, Stanley Armitage was a strong old bugger. Once he'd taken my measure and found me wanting, he winked and said, "Follow me. We can speak in my office."

I trailed him through the school, noting the position of the cameras and, whenever possible, their proximity to the various crime scenes. The coverage was extensive, as I expected. Eventually, we arrived at a heavy oak-panelled door, and I followed him inside.

Stanley Armitage's office was surprisingly small, given the grandeur of the rest of the school. It seemed that the head of security had been put in the equivalent of a broom cupboard.

There was only one window – small, lead-cased and set high up in the wall – allowing only a meagre amount of weak, grey light through that was rendered moot by the glare of an overhead fluorescent tube. An elderly computer with a CRT monitor was perched on a cluttered desk, and a small bookcase sat at its side, filled with dog-eared paperbacks. Clive Cussler, Dan Brown and James Patterson were all present and correct in his collection of thrillers. I deduced that Stanley had rather a lot of time on his hands during the standard working week.

He removed an Android phone from his pocket that was even older than mine, plugged it into the charger and balanced it precariously on the radiator. Then he leaned back in his chair and said, "So, Mr Carson, what can I do for you?"

I didn't bother correcting him the second time. Either he had bad hearing, or he was trying to get a rise out of me. Neither warranted comment. Instead, I smiled and told him why I was there.

He nodded. "Oh, yes. Terrible it was. But I'm not sure what I can do to help you. The police already have my full statement."

"So, you were on site on the evening of December fourteenth?"

"No. As I told the police, I'd taken the night off. Gone to see the pantomime at the Palladium with the grandkids. Can't say I thought much of it, to be honest. How anyone could cast Julian Clary as Robin Hood is beyond me. Filth monger. The little 'uns liked it well enough, mind."

"I see. So, was there someone else on duty?"

"We were meant to have an agency lad on, but he didn't show up. They did call me, but because it was outside of term time, we figured there wouldn't be a problem. There wasn't supposed to be anyone there, you see. Most of the staff and students had gone home already."

"I see. So, you found out about the incident when, exactly?"

"The coppers dragged me out of bed in the early hours. Had to drive in from Ealing. Of course, by then there were police all over the place. Forensics mostly."

"They wanted to see the CCTV footage, I assume?"

"Yeah, I brought this one copper down here and left him to it. He went through the recordings, then the forensics lads came down and wanted to take it all away. Computer, hard drives, the whole bloody lot. I told them, you can't have all of that. We'd have no bloody security system. In the end, they just took copies of the footage, but I had to kick right off before anyone would listen."

"Were there any other backups of the files? Cloud storage, perhaps?"

He laughed. "Bleeding hell, what do you think? The bloody computer here's nearly as old as I am. Cloud storage? Pull the other one."

"Do you still have those recordings, Mr Armitage?"

"Nah, once the rozzers had what they needed, the files got deleted. Overwritten a week later. Like I say, we don't have a modern system here, Mr Carson. None of that fancy stuff. We don't keep things more than a week."

I was a little out of practice in my interview techniques, but I was pretty convinced Armitage was lying through his fucking teeth. For one thing, the camera system I'd noticed in the hallways and common areas looked brand new. State of the art. And there was no way that a system like that was run from an ancient PC like this. There would be a dedicated server somewhere in the building with offsite backups as part of the package.

"Did you watch the recordings, Mr Armitage?"

The colour washed from Stanley's face, and he looked as if he were about to throw up. "No, of course not. Why would I want to see that mess? It'd give me nightmares for the rest of my life."

That would be a yes, then.

"Are you sure you didn't have a little peek? I would have thought the temptation would be quite overwhelming."

He ignored my last question and said, "If that's all, Mr Carson, I have to be getting on. I'm a busy man, and I can't afford to neglect my duties." He got to his feet and opened the door.

"That's fine, Mr Armitage," I said. "Thank you for your time. I'll see myself back to reception."

He nodded and thankfully didn't offer to shake my hand again. Then the door slammed closed behind me. Strange that the head of security wouldn't escort an unwanted visitor off the premises. But I wasn't complaining.

I walked through the corridors and ran my fingers over Stanley's telephone, which had somehow fallen into my jacket pocket as I left. I slipped into an alcove in a CCTV blind spot, fished the device out of my pocket and checked the touchscreen. Sure enough, Stanley's unlock pattern was streaked in grease across the screen. I quickly verified that it worked, then put my elbow through the nearest fire alarm panel. Oops. Clumsy me.

The classrooms and dormitories emptied as dozens of Stepford Children filed downstairs and out toward their fire assembly points. This gave me some time – maybe thirty minutes at most – before the fire service arrived to check the place out and issue the all-clear. Valuable time. Because if Stanley Armitage was standing out on a playing field in the cold and the wet, he wasn't locking down his email and online banking accounts.

I left through reception among the hordes of staff and children, logged into Stanley's phone and scrolled through the emails. Unfortunately, if anything untoward had occurred between the fourteenth of December and the end of the year, it had been well hidden, with nothing of note in the sent items or trash can. The same went for the call records and text messages. Nothing suspicious at all. I went for his online banking next. I requested a PIN and Password reset, which, of course, then came through to his phone, then I worked my magic.

This was where things got interesting. Between the fifteenth of December and the fifteenth of January, there were five transactions into Stanley's current account for the sum of five thousand pounds a time. There was no name associated with the account, but something about the account number and sort code rankled me. I downloaded the statement as a PDF, transferred it to my own phone via Bluetooth, and then dropped the stolen phone down the nearest drain.

Someone had paid Stanley Armitage off to the tune of twenty-five grand. The questions at the forefront of my mind were: who and why?

***

I'd arranged to meet Chloë in Hampton Hill, an exclusive suburb whose house prices would have made most people's eyes water. Not that I'd have wanted to live in a place like this. The high street was full of pretentious artisanal shops with no sign of a single recognisable chain store or brand. One of the places seemed to sell nothing but specialist beard oil, for fuck's sake. Everywhere I looked I saw overpriced crap with little to no practical value. I wondered at that. Perhaps this was what gave wealthy people their biggest hard-ons: the ability to waste money while everyone else struggled. The whole place spoke of a client base so far removed from the realities of life that it beggared belief. Naturally, even in my freshly ironed clothes, I stood out like a fresh turd on a snow drift. It was astonishing that I made it the length of the high street without being bundled into a police car.

I eventually arrived at The Roebuck and had a look around. It had probably been a nice, traditional and unassuming drinking spot before the area got gentrifucked. Now, the traditional beige exterior had been painted bright red, and the inside décor made it look less like a pub and more like a house clearance sale. Wicker bicycles hung from the ceiling alongside pots, pans and ornamental maritime steering wheels. There was no discernible theme that I could make out, but I supposed it must hold a charm for some. This extended to the offerings behind the bar.

I didn't recognise a single beer. They were all specialist micro-brewery bollocks with names like "old badger's arsehole" and "crotch goblin's yeast infection". It gave me a powerful longing for the simple delights of The Dolphin.

I found Chloë Davidson sitting in the corner of the bar beneath a plastic-mounted fish that looked horribly likely to sing if anyone was foolish enough to insert batteries. I took the seat across from her and introduced myself. She was a short girl with dirty blonde hair, round-framed glasses and a quizzical look that somehow made me think of a vole. She pushed her glasses up from the bridge of her nose and told me I looked like shit.

"Yeah, I've been getting that a lot this week. Can I get you a drink?"

The girl put her hand across the top of her bottle and pulled a face that spoke vividly of disgust. "Erm, no-oo-oo. As if! And just so you know, I've told four people where I'm going, and who you are, so you can get any of *those* ideas out of your head. Did you bring my money?"

I leant back in my seat so that I could get out of her personal space and fished the cash out of my wallet. "Here's half now. You can have the rest afterwards. But look, you have to know, I'd never try anything like—"

"Yeah, whatever, skank. Any perv could say that. Ask your stupid questions and get lost. I've got other stuff to do."

I got to my feet and moved back from the table. "Okay. But I've got to get a drink for myself first. They'll probably kick me out if I don't buy something."

Chloë rolled her eyes and grumbled, "If you must. But don't take too long."

I shuffled to the bar and returned a few moments later with a pint of something I couldn't pronounce that tasted like someone had strained

Foster's Lager through a pair of dirty socks. Considering how much it cost, though, I resolved to drink every drop.

"Right, you've got your piss water," Chloë sighed with exaggerated impatience. "Now, what do you want to know?"

I took another mouthful of my beer and almost coughed at a vinegary undertone I'd missed the first time. "I take it you didn't like your classmates much?"

"What gave me away?"

I flipped my notebook open and read from it blandly. "'The whole bunch of bastards had it coming. I'm glad they're dead. I hope she's next.' You caught some grief for that, I gather?"

"Yeah, well, balls to them and their simps. They were cunts, all of them. Not just to me, either; they treated everyone like shit. Then what? Just because they're dead, the whole school was suddenly all 'Oh, we can't believe you're gone!' and 'Heaven has some new angels tonight' and all that shit. It made me sick. Bunch of fucking hypocrites."

In many respects, it hardly seemed shocking that a clique of privileged children had acted like arseholes, but in the moment, I did wonder if I'd blown my cash on a dead end. I probed the horrible gap, trying to find something – anything – to make this trip worth it.

"What sort of things did they do?"

"Oh, mostly it was just low-grade bitchiness. Sometimes, they'd cross the line into flat-out bastard territory." She wrapped her arms around herself when she said that; an unconscious action that made me wonder just how far their bullying had gone. "There was a boy here last year that Darby took against. He made his life hell. The kid had to be taken out of school in the end. Lost his shit completely and ended up running around the quad without his pants on. The school kept it out of the news, but it was all anyone talked about in college for days."

"Oooooo-kay," I mused. "You say 'ended up running.' What did people think happened? Was it some kind of humiliation ritual, drugs, a mental breakdown?"

Chloë's gaze darted around the pub, then she leaned in conspiratorially and whispered, "I heard Darby drove him mad with black magic."

"Look, if you're gonna take the piss I'll have my money back. This is a serious matter."

"I am being serious!" she snapped in self-righteous fury. She picked up her drink and took a long, sulky swig. "That whole group of them was right into the spooky shit. One of the teachers caught Darby and Cassandra trying to do a ritual with a dead cat one weekend. Really dark stuff. They'd cut it open and drawn a pentagram with its blood. Mr Anderson lost his mind. He was a proper old holy roller, was Anderson. Dragged Darby out of there by his hair. Of course, his father's richer than God. Made it all go away, along with Mr Anderson. The way I hear it, he's teaching at a comprehensive school in Grimsby now."

"So, they were all into this stuff?"

"The boys, for sure. Darby and Aldous thought of themselves as dark wizards, and I'm talking Alistair Crowley here, not fucking Salazar Slytherin."

I nodded along and resisted the urge to roll my eyes. Too many years of listening to Billie talk out of her arse left me predisposed to dismiss the supernatural out of hand. But Crowley and the like were real people who acted according to their beliefs. It was an interesting angle that could certainly lend credence to the narrative I was building. As far as dirt went, black magic was right up there.

"I don't know how much Cassandra and Anastasia were into it, but they followed those two around like puppies. They'd do anything to impress them."

"What about Alice?"

Chloë frowned. "She was different. Not so obvious, you know? Kept to herself mostly, when I first met her. We were nearly friends, but then she started hanging around with those dickheads, through Cassandra. Turned into an arsehole as well. Shame, really. She used to be alright for a rich bitch."

"Okay, I'm building a picture here. What's the word around the college? Do people think she did it?"

Chloë laughed. "No way! Darby and Jerome were twice her size. I reckon it was those two knobbers, off their tits on something. Alice probably got a lucky shot in at the end after they killed the others."

I took another drink from my pint, which now revealed an ashtray after-taste. I winced but forced it down, draining half of the rank liquid in a single go. "It's a nice theory. Shame there's no evidence to back it up."

Chloë smiled. "Oh, I wouldn't say that. For another hundred, I'll tell you all about their secret shagging pad. As far as I know, the police never went anywhere near it. Who knows what you might find there...?"

***

I drained the rest of my beer, determined not to waste a single drop, and left The Roebuck with Chloë. "The nearest cashpoint is around the corner," she said merrily.

I withdrew the last bit of money in my account and stuffed it in my pocket, then gave her the other fifty I owed her. "I'll give you the other hundred once we get there, okay?"

"Right, follow me. It's not far."

I followed her along the main road, then down into a set of tree-lined side streets, with high privet hedges hiding large red-brick houses behind them. A few of them seemed to have been converted into dentists' surgeries, accountants' offices and the like. The cars parked outside were all less than two years old – BMWs in the main, but enough Audi and Mercedes mixed in to break up the impression this was some cheekily disguised local car dealership. Eventually, she stopped outside a house, looking up at a window on the top floor.

"Here we are." She grinned tightly.

She could have taken me to any house, and I was very conscious of that. "Are you sure that it's this one?"

Chloë rolled her eyes. "What were you expecting? Pentagrams on the windows? A big ol' statue of Baphomet in the front garden? They wanted somewhere close to the town where they could bring their conquests, but not in some scummy area."

"How do you know the police didn't know about this place?"

"I heard Darby bragging about it once. They said they'd set up a fake property management company in the Cayman Islands and bought it for cash."

"Cash? This place must have cost half a million quid!"

"Seven hundred, I think. I told you that prick's father isn't just a little bit rich. Anything less than a million to that family is basically pocket change."

I gave the house my full attention. No CCTV that I could see, and the alarm box on the wall was fake. I recognised the logo and design. There were no cameras on any of the neighbouring houses that I could see either, and the hedge obscured the view of the front door from the street.

"I thought you had stuff to do with the four people you gave my details to?"

She let out a sardonic laugh at that. "Nah, that was just to put you off in case you were a creep. These pricks wouldn't have anything to do with me, even before I slagged off King Cunt and his followers on Facebook." When I looked confused at this, she explained, "I'm here on a scholarship. All the joys of being a brainy middle-class kid in a school full of inbred numbskulls. The college only lets kids like me join to push up the average grade. The rich kids avoided me like they might catch cooties from the first day."

I stood there, sideswiped for a moment. Her eyes twinkled.

"Are you going to break in, then?"

"What? No, of course not! But thanks for showing me this place," I said, and handed her five more twenties. "You've got your money, so best you get going. I'll message you on Instagram if I need to ask you anything else."

"You *are* breaking in. I knew it!" She grinned. "Well, don't just stand here looking dodgy. Get on with it."

"Erm... what?"

"Well, I'm coming in there with you, obviously. I've always wanted to see what the famous Darby Love-Shack looked like inside."

"This isn't a game, Chloë," I hissed, placing a hand on her shoulder. "Look at me. My life is so badly fucked that a stretch inside for burglary would honestly feel like a nice rest at this point. I don't want you to screw up your life as well."

She smacked my hand away. "Then stop drawing attention to us and get on with it, you knob."

I glanced around the street, but there didn't seem to be anyone watching us apart from a massive black crow on the roof of the house opposite. Or was it a raven? I remembered my dream and shuddered. Then I flipped the bird at the bird and made my decision.

The widespread belief is that most burglaries happen in the dead of night, with a group of masked men sneaking around. In fact, the opposite is true. People wake up at all hours of the night to go to the loo, and they're hyper-alert for unexpected noises. There are hardly any regular people on the street, so those that are there stand out and get noticed. But during the daytime? Unexpected noises like breaking glass could be builders or accident-prone children. And that stranger walking up to the front door of that house could be a delivery driver or a tradesman. Which all means that, as long as you don't act suspiciously, the chances are most people won't pay any attention to a daytime burglar at all.

The first thing I did was to ring the doorbell and listen for any movement inside. I still wasn't entirely certain that Chloë was on the level and if someone did answer, I could always pretend to be lost and ask for directions. However, the house was silent. I rang it again, just to be on the safe side, but it soon became clear there was nobody home.

The lock was a simple Yale, the kind that would probably pop open with a well-placed kick but, given the general state of my body right now, I decided to pick the lock instead. It took me all of three seconds to open it, only slightly longer than it would have taken me if I'd been using a key. People really should take their home security more seriously.

Once Chloë and I were through the front door, I stopped and listened, gesturing at her to do the same. You really don't want any surprises if you're breaking into a property. There could be any number of reasons why someone hadn't answered the doorbell, so I wanted to be certain the place was empty. We stood there for a few minutes, but the only sound inside was a compressor in the refrigerator coming on.

"Okay, it looks like we are in the clear. Stay with me, and don't touch anything. If the police do come here at some point, the last thing you want is for them to find your fingerprints all over the place or bits of DNA lying around."

She nodded firmly and shot a glance up the stairs. My first instinct was to check the ground floor first, though. Thorough, methodical, quick. I pushed open the door to what I assumed was the living room and found a long, open-plan living space extending through to the rear of the property. There was what looked to be an original 1930s metal fireplace in the centre of the room, with a large oil painting dominating the space above it. The painting was disturbing, to say the least. It looked old. Really old and showed dozens of naked people falling from the clouds into a dark pit only to be consumed by hellish creatures: serpents with the heads of lions, men with the heads of wolves, and other creatures who genuinely defied description.

"That's Rubens' Fall of the Damned," Chloë murmured. "Not the original, of course. Someone destroyed that in the 1950s. It's an 18th-century knockoff. Quite a good one, though."

I tore my gaze from the painting. "And how would you know that, Chloë?"

"I'm an art student," she said archly. "They teach us these things."

I let it drop for now, but I had the feeling Chloë wasn't telling me the whole truth.

One thing that was becoming very clear to me as we searched was that the place was utterly spotless. Expensive leather sofas took up most of the living room, with other occult-looking ornaments positioned by the fireplace. None of those ornaments had so much as a speck of dust on them, despite the fact Darby and Jerome had been dead for a couple of months now. It made me nervous that some cleaner would come blundering in to find us poking around. There were no plates, glasses or cups on the kitchen worksurfaces, and the dishwasher was empty. I looked inside the fridge and found it filled with expensive bottles of champagne, caviar and a punnet of strawberries. Fresh ones. That sealed it. Someone was cleaning this place regularly and keeping the fridge well stocked.

"Come on," I said, the hairs rising on the back of my neck. "We need to be quick."

I made my way upstairs, with Chloë following fast on my heels. There were two bedrooms and a bathroom on the upper floor. The bathroom seemed relatively normal. Spotless, like the rest of the place, with black marble walls and flooring and a walk-in shower enclosure at the far end. The main bedroom was another matter. I found an array of elaborate equipment that would have made the Marquis de Sade blush. There was a bed – king sized, dressed in black satin sheets – but it had been pushed into the corner to make space for the central feature: a large metal frame that stretched from floor to ceiling. There were steel manacles anchored with chains to the frame at all four corners. Displayed on the walls were all manner of flails, blades, and other torturous pieces of equipment. Leather whips with steel studs at the end were the least of them. There were metal dildos with vicious-looking spikes on them. Gags. Apparatus that would not look out of place in a gynaecologist's office. A spice rack of lubricants and irritants. One vivarium housing an ant colony, another containing spiders and a third with some kind of snake coiled up.

I felt sick. This went beyond a bit of simple S&M. A good deal of the things on display here could do serious, permanent damage to a human body. I turned to hustle Chloë out of the room, tell her not to look, only to find that she had vanished already. I couldn't blame her. But then a nasty little thought wormed into my brain. I raced through to the next bedroom, which was almost identical in set-up, to find her standing over a laptop, tapping away.

I grabbed the computer from her hands, and she screamed at me, lashing out as she tried to take it back. Fingernails raked the side of my face, and I felt the warmth of fresh blood trickle down my cheek.

I held her back with one arm and glanced at the laptop screen. Understanding dawned, and a cavern of pity opened up in my chest.

There was a video file open, frozen in place. Pictured was a young woman strapped into the metal frame, facing away from the camera. Her bare back and buttocks were streaked with bloody gashes, presumably inflicted by one of the barbed whips.

"Oh god, Chloë. I'm so sorry."

She lunged for the laptop again. "Give it to me. I need to delete it! Get rid of them all."

I closed the window and saw it was just one of dozens in a folder titled "Chloë." There were other folders – lots of others – each with different names: Suzanna, Gemma, Phoebe, and more. They were all young women brought to this place and subjected to things that would haunt them for the rest of their lives. I highlighted the folder with Chloë's name on it and clicked delete.

"That's not enough," she protested in tears. "It needs to be destroyed. All of it. It needs to be fucking burned."

"It will be, Chloë. I promise you. No one will ever see these. I'll make sure that they're gone from the machine, and any cloud accounts they're backed up to. But right now, I need this laptop, and we don't have time to deal with it all here. LISTEN!" I hissed as she tried to grab it off me again. "There might be other things on here, things that could explain what happened at the school. The murders. It could be vital evidence. Once I've gone through it all, figured this shit out, I'll destroy it, I promise. Trust me. You have my word."

"No one can ever know," she sobbed. I've never been any good at dealing with crying women; I had this overriding urge to try to fix whatever had upset them, and usually ended up saying the wrong thing. This time, I had the good sense to stay silent until her tears had subsided. Then she straightened her back and wiped her eyes.

"Aw, shit." She sniffed. "I've scratched your face."

"Don't worry about it," I said with a wink. "It's probably an improvement."

"Shall we get the hell out of this place before the cleaners turn up?" she asked, her mask of indifference sliding back into place.

I nodded my agreement, slid the laptop into a backpack, and followed her down the stairs.

The street was still empty as we stepped out into the freezing air, the snow falling in big, fat flakes. The only witness to our exit was the black crow, still watching us from the rooftop of the building opposite.

I closed the door behind me and followed Chloë down the path. She reached the pavement, then gasped. She turned around stiffly to face me.

"Jack? H-help!" she stammered, her voice wavering.

Chloë's body was ramrod straight, muscles tense. Her eyes were red-rimmed, fresh tears streaming down her cheeks. Every part of her spoke of fear and confusion except her mouth, which was curled into a strange, lopsided, slightly manic grin.

Then Chloë Davidson stepped backwards into the path of a double-decker bus.

Chapter Ten

It was early evening by the time I made it back to my flat. I'd resisted the urge to flee the scene and waited for the emergency services to arrive. I'd given a statement to one of the attending officers while the fire service untangled Chloë's mangled corpse from beneath the wheels of the bus. The ambulance crew had stood around smoking cigarettes until it was time to remove the pieces of her body from the scene. A dozen passengers on the bus had seen her step out into the road so, as far as the officers were concerned, there was no sign of foul play. However, I knew differently.

Jack? H-help! Those two words haunted me, replayed in my mind as I went back over the incident again and again. I didn't know what the fuck it had been, but that wasn't suicide. Chloë was terrified and her movements had been odd. Forced. As if she'd been a puppet controlled by unseen hands. And that grin on her face. I'd seen that fucking grin before! On Marcus, right before he hit the pavement. What the fuck!?

I had a fight on my hands. I had to follow the evidence, build up the bigger picture without prejudice, without trying to form a narrative of explanation; that's the lawyers' purview. The detective, private or otherwise, is just there to gather data. I couldn't let myself get lured into the kind of thoughts my whole being was screaming – that there really was black magic at work. Not while there were other things, more rational things to consider. Like drugs. Marcus had been behaving erratically before he ended his life, which could indicate substance abuse.

Chloë had seemed fine, as far as that went, but I didn't know her, and there could be some dodgy new drug on the market. Post hypnotic suggestion? Maybe. I'd heard of it but had no real idea how it worked. Chloë had clearly been subjected to torture and degradation, though. Was it possible that Darby had gotten into her mind somehow? Seeing those recordings – and being back in that place – would almost certainly have triggered a strong traumatic response in the girl, but could it have triggered something else? Something planted there deliberately? But then, how could Marcus have been influenced in the same way?

I was clutching at straws, and I knew it. I was getting caught up in the means when I should have been concentrating on the motive and opportunity. I could only hope the answers would be found on Jarod Darby's laptop.

I sat at my desk, downed a large glass of brandy, then poured myself another one. I'd need to be a little bit numb to wade through the sewer of Darby's world – at least, that's the lie I told myself. What I really wanted to do was down the entire bottle to blot out Chloë's death, but I needed answers. Fast. If I didn't force myself to dig through the horrors on that laptop now, I'd find it twice as difficult tomorrow.

Despite best intentions, the bottle was half empty several hours later as I slammed the laptop lid closed, blinking tears from my eyes. I'd seen some nasty shit when I was on the Force. Things that made me lose faith in humanity and half-wish for a plague or meteor to wipe us out. But I'd never seen anything like the things contained on that laptop. The callous disregard for their victims sickened me to the core. Jarod Darby and Aldous Jerome hadn't just left permanent, physical scars on their victims. They'd mocked them as they did it. The little bastards laughed as they cut these girls, diminished their humanity, stripped away every last fragment of dignity or self-worth. There was not an ounce of empathy in either of them, no shred of compassion for these young women who'd begged and pleaded for them to stop. To these monsters, the girls were little more than pretty toys to be discarded, broken and bleeding, once they'd had their fun. I was glad they were both dead. If they'd still been drawing breath, I might have taken steps to remedy that.

None of those videos, however, had given me anything connected to the King's College massacre. I found that stuff later, hidden away on a private cloud account, stored on a Russian server. It was bizarre. The main content was high-resolution photographs of a book – a very old book. Every page had been carefully copied and saved to the account, along with dozens of text files that seemed to be notes and partial translations of the arcane symbols and drawings. I had no clue what this meant, in a literal sense, but there was something familiar there. I cross-referenced it with the crime scene photographs and saw that some of the drawings in the book had been replicated on site. *This was it!* Evidence that the boys had a direct connection to the ritual killings – though it remained to be seen how it all went so wrong for them. I'd bet good money Aldous Jerome never imagined himself crucified like this, tied to the cross with his own intestines. There were other images, many of which were far, far worse: a screaming woman being slowly skinned and carved by smiling assailants; a person being literally torn limb from limb by a naked howling mob; gleeful cannibalism. It put the Rubens to shame in sick imagination. I had no idea what it meant beyond the fact that somebody had clearly used it as a template at King's. It was all beyond me, but I did know someone who might be able to comprehend it; someone who knew a great deal more about monsters than I ever would.

***

"Jesus, fuck. How many have you had, Jack?" Billie asked from the doorway of her flat, wiping the sleep from her eyes. It was almost one o'clock in the morning. I'd been unable to reach her by phone, so I'd packed up the laptop and gone to see her in person.

"Half a bottle," I said, guiltily. Because she often drank with Chris and me, I'd assumed that she'd consider one a.m. an early night.

Her hands went to her hips, and she glared at me. "Half a bottle of what? Beer? Wine, maybe?"

"Brandy," I admitted.

She shook her head and shoved me away. "Go home and sleep it off, Jack. I'm not in the mood for your shit. And if you're hoping for a bootie call, you're bang out of luck. Especially the way you spoke to me the other day. Piss off. I'll talk to you in the week."

I'd already shoved my foot in the doorway. "It's not that, I swear. I need your help, Bill. A girl killed herself today, right in front of me."

Billie's expression softened with empathy. "That's horrible. I'm really sorry you had to see that, especially after what happened to your friends. But, Jack… I can't help you. Not now. Not when you're like this. Go home. I'll talk to you tomorrow, okay?"

I pressed the laptop into her hands. "Wait! I found stuff on this that's related. To the girl. And to my case. Things I don't understand.

Occult stuff. It's scaring the shit out of me. That's why I'm here. I'd never... you know..."

She stood back, weighed me up. Then, finally, she stepped aside and waved me in. "Fine. But if you so much as look at my tits, I'll drag you out by the nutsack. Got it?"

"Billie, I promise. It's nothing like that. I just really need your help because... I just... I don't know what I'm looking at."

"Okay, okay, I'll take a look. But not for long. I'm meant to be meeting my mother for lunch tomorrow, and I can do without her adding 'you look tired' to the usual stack of critical bullshit she's going to throw at me."

I'd only been to Billie's flat once before, when she'd brought Chris and me back after the pub closed. The night had gotten messy, and I'd ended up destroying her toilet after one of Chris's specially loaded joints and a whitey of epic proportions. The damn things could sit a rhino on its arse. While I'd been hugging the porcelain, Chris drank everything in the house, then pissed himself on Billie's sofa. Neither one of us had been invited back again, which was hardly surprising.

Billie's place was a nice ground-floor apartment in an old Victorian house on Broadwater Road. The front door led straight into a large living area containing two comfortable leather sofas and a large wooden chest of drawers that had been roughly sanded back and painted blue. A modest TV sat on top of this, and a few Banksy prints adorned the walls. The wooden floorboards had been varnished, and a large, fluffy beige rug covered much of the floor between the sofas and the TV. I went to sit down, but she shook her head.

"Not in here. Step into my office."

I followed her down a short corridor, past her bedroom – the door open, covers thrown back – to her workspace. The door was different to the others in her flat. While the living room and bedroom doors were the traditional wood-panel, the door to what would have originally been the second bedroom was made of solid steel, sealed with a biometric lock, and painted white so that it didn't stand out 'too much' to the casual glance, but I knew from looking at it that it would be easier to knock the wall down than try to force that door.

"I know what you're thinking," she said, "but those are load-bearing walls. If some troglodyte tries to go through those with a sledgehammer, he's likely to have the building fall on his head."

Billie pressed her thumb to the sensor, then tapped a lengthy code into the keypad. There came several solid clunks as the locks disengaged, then Billie pulled the door open, and we stepped inside.

I don't know quite what I was expecting the 'office' to look like, but I hadn't pegged her as a supervillain in design aesthetic. A large desk was positioned against the far wall, with four huge monitors fixed on a metal stand in an inverted T shape. These flickered to life as we entered the room, and I briefly glimpsed a series of maps – the northwest of England, by the looks of it. Red pins dotted it from Liverpool up to Preston on one screen. The other seemed to be a satellite image of part of the northeast. There was what seemed to be a large town filling the screen but without any roads leading to it. Before I could look closer, Billie called out, "Alexa, kill screens!" and all four of them winked out, leaving ghost images that quickly faded.

"Most people worry about being caught looking at porn. I've never seen anyone fret over maps before."

"Yeah, well, that's private stuff. Some 'cases' of my own, and the less you know about it, the better. Got it?"

I was taken aback by this, but she held my gaze firmly. I smiled tightly and nodded.

"Right then, let's have a look at this laptop."

I sat myself uncomfortably on a small filing cabinet while Billie settled into an oversized gaming chair. As she booted it up, I gave her the précis.

"The obvious shit on the laptop is sex stuff. Dark and nasty. You don't need to see that. What I want you to take a look at is on a server overseas. Russian, by the looks of it."

Billie's eyes widened. "You hooked this up to the internet from your flat? Fuck's sake, Jack, I thought you'd worked in cybercrime."

"For about six months. Why?"

"Hang on!" Her hands flew over the keys for a minute, then she started to explain. "Any decent cybercriminal would have whitelisted the IP addresses they wanted to be able to access the files, but they could also set traps – maybe even a self-destruct code if any other IP tries to get in. I'm just checking the access logs now."

Billie hunched over the machine and scrolled through a series of configuration files before turning on her own PC. After another few uncomfortable minutes, she sat back and said, "Right, we're okay. I've spoofed the original IP address from my home network, so the server thinks we're back wherever you stole this from. Now we can hook it up, assuming you've not already burned the data by floundering around."

She tapped away on the machine for a few more minutes while I got us some refreshments. As I returned, I noticed her shoulders had stiffened and her head was in her hands.

"What?" I asked, craning my head to look.

"Shit, Jack. This is bad. It's Really Fucking Bad. I— I don't know what to do with this. I mean... there are some people I can ask, but fuuuck!" She swivelled her chair around to face me. "Please tell me you didn't read any of the translations out loud?"

I looked past her at the screen, "What? Klaatu... Verata...? Ow!"

I rubbed my shin. I'd never seen Billie take a joke so poorly. I mean, she was five foot two and seven stone soaking wet, but suddenly my friend was scaring the shit out of me.

"DO NOT FUCK ABOUT, JACK!" she screamed, eyes wild, spittle flying. "When I say this is bad shit, I fucking mean it. You don't mess with this stuff, even as a joke. And you Don't Fucking Do It In My House!" she railed, poking my shoulder to punctuate each word.

"Wow. Shit, Billie, I'm sorry. I didn't know."

"No," she sighed. "You probably didn't. Look, you need to leave now. I'm going to have to talk to some people about this. It's gonna be a long night."

I reached for the laptop, but she slapped my hand away. "That stays here," she said. The steel in her voice brooked no argument, but I had to try.

"It's evidence, Bill. I need it for my case, and time's running out. Some of the pictures on it match the bodies at King's College. It proves premeditated murder!"

She shook her head. "It's worse than that, Jack. It looks like a sacrificial ritual. We need to find out why." She rubbed her eyes. "Go home. Try to sleep. I'll talk to you tomorrow."

I tried to object, but Billie was having none of it and before I knew what was happening, I found myself out on the street.

"Right," I said to the closed door. "I'll just... go home and wait then, shall I?"

The door didn't feel inclined to answer, so I trudged homeward through the snow. I was about halfway back to my flat when the hairs rose on my neck. I had the overwhelming feeling I was being watched. The sensation was so strong that I stopped and pushed the hood of my coat back, scanning the doors and windows for threats. There was no sign of anyone. There weren't even any taxis on the streets in these early hours. The snow wrapped the cars in white cotton wool, but there were no tyre tracks or footprints to indicate any intrusion. The world felt hushed – muted somehow, as if fearful that the leaden skies might fall should anything dare make a sound.

Then I saw it: the raven, watching me from the roof of a nearby house. The reflected glow of the streetlights stained its glossy black feathers with an orange hue and sparked fires in its beady eyes. It tilted its head to regard me, then took to the air with a throaty croak. Within seconds, the shadow of its wings had vanished into the flurry of fat falling snowflakes.

I hurried back to the relative safety of my flat, barely slowing my pace until I was safely through the door. Ten minutes later, my heart was still racing, and the very thought of sleep made me shudder. After the day I'd had, the last thing I wanted was to return to *that* dream.

I fished out my phone and was about to start doomscrolling Facebook when I remembered Stanley Armitage's online banking statement, nestled safely in my downloaded items. There'd been something about it that had been bugging me all day, but it had been pushed to the back of my mind as events overtook me.

Something about the account number and sort code felt familiar.

On impulse, I opened my own online banking app and input the details. I'd intended to set them up as a new payee, then try to send a small deposit to them to see how it appeared on my statement. As it happened, I didn't need to go that far. I already had the details recorded in there.

Stanley Armitage had been paid off by Hartington, Hartington and Jones.

It was all too much for me to get my head around. I'd been awake for almost twenty-four hours and this fresh discovery raised far more questions than I'd been anticipating. I couldn't think it through. Not now.

I picked up the bottle of brandy, sat in my armchair, and waited for the night to bleed into dawn.

Chapter Eleven

Consciousness is overrated. It took me a few moments to realise someone was banging on my front door, as it synchronised with the hammering in my skull. Just because the booze is expensive and smooth, it doesn't mean its effects are any less cruel the morning after— a fact I was only too keenly aware of in the moment. It didn't help that I'd eventually blacked out in my armchair, slumped to the side. My body was cramped and when I tried to spur myself into motion, my ribs complained bitterly. Biting back a string of expletives, I dragged myself to the top of the stairs and half walked, half slid to the bottom.

I'd already dragged the door half open when it occurred to me that I hadn't checked to see who was there first. If it was Arthur and the goon squad come early, I was fucked, though right now being beaten to death in the street might have been a blessed relief. Instead, it was Billie pushing her way in out of the snow.

She looked exhausted. Dark rings hung beneath her eyes, and her face was pale and pasty. This was despite the uncharacteristic use of makeup. She was wearing a floral dress beneath her coat, too. *Weird.*

I'd never seen her in a dress before. I was about to comment, then I remembered she was meeting her mother for lunch. Even I know when to keep my mouth shut sometimes.

"Where the hell have you been?" she asked, elbowing me in the ribs as she pushed past me. "I've been trying to call you for an hour. I thought something had happened to you."

"Brandy," I croaked. "All whispers are appreciated. Make yourself at home."

I followed her up the stairs as fast as my condition would allow while my mind scrambled to remember if there was anything gross on display. Fortunately, I'd not spent much time in my home since Robyn cleaned me out. Still, Billie looked concerned at the evidence remaining.

"When was the last time you ate anything that didn't come from a burger van, Jack?"

"Last week," I replied, a little defensively. "I had some money, so I ate at The Dolphin."

Billie arched her right eyebrow at me. "And what did you have from the pub? Salad maybe? Veggie lasagne?"

"A burger," I mumbled.

She shook her head. "You need to start taking care of yourself, mate. Seriously, you keep treating your body like this, you're not going to be around for much longer."

"It's not that easy. Have you seen the cost of food these days? I can't afford the good stuff, let alone find the time to cook it."

Billie picked up the empty brandy bottle and glared at me. "But you can afford the essentials, right?"

I practised my best kicked puppy look, and she sighed. She'd seen it all before. "Christ, Jack, I'm not your mum. You've got to start looking after yourself. Which brings me to the reason for my visit."

She handed the laptop back to me, her face etched with revulsion. "This is nasty stuff. Dark as Hell. I'd tell you to walk away from this, but I know you're not going to."

I shook my head then regretted it as the room spun. I eased myself into a chair and said, "No. Not now. Not after what happened to Chloë yesterday. You should have seen her face, Billie. She was terrified. She begged for help before she went under that bus. She knew what was happening to her, but she couldn't stop herself. I've been going over it in my head, and I can't make sense of it. Something those two bastards did to her, maybe. I don't know how, but I'm fucking well gonna find out."

Billie nodded. "I understand, Jack. I probably wouldn't have before last night, but now... yeah, I get it." She handed me a small metal box. "Here you go, then. This is the original hard drive. I deleted all of those fucking videos, then cloned it. The clone is in the laptop. That way, when you hand it over, they won't be able to recover any of the deleted files. No one should see those ever again."

"You watched them?"

She nodded, "I went through everything on there. Then ran some utilities on the thing to find any hidden or deleted files. It turned a bunch of other stuff up. It's all there on the original. But promise me this – when your job is done, you'll shred the fucking thing."

"Of course. I promise. Those girls will keep their anonymity. You said you found other things?"

"More of the same stuff. Rituals, scans of other old books, and some photographs. Old ones. Black and white, showing the same sort of murders as you found in the book."

"You think these little pricks are copycats?"

"I don't know. Could be. Or they could have summoned up something a fuck load scarier. I've sent the relevant files to some people I trust who know a lot more about this stuff than I do. We'll have to wait to see what they say."

I managed a bleak smile. "There was me thinking you were the foremost authority on weird shit."

"Far from it." She wiped her hand down her face and took a sip of her coffee. "I know just about enough to rattle some cages and put myself in danger, but Jack – this thing is way outside of my experience. I don't know what's at the heart of it, but it's bad. Really fucking bad. If you won't drop this, then at least promise me you'll be careful."

"Don't worry. I have no intention of kicking any buckets in the near future."

She stood up and pecked me on the cheek. "You'd better not. Could you imagine what life would be like if Chris was my only friend? My liver couldn't take it. Right, I have to go. I need to face evil in another form."

When I looked confused, she grinned and said, "My mother. Sunday dinner. Where I shall be quizzed on why I look so knackered. To which I shall reply, 'My arsehole friend, Jack, kept me up all night.' And *that* will lead to a whole other deeply tedious conversation about relationships, ticking clocks, and the like— But don't worry, that gets thrown at me every week regardless."

I snorted and walked her down the stairs to the front door. "Thanks, Billie. I really appreciate your help on this. I didn't know who else to ask."

"Yeah, well I can't exactly say it's been a pleasure. You owe me big time for this," she groused. "I'll be in touch when I find anything out, though."

Billie stepped out into the snow and almost collided with another woman. Robyn. Because my day was long overdue going to dogshit.

"Oh, Hi, Jack. I hope I'm not... interrupting anything," she said, with a meaningful glance at Billie. She held out a limp hand. "Hello, there. I'm Robyn."

"I know who you are," Billie replied in a tone that would cut glass. Then she turned her back on the other woman and jabbed a finger at me. "Be careful, Jack. Please." And then she walked away.

"She seems nice," said Robyn, dripping sarcasm.

"Make it quick. I'm not in the mood."

"The mood for what?" she asked with a sly little grin.

"For any of it. I've had a shitty few days, no sleep, and I'm probably going to get killed later tonight unless you've brought my money."

Robyn ignored me, went through to my living room, swept some junk onto the floor and sat on my sofa. She reached into her oversized Mulberry bag and produced a large brown envelope. "OK, first of all, let's get this out of the way. I couldn't get hold of *all* the cash because the banks are closed, but I've managed to pull together something like six thousand for you. I trust that'll keep your debtors off your back for a while longer?"

I snatched the envelope from her and checked the contents. It should just about cover the debt if I could get it to Eddie before the end of the day. I counted the notes twice, to be sure, making a show of checking random notes for their watermarks and metallic strips. The newer plastic notes were harder to forge than the old-style paper ones, but I wouldn't put anything past Hartington.

Finally, I sat opposite her, the envelope in my hands. "OK, thank you for returning *some* of the money you stole. I'll expect the rest first thing tomorrow when the banks open."

I gestured to the door, but she just sat there, shifting uncomfortably on the sofa.

"Was there something else?"

"Well, I wanted to see if you'd gotten anywhere with the case?"

"Fuck's sake, you only saw me two days ago. These things take time. This really isn't going to work if you keep riding my arse every two minutes for an update."

Her attitude changed as I spoke, the bravado melting away under my scorn to reveal something much more vulnerable. Almost tearful.

"I'm sorry, Jack. It's just... I asked Stuart about the CCTV footage – like you said – and he bit my head off. Told me to keep my nose out of things that don't concern me. It seemed important, so I hung around after work yesterday to dig around. I thought everyone else had gone, but I had an email from him last night that just said, 'I'm watching you.' Ever since then, it's like I can feel him over my shoulder the whole time."

I rolled my eyes. "He's just trying to scare you off. Don't worry about it—"

"But I am worried. You don't know what he's capable of. Every time I turn around there's someone looking at me. Different people, but always eyes. Even when I'm at home by myself I feel like I'm being watched. And I keep seeing this crow—"

"What?" I snapped, my bubble of cynicism suddenly popping. "What crow?"

She shook her head, "I don't know. It sounds stupid, I know. There are crows everywhere. But I keep seeing the same one, I swear. Bloody huge thing."

"A raven?" I said.

"Maybe. I don't know. I've never done the whole Tower of London thing. But listen, everywhere I go, it seems like it's sitting on a rooftop or a lamppost nearby, just... watching me."

I rubbed at my jaw and Robyn laughed.

"Sorry. Just saying it out loud makes me realise how ridiculous it sounds. I'm sorry. You're probably right. I'm just being paranoid."

"No. You're not being paranoid," I said, nausea washing over me. "I've been seeing it as well. And there *have* been some... developments in the case as it happens. It seems that Jarod Darby and his buddy Aldous Jerome were messing with some occult crap, and they had a sideline in mutilating teenage girls."

Robyn's eyes widened in shock. "What? Are you serious?"

"Deadly. Yesterday I—"

"Hold on," she said, reaching into her bag. "I get the feeling I'm going to need a drink before I hear the rest of this." She produced another bottle of expensive brandy, the twin of the one I'd polished off the night before.

When I appeared reticent, she rolled her eyes, removed the metal seat from the bottle, and then took a swig straight from the neck of the thing. "There you go. Satisfied? Now, are you getting us some glasses, or are we doing this straight from the bottle."

I took the brandy from her and took a swig of my own. It felt wrong, somehow, to treat something as refined as this with such a lack of respect. This was a drink to be sipped and savoured, not glugged like a bottle of own-brand crap. But part of me revelled in that. I handed her the bottle back and then told her about the previous day.

By the time I'd finished recounting what I'd learned so far, the bottle was half empty, and Robyn was in tears. I was experiencing a conflicted emotional state at this. While I'd more or less accepted that Robyn had been put in the firing line by Hartington from day one, I'd never found it easy to forgive and forget. Still, she seemed genuinely scared by what I'd told her, what she'd seen on the laptop and how it tied into her own experiences. And I never could stand to see a woman cry. Do these sound like excuses to you too? Well, we all do stupid shit.

I moved to sit beside her, placed a tentative hand on her shoulder and said, "I know it's messed up, but we'll get to the bottom of this. It'll be okay."

She looked at me with red-rimmed, puffy eyes and said, "How can you know that? We don't know what the fuck is going on."

"I don't know. I suppose I just have… faith that there's some kind of rational explanation for this shit. We'll work it out, and then it'll be done."

Robyn threw her arms around my neck, pulled herself against me and sobbed. The awkwardness jumped several levels, and I became intensely aware of her breath against my neck, the scent of her perfume and the warmth of her body pressed against mine. I returned the hug awkwardly, holding her until her tears subsided. She pulled away a fraction, her face inches from mine, and looked deep into my eyes. She seemed to be searching for something. Anything she could believe in and draw comfort from. Then she leaned in and kissed me deeply.

The kiss was hard. Fuelled by passion and fear. Soft and yielding at first, then almost painful against my split lip. Her tongue flicked against mine, and I could taste her vanilla lip gloss. All of those feelings I'd been trying to suppress came roaring back with a vengeance, but I pushed them down with a herculean effort and pulled away from her, gasping for breath. "Robyn, I know you're scared and upset, but I'm not sure if this is—"

"Jack," she said, as she pushed me back against the sofa and wriggled onto my lap, grinding against me. "Shut the fuck up."

My objections duly silenced, I returned the kiss, my hands sliding up her back. She reciprocated by pulling my t-shirt up over my head.

My right hand found the clasp of her bra strap, and I undid it with a click of my fingers – a trick I'd learned in college – and this time, it was Robyn's turn to gasp in surprise. My hands slipped beneath the sheer fabric of her blouse and slid across her back's warm skin, tracing little lines with my fingernails against the sensitive flesh. She pulled away and slowly unbuttoned her top, taking her time, fixing me with a gaze that set my heart racing. Then she removed the blouse and bra, throwing them onto my living room floor. She undid my fly, then raised herself up on her knees, letting her skirt fall away. My hands slid up her thighs to her silky black panties. I pushed the fabric to one side and felt her hotness against my fingertips. She pushed my hand away, then kissed me hard as she guided me inside her body. She pushed down hard, and I reciprocated, moving my body against hers, into hers, harder and faster, sweating and groaning in carnal ecstasy until, finally, we collapsed in sweet release, our bodies covered in a sheen of sweat. We lay there panting, grinning, caressing for a while, then she leaned over and kissed me on the brow.

"I knew there was something I liked about you," she said. "Thank you. I needed to feel something other than fear."

I pushed myself up from the sofa and limped across the living room to where Chris's laptop rested on a coffee table.

"What are you doing?" she asked, propping herself up on an elbow.

I winked at her, powered up the machine and logged into Chris's infested Windows XP installation. "Getting to the bottom of this shit and going on the offensive." I slotted the pen drive Hartington had given me into the laptop. "I don't suppose you know the name of the company your office uses to deal with IT problems, do you?"

***

As much as Hartington had managed to steer me in the direction he wanted, the arsehole seemed to have forgotten that I knew him just as well as he knew me. I might have succumbed to alcoholism, but I could still be a devious bastard when I wanted to be. I'd already put Step 1 of my plan into motion shortly after he'd given me the evidence package.

I'd suspected from the beginning that the Shart had laced the drive with malware, because I'd seen him use this trick on people before. Hell, I'd helped him do it. It hadn't taken me long to find the custom trojan horse application hidden within the files. It seemed this would have given him full and open access to my machine if I'd been stupid enough to plug it into my own laptop, which is why I'd used that barebones installation with no network connection. Now, I plugged the device into an unprotected machine. No firewall, no antivirus. And crawling with every nasty bit of malware that had made it into the wild over the last couple of decades. I was astonished the damned thing even functioned; it was so horribly infested. And I'd just stuck Hartington's virtual dick into it.

Whatever machine Stuart Hartington was using to spy on me had been given a massive dose of digital clap.

Now it was time for Step 2.

I sat in a cafe across the street from the offices of Hartington, Hartington and Jones. It was a modernist nightmare of glass and steel that clashed with every building in the area, drawing appalled gazes from everyone who passed by. The structure was the architectural equivalent of a Ford Mustang with a fibreglass spoiler the size of a small aircraft wing, neon LED lights, go-faster stripes, and a set of pink fluffy dice. It was horribly crass, and everyone knew it except the smug fannies sitting inside. I felt a little bit of my soul shrivel up and die whenever I looked at it. It was my own personal Heart of Darkness. But I needed to get inside.

NIGHT BLEEDS INTO DAWN

Fortunately, Hartington, Hartington and Jones were just the sort of bastard company that made people work all over the weekend. This meant that the offices would be open, and the receptionist almost certainly hungover, seething with resentment. Of course, the senior partners would not have given up their weekends for anything. This would be a skeleton staff of office juniors and interns for the most part. Nobodies, save for the occasional exec pretending to work so they could avoid their kid's birthday party. Fundamentally, the chances of me running into anyone who actually knew me was remote.

"Are you sure this is going to work?" Robyn asked, her face creased with concern.

"Not in the slightest," I said as I pulled on the black cap. "How do I look?"

Robyn frowned as she took in my improvised outfit. Hartington, Hartington and Jones outsourced all their IT to a firm called Capital Systems, a massive conglomerate whose main office was in Bangalore. It had taken me a matter of minutes to grab their company logo from their website and download it to my antique smartphone. We'd made a quick stop off at a novelty T-Shirt printing company in a nearby shopping centre, and Bob's your uncle. I'd emerged with a black T-shirt and cap emblazoned with their logo, slapped more or less in the right place. It wouldn't stand up to close scrutiny, but I was betting it would get me past reception on a cold, snowy Sunday afternoon.

Robyn pulled a face and said, "You look like shit. You've got black eyes and a split lip, and your uniform looks dodgy as hell.' Hold on a moment." Robyn took her phone from her bag and called a number. "Yes, hello? This is Miss Whittaker. I'll be coming into the office in a moment. Is Mr Hartington available? Uh-huh. Well, when do you expect him back? Fine, thank you."

She turned to me. "Your outfit might not fool a child, but Heidi's in reception today, and she's an idiot. Good news – Hartington is out. He dropped his laptop off an hour ago." She smiled at me. "On balance I have to say, Jack, I'm impressed!"

"I do have my moments," I said with a grin. I put on my cheap cap, adjusting the peak to shadow my bruised face. "Not many, I'll admit, but I do have them."

She smiled. "So it would seem. Okay, you go first. I'll follow on behind you in a couple of minutes."

I left the cafe and hurried across the street to the entrance of the building. The snow was still falling, though not as heavily as before. There weren't many cars on the road. London drivers can barely cope with a centimetre of snow; their cars are used so infrequently that they generally have no clue how to drive in those conditions. There was considerably more than a centimetre covering the capital now, piled up in great slushy slabs on the edge of the roads, making the surfaces slippery and hard to navigate. You'd have thought that more of the city's residents would have relished the chance to put their four-wheel drives to good use, but they either huddled inside or wandered down to the local parks with their children.

I stepped through the smoked glass sliding doors into the foyer of Hartington, Hartington, and Jones, stamping the snow from my feet. Then, conscious of the CCTV and keeping my face down, I sauntered over to the reception desk.

Heidi looked up at me with an expression of boredom and disinterest so profound I feared that she'd lapse into a coma before I could introduce myself.

"Hi," I said brightly. I'm here from Capital Systems. Got a laptop to fix, I understand for Mr…" I made a show of referring to my phone. "Hartington?"

Heidi grunted and pushed a pad across to me. "You'll need to sign in." She'd already turned her attention back to her screen before I'd picked up the pen.

I scrawled some fake details onto the pad, then stepped past the desk towards the stairs.

"Wait!" said Heidi, and my heart lurched. Had she recognised me? I'd more or less worked out of this office for several years and had been married to one of the senior lawyers after all. I half-turned towards her, shoulders tense, to see a plastic wallet being waved at me. "You need your *pass*," she snapped, rolling her eyes at my incompetence.

I took the lanyard from her and was pretty sure I heard her mutter, "pisshead" under her breath as I left. I scurried through the turnstile and made my way to the elevator. I was mildly disturbed to realise that a well-dressed man had followed me to the elevator. A quick glance in the mirror as we stepped inside was enough to verify he was no-one I knew, but I did see him wrinkle his nose in distaste. While the T-shirt was new, I'd not showered since yesterday morning and was a little on the ripe side. A small voice in the back of my mind told me that there was a remote chance that this was one of those drunken ideas that had seemed perfectly sensible to my pickled brain but was actually about as stupid as it got. I pushed that voice aside firmly. I didn't need that sort of negativity right now. Besides, the plan was working so far.

I hurried along the corridors, confident in my invisibility as a mere manual worker in an office environment and let myself into Hartington's office.

It hadn't changed much since I'd handed in my resignation. The chair was new – a large, leather-bound monstrosity closer to a throne than an office chair. The desk was the same massive slab of antique oak he'd had for years. Apparently, it had belonged to his grandfather. It was the only thing I could ever remember him being sentimental over. I found myself wondering again if Sarah really had been seeing him behind my back and fought the urge to carve an expletive into its surface. Instead, I sat down in the chair to begin my work.

Hartington's laptop was sitting on the desk with a pink Post-it note attached to its lid, that simply read, 'Fix it!' I wasn't interested in the laptop, though. I was after the huge iMac desktop which dominated the room— the 'Command Centre,' as Hartington had once called it. *Prick.* I powered the machine up, crossed my fingers, then typed in the Shart's old password.

My gamble paid off. Hartington was one of those people who thought he was above key advice like 'change your passwords regularly' or 'if you are going to create a VPN connection between your machine and an unknown machine, you might just want to take some precautions against viruses'. In this instance, it seemed that he'd been reluctant to give up his 'Stew!3i5ag0d!' password that he'd been so proud of a few years ago. I made a mental note to investigate what other devices and accounts the dickhead used this for, then returned my attention to the job at hand.

I'd describe his filing system as chaotic and childlike, but that would be too kind. Imagine a number of chimpanzees getting hold of some edibles, then shortly afterwards deciding to be 'helpful'. Most of his files were scattered across his desktop, along with links to various websites and applications. It took me a few minutes to sift through the garbage on the hard drive before coming across a folder entitled 'King's College'. A subfolder was called 'For Jack' and contained all the files I'd been given on the USB drive. The rest of the folder contained a whole raft of material I'd not been privy to. So much for our transparent working relationship. And there were *gigabytes* of data in there, far more than I could wade through safely here. I plugged in a clean pen drive and started copying the files across. Then my phone buzzed in my pocket. I fished the device out and saw Robyn's warning: 'He's Back!'

I glanced at the progress bar and discovered it was less than halfway across. 'Stall him!' I replied, then ducked behind the desk and prayed for a miracle.

A shadow passed in front of the opaque glass door, and I heard the unmistakable click of a door handle. Suddenly, my genius idea didn't seem so clever. There was no way to explain this away. I'd effectively broken into my employer's offices to steal restricted information. The fact I should have been given it from the start was immaterial, as was the fact that Stuart Fucking Hartington had paid off the security guard at King's College to obtain it. Hartington would sack me out of hand and then make good on every threat he'd made against me. I'd be out on the street, probably never work again and, worst of all, have my access to Steph revoked. I held my breath as the door swung open.

Then Robyn's voice broke through the silence. "Hi, Stuart. I was hoping I could have a minute?"

"Not now, Robyn," he said curtly, "I'm due on a conference call in five minutes."

"Ah, damn. Sorry. It's just that I saw Jack earlier, and said he'd retrieved a laptop that belonged to Jarod Darby. There were some... interesting things on it, apparently. He also mentioned a flat that the police were unaware of?"

"Jesus!" Hartington hissed. "Do you have the machine?"

"Yes, it's in my office. I thought you might want to see it before I handed it over to the police. Was that wrong?"

The door clicked closed again and as their footsteps receded, I could hear Hartington muttering to Robyn rapidly in hushed tones. I couldn't make out the details, but he did *not* sound happy. I checked that the download had finished, grabbed the pen drive from the Mac, then got the fuck out of Dodge.

Chapter Twelve

Robyn and I were in a jubilant mood when we entered The Dolphin. She seemed almost ready to pounce on me again, right there in the foyer by the toilets.

"Oh my god, I can't believe we did that," she said, a mischievous grin plastered across her face. "I can't believe *I* did that. My god, if he'd caught us, I'd have been sacked. Maybe even disbarred."

"Yeah, but we didn't get caught, and now we've got all of his dirty little secrets – at least as far as this case is concerned."

She took my hands in hers and then kissed me. "You are a bad influence, Jack Carlton."

"Yeah, because you never did anything illegal or immoral before you met me."

"It's true!" She grinned. "I was a paragon of virtue before you corrupted me."

Hand in hand, we pushed the doors open and stepped into the pub.

"Well, well," boomed a scornful voice from the bar, "if it isn't Robbin Cunt and her pet fuckin' eejit."

I looked up and found Chris and Billie sitting on bar stools, glaring at us both. Billie shook her head in disgust and turned her back.

Shit.

"Hey, guys. Look, it's not what you think."

"Oh, so yeh haven't been playing hide the sausage with the thieving bitch then?"

This wasn't going to plan. "No, I mean, she's not the person we thought she was."

"Oh, do tell," Chris snarked. "She's undercover, is she? Working for a secret governmental agency, yeah? Keeping you skint for your own good so you don't die of cirrhosis? Very charitable!"

"Well, she did... I mean, yeah, that happened, but we've worked it out."

Chris glugged his pint and waved to Jean behind the bar to replace it. "Fuck's sake. I'm hardly one to lecture a bloke about thinking with the little head instead o' the big 'un, but there *are* limits, pal. Even yer evil ex would be better than this toxic slag."

Robyn pulled her hand free from mine, mortified. "I think it would be better if I left," she said quietly.

"Aye, off ye fuck, love. Try not te drug anyone on the way out, eh?"

I grabbed Robyn's wrist before she could leave. "No, Robyn, you stay. We came here to celebrate, and that's exactly what we're going to do. Go and grab a table. I'll get the drinks in. Please." I turned to Chris and gave him a hard stare. He glared right back at me, eyes bright with hurt and defiance. I sighed and clapped him on the shoulder. "Listen, mate, I appreciate your concern, but you need to back off. She's here because I invited her. I'm working this case with her, and she just helped me get crucial evidence from the Shart. This could make all the difference. If you can't be happy for me, feel free to stay out of my way."

Billie turned to face me, eyes pained. "Jack, you can't blame Chris for being worried about you. That... woman hasn't exactly had your best interests at heart. We don't want to see you getting stitched up again. Or hurt."

I could feel my temper beginning to fray. "I know the risks, Billie. Honestly. But things are happening to me – things I can't explain. And now they're happening to her, too. She's not just Hartington's pet anymore; she's got skin in the game." My voice dropped down to a whisper, to prevent anyone else hearing. "And like I say, she just helped me get into the fucker's office and grab the CCTV footage he'd been keeping from me. She even ran interference when he turned up unexpectedly, so can we all please give the fucking hostility a rest?"

Billie's shoulders sagged, and she held up a finger to quieten Chris's objections. "Okay, Jack. I hope you know what you're doing. I won't pretend to be happy about it, but I trust you. Listen, though. Before you go over there to celebrate or whatever, I need to talk to you. One of my contacts got back in touch, and it's not good news. This ritualistic stuff isn't just sadistic, it's demonic."

"Yeah, I figured. I mean, we already know the scumbags were into the whole heavy-metal Satanist garbage."

"I'm not talking about the plastic occultist crap; this is the real stuff. Benjamin's a bit of an arrogant twat normally, to tell you the truth, but he sounded proper scared when he got back to me. Shaken. He's already in the car, on his way from Leeds. Whatever he found out, he's taking it really seriously."

Great, I thought. I needed another conspiracy nutter like I needed an extra bollock. But I kept my thoughts to myself and thanked her. I didn't want to upset Billie any more than I already had done. She'd put up with a lot of shit from me over the years, but she kept coming through. Whether it was bullshit or not, the killers believed it was real. Fundamentally, that was all that mattered right now.

"Ye gonna look at the footage now?" asked Chris in a subdued tone.

"Don't be daft. A pub's hardly the sort of place to go through shit like that. We were just going to have a quick drink, then go back to mine to check it out."

"Hey, Jean," Chris yelled. "Can we use the function room for a couple of hours?"

"Knock yourself out, love," Jean called back. "Just don't make a mess in there. And if I catch you doing lines on the mirrors again, you'll be barred, Chris. For *life* this time."

"Aw, Jean, ye know ah love ye. There'll be no shenanigans, ah swear."

Jean didn't look particularly convinced by this, but she came to unlock the double doors at the far end of the room.

Chris bowed and waved us over with a flourish. "Ta-da! Problem solved."

I was a long way from being sure about this. At least in the open bar, Jean might be able to stop Chris and Robyn from killing each other. Plus, I really had no idea what was on the files we'd grabbed. Billie would be discreet, I was sure, but Chris? Get a few drinks in him, the details would be common knowledge all over North London.

"Chris, while I appreciate the effort, I don't have a laptop here. It's just a pen drive," I said weakly, holding up the device.

"Gotcha covered," said Billie as she produced a laptop from her bag. She snatched the flash drive from my fingers, drained her drink and marched off towards the function room. She paused by the doors, turned back to the three of us and said, "Well, are you lot coming or what?"

Chris needed no encouragement and followed Billie into the function room. Robyn grabbed my arm and hissed, "What the fuck, Jack?"

I shrugged. "Billie's been helping me. She's fine, honestly."

"And your charming Scottish mate?"

"Yeah... Chris is— I mean, he's... He'll get bored and wander off within five minutes. Don't worry about it."

"Jack, I put my career at risk to get those files. I'm not happy showing them to some loudmouthed idiot. We haven't even seen what's on there ourselves yet!"

I sighed. "It is what it is. I'll keep him under control, I promise. Let's just get in there or they might start without us."

I paid for our drinks, and we joined Chris and Billie in the back.

The Dolphin's function room was not somewhere I'd ventured often. It was reserved for private parties for the most part, and I didn't tend to get invited to many of those. Not that anyone saw The Dolphin as an ideal venue for parties, it was more that it was safe ground. Familiar comfort for our small community of losers. About a year and a half ago, someone had their wedding reception there and, from the look on the bride's face, the marriage was on the rocks before the happy couple cut the cake. The wallpaper was nominally posher in here, but at least as old as the rest of the decor, peeling in places, ripped in others, and someone had drawn a large phallus on a painting of King George VI. Collapsible tables and some rather unstable-looking chairs were stacked at the far end of the room. The place had an unpleasant, musty smell, like clothes left in a washing machine for too long. Billie and Chris had already dragged out one of the tables along with four chairs and were now sitting in front of a large expensive-looking laptop. I walked over and tapped Chris on the shoulder. "Move your arse," I said, thumbing over to one of the chairs off to the side.

"Ah, shite. Consigned te the cheap seats, am ah? I don't suppose ye thought te bring popcorn?"

I shook my head and sat next to Billie while Chris and Robyn jostled for position behind my shoulders. Billie rolled her eyes, shifted over, then slotted the drive into a port on her computer.

"Where did you say you got this, Jack?" she asked without looking up.

"Hartington's office. Straight from his hard drive."

"Breaking, entering *and* hacking. I'm impressed. The state you were in when you left mine last night, I'm honestly surprised you were capable of getting out of bed, let alone cybercrime."

"It was hardly Mission: Impossible," I said sheepishly. "And I had help."

"Alka Seltzer?"

"That, too. Smartarse."

Billie spent another few moments doing the digital equivalent of sealing the video files in a lead box, then selected one at random from the crowded directory.

"Right, then," she said. "Let's see what we have here."

The video was from a camera set high up with a view of a familiar grand entrance hall. King's College. An ornate double staircase dominated the room, and on either side of the staircase, around twenty feet in the air, were two marble statues of angels, one with a sword held in a double-handed grip, the other with its arms outstretched. This was the second crime scene. Where Aldous Jerome was crucified. To say I was conflicted would be an understatement. After witnessing what the nasty little shit stain had done to those girls at his S&M den, I had very little sympathy for him. I was glad that he paid for his crimes. But I wasn't exactly looking forward to watching it unfold. What I felt was more of a nagging, morbid curiosity as to exactly how it had been accomplished. Of the four killings, this was the one that seemed to defy rational explanation – not in intent, necessarily, but in the practical mechanics. As my mind began recalling details from the still photographs, I began to feel less and less sure I was ready to watch the full show in high-def, technicolour video.

"Guys, I don't think we should be doing this. The photos were awful and watching this play out is going to be beyond disturbing."

"Aw, stop being a fuckin' pussy and get on wi' it," said Chris. He'd managed to pop out to the bar and get a packet of pork scratchings in lieu of popcorn. He plucked out a large one that looked like an infected toenail and popped it into his mouth, crunching loudly.

"Fine," I said. "Don't say I didn't warn you."

At first, there wasn't much to see. The entrance hall was illuminated by shafts of moonlight streaming through the windows at the top of the staircase, casting a silver glow across the foyer. It was a peaceful, if slightly spooky, scene. I half expected to see Bela Lugosi appear. Then a burst of static flickered across the video, and I saw movement at the bottom of the screen. Four figures entered the frame, and it was immediately apparent that there was something very wrong with them. They didn't *move* like people should. There was something insectile about them. They scurried and scuttled across the polished wooden floor of the hallway as if their movements were illuminated by strobe instead of the cool, white light of the gibbous moon. The movement of their limbs was wrong somehow, and they left bloody footprints behind them on the polished wooden floor. If I had the timeline right, this would have been just after Anastasia Grier-Snelling had been torn apart – by all four of these bastards, apparently!

They reached the foot of the staircase and then as one, they turned their heads to look directly at the camera. Aldous Jerome, Jarod Darby, Cassandra Foss and Alice Wells, each with jet-black eyes, a single silver pinprick of light shining in each pupil. I shuddered. It felt like they were looking straight at me through the camera. The black eyes could have been contact lenses or a trick of the light, but the effect was unsettling, to say the least.

Then Aldous Jerome tore his blood-soaked shirt from his body and, still holding my gaze, ran one of his fingernails across his midsection. His flesh parted as if he'd used a scalpel. Skin and muscle tissue opened smoothly to display the coiled purple tubes within. Blood spilled from the open wound, pooling on the floor beneath him, but Jerome's face was a mask of joy. His mouth spread in a triumphant, maniacal grin, but his eyes told a different story. The blackness drained from them, leaving the stark terror of a teenage boy to peer out from this mask.

Chloë had looked much the same as she stepped in front of that bus. They were the eyes of someone fully aware of the horrors being inflicted on them but powerless to prevent it.

I bit my cheek and groaned as Jerome plunged both hands into the open wound and began tugging spool after spool of intestines out, letting them unravel on the floor by his feet. Billie and Robyn made their own sounds of horror and disgust, while Chris crunched down on another pork scratching. I couldn't look away. Because at this point, things went from strange and horrible to utter madness.

Alice Wells grabbed the mortally wounded boy by the throat with one hand and began crawling up the wall like fucking Spider-Man, trailing a bloody streak behind her. As she reached the stone angel, Darby and Foss stretched their arms out and *floated* up to meet her. Aldous Jerome was now screaming, and somehow the lack of an audio feed made the whole scene worse. Cassandra Foss took great loops of the boy's guts and wrapped them around the angel like ropes while Alice and Darby rammed the boy's triceps through the pointed marble fingers of the statue, hanging him from them like Christ. Then Alice removed Jerome's pants and tore his penis off with her bare hands, stuffing it into his mouth like a gag. She floated down a little, showering in the blood as it gushed from the boy's torn root, rubbing her arms, face and breasts in the hot red spray.

Jerome's body finally slumped and was still. The three remaining monsters then floated back down to the floor by the staircase and scurried out of frame, presumably towards the kitchen and the next horrific murder.

Ashen faced, Billie slammed the lid down on the laptop, swearing and sobbing, and thrust the machine away from her. Tears were running down Robyn's face, too, along with her makeup. A crunch from over my shoulder confirmed that Chris was still working his way through the pork scratchings. I shook my head in disgust.

"So, Billie," I said, my voice shakier than I'd expected. "You were saying something about demons?"

We hadn't been able to watch any more of the footage. Chris maintained that he'd seen better special effects in any nineteen-eighties horror movie and remained unconvinced, but then, Chris was an idiot.

Robyn left the function room while Billie and I sat in stunned silence, and Chris munched his way through the rest of his snacks. She returned with a full bottle of brandy, no doubt purchased from Jean at an extortionate price. She poured about half of the bottle into four glasses and passed them to each of us.

No one said anything for a while, but eventually, the alcohol enabled Billie to find her voice. "I fucking knew it," she growled. "Everything I've been saying for years is true. It's all fucking true. Why isn't this all over the news? I mean, this is evidence – actual evidence – of the supernatural. Why aren't the CPS using this? Do they even have it? Or has it all been covered up by the fucking government?"

Robyn looked up from her drink and said, "Jack knows, don't you?"

I sighed. "It's not some government conspiracy. The CPS and the police wouldn't use it. It's 'not in the public interest' to cause panic. Alice is the only survivor, and she was involved in the murders. If they have enough forensic evidence to pin it on her anyway, there's no need to make the footage public. At least so far as this case is concerned."

"Not in the public interest?" Billie snarled. "Don't people have the right to know these *things* exist?"

"Can you imagine what would happen if people knew that demons were actually real? The churches would fill up with people praying for their souls, sure, but you'd get just as many sick bastards heading out to lynch people, convinced they were possessed."

"It'd be the witch hunts all over again," Robyn added.

"Yeah. And that's before you looked at the real fucking nutjobs who'd actually try to summon the things. Christ, a bunch of entitled teenagers managed it, so the ritual itself can't be all that difficult. If the details got out, if more of these things got into our world... Well, could you imagine it? You've seen what they're capable of!"

Billie shook her head vigorously, her face contorted with rage. "People have a right to know, Jack. If they're covering this up, who knows what else is out there?!"

An ice finger traced a path down my spine, and I decided that I really didn't want to know what else was out there. I was going to have enough trouble sleeping as it was.

We finished the rest of the bottle in silence. Chris, Robyn and I went through the fire door and chain-smoked cigarettes while Billie sucked on her asthma inhaler as if it were a vape. I took the pen drive despite Billie's objections. If I'd left it with her, those videos would have been all over the internet before I got home, I was sure. We all shared a taxi from The Dolphin, dropping Billie off first, then Chris, before Robyn and I went back to my place. I didn't want anyone walking back home on their own. I kept scanning the rooftops for the raven, but all I could see was the glow of sodium streetlights reflected back from the leaden sky.

Robyn and I fell into bed together. This time, the sex was driven less by desire and more by a desperate kind of need to affirm that we were both still alive despite the horrors we'd witnessed. We fell asleep in each other's arms a little after midnight.

Chapter Thirteen

I awoke with a cry, sitting bolt upright in bed, my hands reaching out to... to what? I didn't know. The dream unravelled like smoke in the wind. I peeled the sodden sheets from my body and fought to catch my breath.

"That must have been a hell of a nightmare," said Robyn from the foot of my bed. She was already up and dressed, with a cup of coffee in her hands, though the first weak rays of morning were only now creeping in through the gaps in my curtains.

"Yeah, it was," I groaned. "I mean, it must have been... I can't remember it. Sorry if I woke you up." I tweaked the curtain and looked across the rooftops. It all seemed so peaceful, but my fingers still tingled with adrenaline.

"Well, it's hardly surprising," she said with a frown. "All things considered. I didn't sleep too well myself."

"I'd try to persuade you to stay in bed with me," I said, holding up the semi-transparent fabric, "but I think I might need to change the bedding."

She smiled then, and it lit up the room. "Believe me, I'm tempted, but I've got to go. I need to be at work in a couple of hours, and I want to go home first."

"You're still going in? After everything we found yesterday?"

Robyn sighed. "I don't have any choice. If I call in sick, they'll know something's wrong. I'm just going to hide in my office, keep my head down, and stay out of Stuart's way."

"I don't think that's a good idea, given what we've found out," I said. "I think you should be staying the fuck away from that place. It's just not safe."

"I know. But there's nothing to connect me to you grabbing those files. Nothing that he can prove, anyway. He might not have even realised that something's going on. I just— I need to get the lay of the land or I'm going to drive myself crazy."

"Don't. Hartington is clearly up to his neck in this. It's not worth the risk."

"Is he, though? All we know for sure is that he paid off the security guard at King's College to get the recordings. Nothing more sinister than how he got the rest of the evidence. Look, the first sign of anything dangerous, and I'll get the hell out of there, okay?"

I clearly wasn't going to win this argument. "Okay," I sighed. "Give me a call if anything happens. See you tonight?"

Her smile returned, "Count on it." She leaned across and kissed me on my sweaty forehead, then left with a little wave.

My head was surprisingly clear, considering how much I'd drunk the day before. Either existential terror was a great way to sober up or, more likely, I was still under the influence. I wouldn't have gotten behind the wheel of a car that day, even if I owned one, that's for sure. I dressed, made myself some coffee and a couple of pieces of toast, fed the cat, then tried to process the previous day's events.

But I couldn't do it. Every time I tried to think about those images, my heart rate spiked, and beads of sweat broke out across my forehead. Everything I knew, everything I'd ever understood about the world was wrong. It was too big to wrap my head around. There was no rational explanation for what I'd seen in that footage, nothing that didn't admit to the supernatural.

I needed to know the rest of it. I needed the full story so I could have a better idea of what I was caught up in. And I hoped the answers were somewhere in the files I'd stolen from Hartington's office. Because if Alice still had one of those things inside her, there was no way I was going to allow it to roam free. And the evidence to support that was more than compelling.

While I made another coffee, I texted Billie and Chris to make sure they were okay. I got a response from Billie almost immediately; she was with Benjamin, her Dark Web contact. Said she'd message me if they turned up anything new. Chris just told me to fuck off. Considering it was before eight in the morning, that was pretty much all I'd expected. I made a fresh pot of coffee, opened my laptop, and got to work.

It took me over five hours to go through it all, and by the end, I had tears streaming down my cheeks. Aldous Jerome and Jarod Darby had been vicious, sociopathic pieces of shit, no doubt. Their home torture kit was evidence enough of that. I had nothing more than Chloë's brief descriptions to tell me about the unpossessed character of Anastasia Grier-Snelling, Cassandra Foss or Alice Wells, but nobody deserved the fates I'd seen on those video files. Nobody.

There was a certain amount of commonality between each death. Whatever demonic influence had driven their actions, they had all taken an active part in their own demise. *Why?* They had wholeheartedly torn themselves apart, only allowing the host personality to surface near the end, presumably so they could fully experience the horror of what was being done to their bodies. Witness the damage at the point when there was no possibility of rescue, no chance they might survive. The screams of those children seemed to fuel the desecration of their bodies, driving the demonic forces into a frenzy. They drank in the suffering and revelled in it. It was obscene. *Evil.* There was no other word for it. Evil.

There had been other pieces of evidence tucked away: emails between Hartington and the Wells family. They'd known what had happened from the start. The entities were explicitly referenced in one of the messages: 'The Nameless', whatever the fuck that meant. I hoped Billie's new acquaintance could shed some light on that the matter. I was so far out of my depth it was frankly hilarious. And Steph and Sarah were living with the prick! That thought almost brought me out in hives. I quickly messaged Steph, asking her to stay away from the house that night if she could. Go stay at a friend's or something. I had a sense that things were coming to a head, and I wanted my daughter to be as far away from this mess as possible.

I felt like getting back in the shower and scrubbing myself raw, but I couldn't afford to turn on the hot water twice in a single day.

That brought my debts back into focus, the money I owed and the people I was supposed to have handed it to the previous day.

Shit!

I pulled open the desk drawer, heart thumping so hard it hurt, but the envelope was still there, right where I'd left it. I counted it again to be sure. I just hoped it would be enough. I grabbed my coat, stuffed the envelope into one of the large inside pockets and was about to leave the flat when my phone rang.

I checked the caller ID and saw it was Hartington, so I hit the reject button. He called back immediately; I let it go to answerphone. Then I got a text.

"Jack, pick up the phone. I need to talk to you. Right now!"

Shit.

Was Hartington onto Robyn and me? Had I set off some kind of silent alarm or something? Hartington was many things, but I had to admit that he wasn't stupid. Which meant that Robyn could be in very real, immediate danger. The phone buzzed in my hand, and this time, I answered.

"Hartington," I said.

"Jack, buddy, I just wanted to congratulate you on a job well done."

"Wait, what?"

"That laptop you obtained from Darby and Jerome's secret sex den. Brilliant work. I've spent all morning with the CPS, and they've agreed to drop the charges against Alice."

"I'm sorry...? They what?"

"Dropped the charges. Between the laptop and the recordings we found on a network hard drive in the apartment, there's enough evidence to pin the whole thing on Darby. They accept the high probability that Alice was acting in self-defence. She's being released from the secure unit into her mother's care as we speak."

"Wait, what? Robyn didn't know where the apartment was."

Hartington sighed. "You aren't the only one who can dig through things on a computer, Jack. We found the delivery receipts for the 'specialist bedroom equipment', and invoices from the cleaner on a webmail account."

"So, what are you telling me here? I'm off the case?"

"Exactly that! You've done us proud. Can you come to Mrs Wells's office now? I can pay you the rest of your fee and your bonus. What was it again? Ten thousand?"

"Twenty," I replied sharply, but my mind was whirling. In some respects, this was good. It seemed I was off the hook and could put this nightmare behind me. Except this wasn't a nightmare, was it? It was deadly fucking real. I thought about what happened to Marcus and Zoe; I thought about the terror in Chloë's eyes as she stepped backwards; I thought about Jerome screaming silently as he was tied to his place of crucifixion; I thought about the likelihood that Alice Wells still had the Nameless entity inside her and any momentary sense of jubilation evaporated. I needed time to think. "Look, Stuart, it's not really a good time for me right now. Can we do it later? I need to see some people quite urgently."

"Sure, Jack. I completely understand. There might be a delay getting the rest of your money to you, though. My calendar is pretty stacked for the next few weeks, and I believe Mrs Wells has some business out of the country. It's just papers to sign, NDAs and all that. The usual stuff."

"Can't you just send Robyn around with them later? I've really got to go."

"Ah, I'm afraid Miss Whittaker is... no longer with us."

"What the fuck do you mean by that, Hartington? Hartington!"

"Be here within the hour, Jack," he said before hanging up.

I tried to call him back, but it went straight to answerphone. I tried to call Robyn and got the same.

Fuck!

I removed the envelope from my jacket and stuffed it behind the refrigerator, then retrieved a set of brass knuckles from beneath a loose floorboard in my bedroom. I wasn't taking any chances.

***

The snow was falling once again and, as a result, half of the underground was operating a reduced service. Quite why snow should affect the operation of trains a couple of hundred feet below the surface remained a mystery to me, but it meant that those trains that did turn up were rammed to capacity with angry, sweaty, impatient passengers. Every time I caught an elbow in my bruised ribs, I grimaced and tightened my grip on the knuckleduster in my pocket. Still, I made it across the capital in record time, all things considered, and found myself standing once more before the imposing facade of Chemosh Property Services.

While most of London looked like some cheesy Christmas card, the blanket of snow somehow made this brown-bricked building seem cold and foreboding. But of course, I knew for a fact now that Wells was tied up in this whole demonic horror. I felt my adrenaline spike. A part of me really wished that I'd had a drink before coming here, but there was no time. Besides, I had the feeling I'd need what few wits I had left to get out of this place unscathed. I was psyching myself to go in when my phone buzzed insistently. It was a message from Steph. It simply read, 'Dad, call me asap xxx' with a follow-up message saying, 'It's important!'

I hadn't been much of a father to Steph. Only a week ago, a message like that would have had me drop everything to respond, regardless of what I was doing. But things were different now. As much as I wanted to call her straight back, I needed to keep on task. Robyn's life might depend on it. I turned the phone off, stuffed my hands deep into my coat pockets, and shouldered my way through the doors.

I ignored Justine, the snotty receptionist, and strode straight up the glass and chrome staircase.

"Wait!" Justine yelled. "You need to sign in. You can't just go up there."

I didn't even give her the courtesy of turning around. I took the stairs two at a time, then shoved the double doors open with my foot, and more force than was strictly necessary.

Margaret Wells was sitting behind an imposing marble-topped desk, talking to her pet lawyer. He glanced up, a fake smile crawling across his face.

"Jack," he said, checking his watch. "Good of you to join us."

I tightened my grip on the brass knuckles in my pocket and envisaged them smashing through his perfect teeth.

"Where is she, Hartington?" I growled.

The grin broadened. "You'll be glad to know that Alice is now safe in her mother's care, thanks to your sterling efforts. Please, take a seat, and we can discuss things like civilised people."

"I'm not talking about Alice or whatever that thing is you've got walking around in her skin. Where's Robyn? What have you done with her?"

Mrs Wells smiled and put her hand on Hartington's. "You were right, Stuart. He is tenacious, even intelligent in a crude manner."

"Yeah, you can fuck off as well, lady. Once I beat this arsehole into a bloody pulp, you and I are gonna have a chat about what happened to Marcus and Zoe Jacobs, as well as Chloë Davidson." I thumped my brass-clad fist against the desk and snarled, "Last chance, fuck-face. Where's Robyn?"

Hartington laughed in my face. "Oh, Jackie-boy, you really have no idea what's going on, do you?"

Screw it, I thought. Maybe the prick would be more talkative after he'd spat a couple of teeth out onto the desk. I didn't telegraph the blow or do a big wind-up. There's really no need to, when you're wearing knuckledusters. Not if you want your target to remain conscious. But Hartington just sat there with a big smirk on his face as my fist stopped, maybe an inch from his mouth.

What the fuck?

My arm was held in an iron grip, invisible, but undoubtedly there. *Something* was coiling its way through my consciousness, burrowing through my cerebral matter like a parasite, sending cold tendrils across my mind. I could feel it snuffing out my will, drinking my psyche until the alien presence dominated.

I knew then what Marcus and Chloë had felt in their final moments. The terror of it clutched at my heart, but my mouth... smiled.

My eyes were the only thing I seemed to be able to control, and they darted from Hartington's face to that of his devilish mistress. Her irises were completely black, save for a cold, silver pinprick of light where her pupils should have been.

Hartington got up from his chair and walked around the desk. He put an arm on my shoulder, leaned close and sighed in delight. "I wish I could say I was sorry it turned out this way, Jack, but that wouldn't be very honest of me. The truth is, this was always going to be your fate. You're a pawn. You always have been. And now it's time to be sacrificed." He looked over at the Wells-creature and said, "Shall we get this over with? I have a lunch appointment in an hour."

The thing smiled and assented. "Of course. I would hate for you to miss lunch with your family. And I have my own preparations to make. Mr Carlton, if you'd be so kind as to lead the way?" Against my will, I found myself turning towards an elevator door set between a pair of bookcases to my right. I wanted to bellow in defiance, to spit my fury and fling myself at the pair of them, but it was no longer my body to command. I howled in the confines of my skull as my body complied, leading them to the elevator and pressing the button like a fucking doorman.

Neither of my captors said a word as the doors closed behind us. Wells stayed behind me, but I could see Hartington at my side tapping away on his phone like he was waiting in line for a coffee. A short while later, the doors slid open, and I was ushered into a circular tunnel lined with white ceramic tiles. It seemed that Chemosh Property Management Services had installed an elevator straight down to an abandoned part of the underground system. From memory, there were about forty disused stations beneath the city. Tour guides operated in some of them, catering to a niche clientele, but I suspected this was a lesser-known development. I'd never heard of any being in this part of the city anyway. My mind trundled on, trying to quell the rising wave of panic that threatened to engulf me, and focused on the one question that really mattered. If they had the power to make me leap off a building or walk into traffic, *why was I still alive?*

"Ah, Mr Carlton, put such concerns aside," said Mrs Wells, apparently reading my mind. "All will become clear."

Great.

Will it? I vocalised in my mind. *Goody. In the meantime, I'm curious. What's behind those black eyes of yours? You're not human, clearly. Or not anymore. What are you? One of those Nameless things that crawled into your daughter?*

Mrs Wells brought herself close to me. At this distance, her breath had an undertone of rotting meat and sulphur that no amount of breath mints could hide.

Don't compare me to such filth! Those stupid children tried to control things they could barely understand. The fact my daughter is host to one of those vile creatures is an insult to our lineage and an outrage we shall soon rectify. She has a far greater destiny than you, or even I.

Oh yeah, what about him? I thought, giving the side-eye to Hartington.

She gave a short, harsh laugh at that, and Hartington turned around, bemused. Wells waved him onwards.

He, too, shall get his reward. But to answer your question, Mr Carlton, you do still have a purpose. You will help me get the creature out of her.

A fresh batch of stress hormones were dumped en masse into my system at this. Whatever those things were, I didn't want to get anywhere near them.

I still don't get it, though: why you went to all this trouble. Why even hire me to investigate if you can make people do whatever you want?

Wells strolled on down the corridor as though our conversation were over, and I felt an invisible tug drag me after her. Her answer rang through my skull like a hissed thought.

It's beyond your capacity to comprehend what is at stake here, Mr Carlton. I will simply say that when my daughter ascends, her name must be spotless. The situation caused by Mr Darby and his friends needs to be dealt with for the public record and then quietly expunged once interest has waned. Your little investigation has given us the means to accomplish this.

And what's with this little tour of the Satanic stations of the London Underground?

She stopped and turned to face me, eyes glinting. *To banish what you would call a demon requires, amongst other things, the true name of the entity. The Nameless – wretched as they are – have no such thing, so banishment is not an option. We need someone else to play host, which is where you come in once again. It ties up all of those loose ends rather elegantly, don't you think? Most of them, anyway.*

As realisation dawned, I fought against her, screaming and thrashing, pushing against the psychic grip with every fibre of my will. I might as well have been trying to demolish a concrete wall with a feather duster. The Wells-thing led me down the labyrinth of featureless corridors, deep under the city. I was becoming more convinced by the moment that this was some old bunker, perhaps from the second World War or the nineteen-fifties. We passed many steel doors within the complex. From behind some, I could hear the hum of heavy machinery. I glimpsed what looked like barracks through one open door – rows of steel-framed bunk beds lining both walls.

And from other rooms, sealed off, I heard the wails of human misery, along with the unmistakable stench of blood, shit and death. Eventually, we emerged into a large octagonal room with a stained concrete floor. The walls were covered with the same unassuming white ceramic tiles as the corridors, with steel pipes running around the entire circumference at head height. The room was tall, extended up through several mezzanine levels accessible via a network of iron staircases. Eight fluorescent tubes per level illuminated the room in a harsh, flickering blue-white light and in the centre of the room was a large, ornate, rectangular stone plinth that had the air of an altar. It was intricately carved with screaming human faces across its sides. The flat top surface had deep grooves cut into it – channels for blood, I surmised. Those channels extended over the side of the altar and inset beneath them were drainage grates. Each corner of the altar had loops with leather straps running through them. It became clear what the stains on the floor came from. God Almighty! How long had this place – these creatures and their followers – been active?

"Remove your clothes, Mr Carlton," Wells said aloud, "then climb on top. Best to strap yourself in."

I complied despite my best efforts. To my internal horror, I even folded my clothes and placed them in a neat little pile for later. Teeth clenched, shuddering with the strain of resistance, I clambered up onto the cold stone and strapped my ankles in place. Hartington secured my wrists. I could almost believe the pity on his face, but it vanished the second his phone began to vibrate.

"Do you mind if I take this? It's a new client."

Wells nodded. "Of course, Stuart. Enjoy your lunch; I'll see you later this evening."

I heard Hartington's footsteps echo away down the corridor, leaving me alone with Wells, or the thing wearing her face at any rate. I had to wonder at that. Was Margaret Wells screaming for freedom somewhere inside like I was, or was she a willing host for the entity? I still couldn't move or speak. All I could do was look up at the smooth, white ceramic ceiling and wait for whatever was to come.

As it happened, I didn't have to wait for long. A new sound reached my ears: the squeaking of what sounded like rubber wheels.

"Ah, here she is. Don't worry, darling. This will all be over soon."

I felt the cold tentacles retract from my mind, and I regained control of my body – not that it made a difference. The straps held me tight to the unholy black monolith. However, I was at least able to move my head and see the new arrival.

It was the girl, Alice Wells, slumped in a wheelchair, head lolling to the side. Her eyes were open but glazed. I noticed that her ankles and wrists were secured by straps like mine. Her hair was greasy, her skin pale and covered with a sheen of sweat. Drool ran from her mouth in rivulets.

An exceptionally large, muscular man in a tailored charcoal suit pushed the wheelchair over to the altar, applied the wheel lock and then, with a curt bow to Wells, turned and walked to the opposite side of the room. He put his hands behind his back in the at-ease posture, betraying a military background.

The thing ran its hand across Alice's cheek, a possessive gesture that seemed more mockery than care. As she did so, she produced a long, vicious-looking dagger with a black blade. The surface did not reflect the light in a normal way; it seemed to swirl like an oil spill on dark water.

"I hope you'll excuse me if we don't stand on ceremony here, Mr Carlton. I have a great many things to prepare before Alice's ascension, so let's make this quick."

With four swift slashes, she sent my blood gushing down the channels. She dipped a finger into the flow and then drew an intricate pattern on Alice's forehead. Taking my hand in her right hand and Alice's in her left, Wells began to chant in some alien language, and I felt my whole being shrink from her. There was something so wrong about the sounds, as if they should never have been formed by a human tongue, let alone be heard by human ears. They echoed around the room, bending and blending in pitch and timbre. It may have been the blood loss, but it seemed to me that the world was darkened and distorted by this discordance. It was as if the ungodly hymn were reshaping reality.

As the chanting reached a crescendo, I felt the words burn through my bones. Next to me, Alice Wells's eyes snapped wide open, and together we screamed. I thought my jaw would break with the force of it. Something boiled forth from her mouth: black smoke with a yellow tinge and a smell like burning tyres. It swelled and churned, this black, leprous, floating tumour. From the main mass, fingers started to poke out, elongating into clawed legs that wriggled and reached towards me. Then, the cancerous flesh parted to reveal dozens of blinking eyeballs. It billowed and spewed towards me, and the cold, slippery legs gripped my cheeks, pulling the mass between my lips and down into my throat. I gagged and thrashed against my bonds, slickening them with even more blood, but I couldn't free myself. I tried to bite down, to sever its grip on my face, but my jaw was locked in place. This was a thousand times worse than the feeling of Wells's fingers in my brain; no less invasive, but much more visceral and violent. I felt its foulness filling me, bloating my flesh and curdling my stomach. Only then did I sense those cold fingers crawl into my mind to steal my autonomy. Suddenly, a needle pierced the flesh of my neck, and ice spread from the wound, numbing my body, sending my senses – and my possessor – into timeless oblivion.

Chapter Fourteen

My mind slowly clawed its way back to some level of consciousness. It took me some moments to realise that the swaying, lurching movement I felt was not entirely due to the waves of disorientation and nausea that threatened to overwhelm me. I was in some kind of vehicle, strapped in, upright, though I couldn't remember how, why, or with whom. I steeled myself and cracked my eyes open. Two large men sat on either side, hemming me in. Historically, this would indicate that things were not going well, but my mind was still searching for context. It was all I could do to stop myself from throwing up, too. Sweat beaded on my forehead, and I felt a strange feeling like cat claws gently kneading my brain. I tried to remember what I'd done to land me in this situation, but my memories swirled and danced away.

"Is he awake yet?"

"Yeah, he came to a couple of minutes ago. He's playing possum at the moment, hoping we don't notice."

Shit.

"Fuck it, in that case, this is close enough. We don't want to be anywhere near him when it happens. Ron, pull over here. Yes, *here*. *Now*. Hurry up, you helmet!"

The car swerved to the left, and I heard horns blaring as it cut in front of the other road users. A cold blast of air washed across my face as the rear passenger door opened, then I was dragged out and dumped by the side of the road in a pile of dirty slush. I opened my eyes to see a black BMW screech away from me, almost colliding with a red Corsa in its haste.

I got to my feet slowly and checked my surroundings. I was on a familiar road, two or three streets away from my flat and, apart from a pair of cold, wet pants and the sense of sickness, I didn't seem all that much the worse for wear than I had been. My injuries from the kicking I'd had from the goon squad a few days ago were still painful, but there didn't seem to be any new ones. Was that them in the car? One of them had said the name Ron, but that didn't ring any bells. I felt around at my back, checking for operation scars in case the bastards had made good on their threats to take a kidney or whatever. Anaesthetic would certainly account for my disorientation, but no, there was nothing. Huh...

I began trudging through the ankle-deep snow back to my flat.

I tried to think, piecing events together like broken crockery. I'd woken up when Robyn had gone into the office. Gone to pay Eddie and get him off my back, but— no. I'd been interrupted. Took that call. That fucking call from Hartington. Memories flashed. The altar; whateverthefuck the thing pretending to be Mrs Wells had been; Alice in the wheelchair. And that pulsating, airborne tumour.

Fuck.

It was inside me. The Nameless monstrosity that had killed those kids at King's College... she'd dragged it out of Alice Wells and poured it down my throat! That stabbing feeling must have been a needle – it *had* been fucking anaesthetic – presumably to keep it under control. But not anymore. That's what the slabs of muscle in the car had been talking about.

Oh, God!

I fished my phone out of my jacket pocket, nestled in with my brass knuckles. I scrolled through the numbers until I found Billie and hit call.

A bored voice answered. "Hello, Pizza Delivery. Can I take your order?"

I terminated the call, looked at the phone, and saw that I'd accidentally highlighted the local takeaway's entry. I squinted at the phone, carefully scrolled back up the numbers until I had the correct one, and stabbed call.

"Hello? D Cars," came a chirpy voice from the other end.

What the hell was going on? I tried to dial Billie's number from memory, taking my time. My eyes kept going out of focus, but I got there, then my thumb just stopped, hovering over the call button.

Yeah, I'm not going to let you do that, Jack.

I recognised the voice from my dream. Alice Wells. I spun around, but there was no one there except a woman twenty yards away, pushing a pram.

Try again! the voice whispered.

I whirled to the right, then spun back around the full three hundred and sixty, but there was nobody else to be seen.

Then it hit me. The voice wasn't coming from outside at all.

Bingo, it said brightly. *Five stars, Jacko. Now, if you're ready, we can have some real fun. Shall we start with Pram Lady, or just go straight to the main event with Stephanie? I know how much you want to see her again...*

My stomach lurched, and I felt the cold probing of my brain resume. It was slower than what Mrs Wells had done to me but no less insistent. I didn't have long, and I couldn't let this thing take control of me – I couldn't let it anywhere near my daughter.

I looked into the road and saw a large red double-decker bus racing to beat the red light. I'd seen what one of those had done to Chloë Davidson. It wasn't pretty, but it *had* been quick. There was no time to think twice. I took a deep breath and threw myself beneath its wheels. Or, at least, I tried to.

The bus rushed straight past me, horn blaring. I looked down to find myself still standing in a pile of dirty snow at the edge of the footpath.

Naughty boy, came Alice's voice in a sultry tone. *I'm going to have to punish you for that one. Do you like being a bad boy, Jack? I think you probably do.*

I cried out and began running through the streets toward my flat. If this Nameless thing could keep me from ending my life, it might already be too late. I had one chance, so far as I could tell. I needed drugs. Enough to knock this thing out, long enough for me to do something. Anything.

I can hear you, you know? it said mockingly. *Do you think I'm going to let you do that? Give up, Jack. Just step aside and let me in. It'll be so much easier in the long run.*

I screamed, "Fuck You!" at the top of my voice, which got me some strange looks from the other pedestrians. The voice in my head began laughing – warmly at first, then with increasing hysteria as I reached the main street and the clot of pedestrians who scattered before me. That suited me just fine. I ran as fast as my jelly legs could take me, savouring the pain, using it to spur me on. I built a wall in my mind with the pain. Visualised it circling me like a protective shield.

Oh, you like pain? it said. *You should have said. I can show you pain like you've never imagined.*

Despite what the demon whispered in my mind, I felt the cold, probing sensation withdraw, at least a little, and the voice seemed farther away. Distant, as if I was hearing it on the other end of a bad telephone connection.

I tore across the road to my flat, half hoping the traffic would take me out, and felt a moment of hope. I was doing it! I was keeping the creature at bay, at least for now.

I reached the door to my flat, fishing the keys from my pocket and totally failed to see the ham-sized fist before it struck my jaw.

Perfect!

I sailed backwards into the snowy street, closely followed by Sheepskin and his jolly band of arseclowns.

"There you are," said Arthur to his pals. "I told you he'd be back. Ye of little faith."

"Not now, you fucking moron!" I snarled. "I've got your money inside, but if you don't get out of my way quick, I'll tear you to fucking shreds!"

Arthur nodded to Herbert, and the fist descended once more.

I swam back to consciousness in the back of the Ford Focus, wedged between the Chuckle Brothers, but inside my skull, the balance of power had shifted. I found myself unable to move, speak or even blink.

Ah, that's better, crooned the Nameless thing in my head. *I have to say, you did better than most at keeping me out. Of course, that might just be the drugs. But I'm in the driver's seat now. Did the bad men hurt you? I think we can do something about that.*

Get the fuck out of my head, I screamed silently.

The demon laughed. *But it'll be so much fun! Besides, I've only just moved in.* The voice receded for a moment, and I could swear I heard it tutting. Then it was back. *I have to say, though, you're not in the best of shape. I mean, wow. Talk about letting yourself go. I'm not sure how this body even functions with the state of your liver. You're a wreck, my friend. If I hadn't taken over, you'd have been dead in a year. Of course, now you'll be dead in a couple of hours, so it'll do until then.*

What are you going to do to me?

Who, me? Nothing at all. You, however, are about to embark on a very violent, very public killing spree. Sad to say, you'll probably end up being slaughtered by armed police, but that's their decision not mine. First things first, though. Let's kill these idiots, move on to your friends and then... yes, let's go visit your lovely daughter.

I screamed in defiance; railed against the mental images this malign creature was feeding me; tried to regain any semblance of control, but all I got was echoing laughter.

Is that the best you can do? Oh dear. I think I must have been right about the drugs. Shall I tell you what I have planned for your daughter, Jack? Well, after she watches you kill her mother, you're going to murder her, too. But I'm going to give you back control of your head so you can cry and scream and beg her forgiveness as your hands tighten around her throat— but we're getting ahead of ourselves. I don't want to give too much away and spoil the ending. Just know that I'm looking forward to it more than you can possibly imagine.

Fuck you! I howled. *Why do this? Why do any of it? You're going to make me slaughter innocent people, get me killed, but then what? What do you actually want?*

I could almost feel the presence smile. *I do it because I enjoy it. Live for it, you might say. Anyway, much as I've enjoyed our chat it looks like we've arrived. Sit back and enjoy the show.*

The Ford turned off the main road into what looked like an abandoned industrial estate. Empty factory units lined either side of the road, and the entrance was blocked by a metal gate. Arthur got out of the vehicle, unlocked the padlock, and then secured it once more when the car passed through.

As he got back in, I took another blast of his rancid breath. "You've been rather quiet, Mr Carlton. None of your usual wit tonight. Perhaps the gravity of the situation has begun to sink in at last?"

The creature controlling my body had nothing to say on the subject, and I had no means to voice my own thoughts. For the next ten terrifying minutes, I would be nothing but a spectator, watching the Nameless at work. I could feel its anticipation. It was plugged into my nervous system which meant what it felt, I felt. And it was excited – more than excited. To my horror, I felt my penis stir into life as the Nameless readied itself.

The car pulled up to one of the abandoned factory units, and a man I didn't recognise pushed open a large, rusted metal door that squealed on its hinges. When the car moved inside, he pushed the door closed again. It clanged with the finality of a judge's gavel, sentencing every single one of these souls to death.

I was shoved from the car by Herbert and walked across the empty concrete floor to where a man was sitting on an office chair. Big Eddie Halliwell, loan shark, East End villain of the old school. The poor sod had no idea what was coming for him.

Eddie put his newspaper to one side, pulled out a cigar that was at least as fat as my thumb, then took his time lighting it.

"Jack Carlton," he said at last. "Ex-policeman turned private investigator. Ex-husband and ex-father turned drunk piece of shit. So good to make your acquaintance in person." He seemed rather bored, but I could tell by the way his fingers twitched that he was eager to proceed. It had clearly been a while since he'd had to get personally involved in this kind of work; perhaps he'd handle the tools himself for old time's sake.

"I hear you've been reluctant to settle your debts with me. In fact, my employees here tell me you've been quite rude, so I thought we should have a little chat. Face to face, as it were. Clear up any... misapprehensions."

The Nameless didn't say anything. It just stood there, flanked by Herbert and Flat-top. Its facial expression was impassive, body relaxed. Eddie got to his feet, noting this, a frown spreading across his face.

"See, at this point, Jack, it's not about the money. Not anymore. It's about trust and respect. They're the oil that keeps organisations like mine running smoothly. I *trust* my debtors will pay what they owe me. I respect their right to forfeit. Similarly, they trust my word when I tell them the consequences of such rudeness and they *respect*" – he spat that last word into my ear – "my retribution when it comes. Some of them even survive it, if they play their cards right. But you, Jack. Oh dear. You've shown nothing but disrespect to my employees, to my organisation, and to *me*. I can't be having that. So—"

His fist slammed into my stomach. I felt the air blast from my lungs, and the pain lanced through my body. I felt it all, but the demon inside was unaffected. The power that flooded my limbs at that moment was beyond description. It raised my head, looked Big Eddie in the eye, and it laughed right in his big sweaty face.

Eddie's complexion flushed beetroot, and he slammed his fist into my nose. It broke with a nasty snapping sound. If anything, this made the Nameless laugh even more.

"Boys," Eddie snarled. "Teach this turd some manners while I get my tools out."

Herbert and Flat-top grabbed an arm each and tried to throw my body to the floor, but they couldn't budge it.

Then everything went to hell. It was devastating. It was glorious.

The Chuckle Brothers were lifted from the floor and slammed together like a pair of cymbals. I heard the distinct wet crack of bone breaking on bone and the pair dropped to the ground, senseless.

Shouts went up from around the warehouse. Angry voices, running feet, all began to close in. Big Eddie, hands in an ominously large bag, had turned around at the crack. His mouth hung open and his stinking cigar lay on the ground in front of him, smoke rising, as calm and lazy as the smile on my face.

While Eddie and I looked on, helpless and horrified, my hands reached down, grabbed the closest thug by his flat-top and tore the top of his head open like a tin of beans. The flesh separated with a wet ripping sound reminiscent of someone peeling an orange, ending with a flourish as the hair and skin came free. The blood-soaked scalp fell to the floor with a wet splat. The next thing I knew, my fingers jabbed into his eye sockets, digging through the sticky gristle and into his brains.

My other hand slashed out at his neck, tearing into soft tissues, wrenching through flesh with unnatural speed and ferocity. Once, twice, leaving little of it left. Then, the skull still gripped like a bowling ball, my Nameless parasite pulled. The last scraps of flesh around the neck stretched, then split; vertebrae cracked; blood sprayed from the wound, and the man's head was torn clean off.

Arthur and three other goons were sprinting toward me, weapons in hand. With a casual grin, my body spun and hurled the bloody head straight at the leader. It struck him in the face with enough force that Flat Top's skull cracked in half. Arthur dropped to the floor and did not get back up.

Then the demon turned its attention to Herbert who was slowly getting to his feet and didn't really seem to understand what was happening. His eyes were glazed, and his right arm was bent at an alarming angle. His concussion was soon going to become the least of his worries.

I felt the Nameless smile, then it raised one blood-soaked hand, and Herbert lifted from the ground, floating two feet from the blood-soaked floor. My wrists flicked and Herbert's limbs spread out to form the shape of an X.

Oh shit, I'd seen this before. This was one of the images in the grimoire.

"What the fuck?" Big Eddie gibbered, finally finding his voice. "What the fuck are you?"

The Nameless ignored him. For the moment, at least. It flicked my wrist again, and Herbert's arm snapped. He screamed in agony, but the monster wasn't done with him yet. Not by a long shot. Another flick saw the tibia of his left leg shatter, the bone breaking with enough force to punch bloody shards through his trousers.

The demon took its time with the man, working its way through all the major bones of his body. Next up were the radius and ulna of his right arm to complement his already shattered humerus. Then the left femur, right collarbone, and on and on. Methodical and cruel. Herbert's screams went up an octave with each snapped bone until he looked less like a man and more like a bin bag filled with blood and bone shards that had split the second someone tried to pick it up. Eventually the Nameless lost interest in him, and the man's devastated body dropped to the concrete in a wet splash.

The rest of the gangsters halted the second Herbert began floating and had beaten a hasty retreat as his screams rang out. They hadn't made it very far. The heavy steel roller doors had so far resisted all attempts to open them. One of Eddie's men had the presence of mind to jump into the Ford Focus we'd arrived in. However, the second the engine roared into life, it took a mere glance from the demon to lock the doors, rupture the fuel line and wreath the car's interior with flame. The smell of burning meat began to fill the warehouse, and saliva washed through my mouth.

Arthur groaned and tried to crawl away from us. One of his eyes bulged out of the socket, his nose was all but paste, and only a few teeth remained in his mouth. Content to let the other henchmen scrabble and tug at the warehouse door, the Nameless launched us up into the air, clearing twenty feet at least, landing astride the gasping mess of a man.

We reached down and dug into the pulped remains of Flat-top's decapitated skull until it found what it was looking for: a sharp fragment of curved bone about the size of a packet of cigarettes. It dropped the pulped remains onto the concrete, flipped Sheepskin over, and began slicing into his abdomen. The flesh parted easily under the demon's makeshift knife, drawing a staccato gurgling cough from the victim. Next, we reached into his slippery innards, pulled out a long loop of intestine, wrapped it around his throat and throttled the last bit of life from him.

Then, it turned our attention to Big Eddie and his two remaining men.

To their credit, the mobsters recognised the threat we posed and, realising escape was impossible, they went on the offensive. The two henchmen positioned themselves between the onrushing horror and their boss. One of them produced a long, stiletto blade from within his jacket, while the other extended a baton that was the twin of the one Arthur had held.

The fact that its intended victims were armed didn't seem to bother the demon one bit. If anything, we scuttled faster toward them, like some monstrous spider. The guy with the knife attacked first, swinging his arm in a wide, panicked arc. We avoided it easily and launched straight upwards, clinging to the warehouse ceiling. We must have flown twenty feet straight up, then skittered off into the shadows to bellowed cries of disbelief.

"What the shit?" cried the guy with the baton. "What the fucking fuck is that thing?"

"Who gives a crap? I just want to know where it's gone," replied his colleague, scanning the rafters for movement. While his men tried to locate the demon, Big Eddie finally seemed to recover from his shock sufficiently to call for reinforcements, pulling an expensive-looking mobile phone from his jacket pocket.

I felt the monster's surge of annoyance at the telephone and hope sparked briefly. I had a sense that, whilst it was frighteningly powerful, the thing was far from invincible. We stalked across the ceiling until we were between the three men and the sealed roller door, then we glanced across the warehouse and sent an empty can clattering against the far wall. All three mobsters whipped their heads around, looking for the source of the sound. And that was when we dropped to the floor behind them.

It placed a hand on either side of the knife-wielding thug's head and twisted it round like a bottle top. Big Eddie fled as the corpse hit the floor, while the demon punched a hole through the other bodyguard's chest. It yanked my arm back out of the corpse, tugging his heart out on the way and then, experimentally, it extended my tongue to taste the organ. Did it hunger, or did it just want to torment me?

Regardless, it stalked towards Big Eddie with a monstrous grin across its bloodied face and waved the heart cheerfully.

"Now, now, Eddie. Hasn't anyone told you it's rude to stare at your phone when you have company?"

The phone burst into flames, searing Eddie's hand. He tried to drop it but found his fingers tightening against his will. Molten lithium dribbled out, melting his flesh and Eddie screamed in agony. I almost shot my load at that point, taken to the brink by the creature's hideous tastes. It hadn't been lying. It *enjoyed* inflicting pain. The worse the anguish, the greater its pleasure. There could be no negotiating with this thing. No plea nor deal that would make a single bit of difference. Whatever lived in Margaret Wells had similar abilities, but this one was worse. Because Margaret's monster was able to defer gratification for the greater cause. For its grand plan. This thing had no such control. It was a creature of chaos, of pure impulse and selfish need.

Eddie, meanwhile, was trying to shuffle away from us, inch by inch. I almost felt sorry for him.

"I thought we should have a little chat, Eddie. Face to face, as it were. Clear up any... misapprehensions," we said in uncanny imitation. "You're not the big man you thought you were, and I'm about to show you why."

It pulled my brass knuckles out, nestled into them and made a fist.

"The thing is, Eddie," we said, "it's *not* about trust or respect; it's about pain."

Then it drove my fist into Big Eddie's kneecap. The noise of his patella snapping was like a gunshot and he howled in agony.

"And if there's one thing I know, Eddie... it's pain."

The knuckleduster flashed again, striking the hand before it could even reach his damaged kneecap. I felt rather than heard those bones shatter like glass, and Eddie's cries became a wail of utter despair. The Nameless drank it in for a minute or two until the gangster's moans sank back to a lesser intensity.

"Wait, please," Eddie gasped at last. "I'll give you anything, whatever you want. Just let me go."

We smiled at him. "Oh, Eddie, you're already giving me everything I could ever want."

Then we really went to work on him.

By the time we were finished he was an unrecognisable mush.

In the dank confines of my mind, the Nameless sighed in post-coital bliss.

Did you enjoy the show, Jack? Well, that was just an amuse bouche, something to fire up the appetite. I don't know about you, but I could do with something more substantial. Where should we go next, do you think? Oh... I know! Pub?

CHAPTER FIFTEEN

The Nameless moved us through the back streets of London, silent and unseen. I could feel the conflict within. There was nothing it wanted more right then than to tear through the innocents it passed. And once, as it skirted the grounds of a primary school, it almost gave in to those urges. We stood between two skips filled with the trash from a building renovation next door and watched as mothers stood at the school gates, chatting and smiling as their excited children played in the snow. The hunger radiated from it in a cloud of malevolence, and it almost broke cover a few times. The monster's mind filled my own with images of the things it wanted to do, staining the snow red in its wake. In the end, though, it slipped away, avoiding temptation by sticking to back streets and alleys as it headed towards The Dolphin. Because the one thing it wanted to do more was to get me killing the people I loved most in this world. I was beginning to understand why. If the pleasure it felt when causing pain to others was sexual, how much more powerful would it be if its host were also feeling that anguish, a helpless witness to the outrage they themselves were perpetrating? It would magnify the feeling a thousandfold. The Nameless was a junkie relentlessly pursuing its next hit of pure smack.

"Don't worry, Jack. We'll be there soon," it whispered in my mind. "Who shall we start with? Good old Chris, perhaps? Or should we build up to the two you really care about? Yeah. We could gut a couple of random drunks and that wrinkly old landlady first. What do you think?"

I'd long since given up trying to argue or break free of its influence. Once I realised it was enjoying my attempts, I ignored it. My chance would come. Somehow. It couldn't pay attention to my every thought and motion.

"Aw, Jack," it sniggered, "What's the matter, sweetie? Do you think sulking's gonna make any difference? Are you having a little pout at what I'm going to make you do to that cute little Billie?"

"Fuck you," I hissed. "I'll find a way to beat you, you fucking parasite."

"Well, if you have some great masterplan, you'd better hurry up and get going. You're due to be gunned down in the street in a couple of hours, remember?"

"See, I get the rest, but not that part," I murmured. "You're nothing but a sad, pathetic spiritual cast-off that can't get it up unless someone's getting hurt. Whatever. I've met plenty like you and it's pretty much always down to mummy issues. Or daddy issues."

No comebacks, no sneers.

"What's the matter – God got your tongue? Here's what I don't get. If you're so blatant you get us killed, won't you just end up getting sent back to whatever hell you came from? If you want to cause pain and suffering on a massive scale, join the fucking Conservative Party. Unless that's all you can manage. A quick bang and you've blown your load. Is that closer to the truth?"

It didn't reply straight away, and I felt a tension that I'd not experienced from it before. At least one of my barbs hit home, closer than it liked to admit. It was a momentary thing, but it was real. And it knew I'd felt it.

"You don't know shit, do you, Jack?" Bluster. *Bravado.* "When your useless fucking flesh gets torn apart, I'll just move home. You think you can beat me? You couldn't fucking breathe without my say so!"

And I couldn't. Right there and then, my chest stopped moving. I panicked, eyes wide, hands clutching at my windpipe, but there was nothing I could do. The world went white around the edges, and I fell to my knees.

Then, just like that, it released me. I breathed in deep, coughed my guts up and slowly but surely began to return to some semblance of normality.

"You're nothing without me. But, when you commit suicide by armed police, I get to start all over again with a fit young copper. One with access to automatic weapons. Imagine the fun I'll have with one of those in that school tomorrow morning. You and your pathetic little family are just the warm-up act, Jack. I'll carve a swathe of death and destruction across this planet for generations to come. Slaughter countless innocents and bathe in their fucking blood. And it's all thanks to you."

My mind spun. The Nameless would say anything that suited its purpose, but nothing it said rang false. Why lie when the truth was so much worse than anything I could imagine. All my hopes died then. I couldn't lie or trick my way to freedom; it could read my mind. I couldn't bargain; there was nothing it wanted more than to make me watch as it murdered everyone I loved. All so it could mainline my despair.

The leaden sky grew darker and the shadows longer as we travelled until, finally, we reached The Dolphin.

"So, Jack, what are we drinking? First one's on me. I think I'll start with a Bloody Billie, then see how I feel after. Sound good?"

I didn't reply. I tried to close my eyes and my mind to the horrors about to happen, but the Nameless wouldn't allow that. It needed me to have a front-row seat to the carnage. We pushed open the doors of The Dolphin and strode inside, yelling, "Honey, I'm home!"

As it happened, the place was fairly empty, much to my relief. There were a few of the old regulars propping the bar up, nursing pints of real ale. Dave was in a booth at the far end with a couple of dodgy-looking teens. And of course, Jean, standing behind the bar with her hands on her hips, a look of disgust on her face.

"Christ's sake, Jack," she said, "We might not be the bloody Ritz, but we do have some standards. You can't come in here looking like that. What is that? Blood? Please, for the love of God, tell me you didn't batter some poor idiot in the car park again."

It grinned at her, "Oh, not the car park. An industrial estate a couple of miles away. I must say, I'm disappointed the place is so... empty."

"Cheeky sod, it's still early. Anyway, you can piss off. I'm not serving you like that. Go and get yourself cleaned up, for goodness' sake. You're getting blood all over the carpet. Come back later, eh? We've got Karaoke."

We smiled and made an elaborate bow, "I think I might do just that, Jeanie. I have a few things to take care of first, but that would round the day off nicely."

We turned and had almost reached the double doors when an all-too-familiar voice rang out across the empty pub. "Jack, ya cunt, what tha hell happened te you?"

I felt a broad grin spreading across my face, then my posture changed. The arrogant stance it had held me in since we strode through the doors changed to a stooped, pained posture. We shuffled round and waved affably. "Chris, I've been looking all over for you. Mate, I need help. Badly. Is Billie here too?"

"Fucks sake," said Chris, and hurried towards us. "What shite have ye gotten yourself into this time, ye daft twat?"

I wanted to scream at him. Tell him to get away. To run and never stop. I could feel the demon playing through the gruesome possibilities of death. Appalling image after image flashed across my mind's eye; I felt the muscles of my body tense and my hands curl into claws. "Chris..." we gasped, "...help me."

He all but ran to my side and put his hand on my shoulder. "God, Jack, what the fuck have ye done?"

We locked eyes with the large Scot and gave him a predatory grin. "There's no God here, Chris," we hissed. Then it punched him in the chest with enough force that he sailed backwards over the bar and disappeared from sight.

Everything I'd felt it do with my body up to that point had somehow felt unreal, as if I were watching it on the big screen. There was even a perverse part of me that enjoyed the theatricality of Big Eddie Halliwell's ending, but seeing my friend slammed across the room with the force of a traffic collision brought it all home. I had become Death. The Nameless responded to my anguish by getting another erection.

"Ah, Jack." It sighed. "That's the stuff. If killing that moron hurts you so much, I can hardly wait until I get to your daughter. It's giving me chills just thinking about it."

We began striding toward the bar, cracking my knuckles. We hopped up onto the bar with barely a twitch of my feet, sending glasses half full of real ale crashing to the floor as the patrons scattered.

On the floor behind the bar, Chris was lying flat on his back, wearing a grin of his own. There was some sort of... pistol? in his hands.

"Suprise, motherfucker," he wheezed, shooting me in the chest three times in rapid succession.

The Nameless looked down at the trio of darts and shrieked in outrage. It tried to hurl us at Chris, but my legs were numb, they gave way beneath us, and my body tumbled to the floor.

"I'll fucking kill you," it hissed as the drugs took hold. I felt arms grab me roughly beneath the armpits and drag us back toward the double doors. The last thing we heard before everything went dark was Jean's voice, shouting, "You're barred, Jack. You're barred for life!"

***

I swam up from the narcotic-induced sleep towards distant sounds and consciousness. Indistinct at first, as if I were hearing them from underwater. Eventually, I was able to separate the sounds into distinct voices. One of them was unfamiliar. High pitched and rather nasal. It grated on me, an irritant to scratch.

"Look, I don't pretend to be an expert in these things," it whined.

"Well, ye fuckin better turn intae one before he wakes up. Did ye see the dent in that Kevlar vest?"

That was a voice I recognised. Chris. I felt a surge of joy and guilt when I heard him, but it took me a second to understand why. Then I remembered it all. A wave of panic washed over me, and my monstrous passenger began to stir in the back of my mind.

"Chris, give it a rest. Benjamin is doing the best he can."

"Aye, well, fuckin Benjamin wasn't the one that nearly had his chest caved in, was he? Is there nothin' at all in those pages?"

Benjamin's whine went up a pitch. "Listen, Mr Barnes. I am doing my best, but I doubt there are more than a dozen people in the world who can read these pages, and even then, it's hardly an exact science. The smallest error could bring disastrous consequences."

"Ah still don't get why we cannae just get a vicar. You know, the whole power of Christ compels you to get tae fuck kinda thing."

Benjamin let out an exasperated sigh. "For one thing, we'd need to convince a catholic priest that this was a real situation, then he'd need to seek agreement and authorisation from the Vatican. We don't have time. The other problem is that Mr Carlton doesn't have a demon in him. Not exactly, anyway. How can I put this...? Alright – to banish a demon, you have to know its True Name; it helps to pin it down, it... leaves it no wiggle room. But the thing in your friend is not a regular demon. There is some conflicting information on them – some texts claim they were demons whose atrocities were so appalling that God stripped them of their names as he cast them out. Others postulate that these things are from before creation. Entities from outside of our universe. It's a lesser being to some extent, because it doesn't have a True Name. The trouble is that makes it harder to pin down. We can't banish it the conventional way. We can't send it back without killing the host, and even then, we'd need to do it indirectly. As I understand it, the Nameless is able to possess the body of the person that dealt the fatal blow. Death as an invitation or something. The text is a little... smudgy on that point."

"If you think you're killing my mate, ye can think again, Pal. You so much as look at him funny, I'll plant my foot so far up yer arse you'll taste leather."

"Wait a second," said Billie, "wasn't there a bible story where Jesus cast a bunch of demons out into some pigs and then drove them into a lake to drown. Is that the sort of thing you mean?"

"Yes, precisely that. If true, we can infer that they were a host of Nameless spirits, rather than demons, inhabiting the possessed man. Unable to banish them to hell, Jesus simply moved them into new hosts and caused their deaths indirectly. There was no killing blow."

"Okay!" said Billie brightly. "So... can you do that? Cast it into a new host?"

I felt the familiar cold tentacles beginning to extend across my mind, subduing me, numbing my limbs. I tried to cry a warning, but a bare groan was all I could manage before the Nameless sealed them shut. Thankfully, it was enough.

"Aw, shite," cried Chris, "How the fuck is he awake? Ah shot him wi' enough ketamine te bring down a horse. Hang on. Two seconds..."

I felt a prick of pain in my arm, and darkness claimed us once more.

***

"What the actual fuck, Chris?"

The first voice I heard this time was Billie's and she used that special tone that indicated a shin kicking was on its way.

"What? It's the best ah could manage on short notice."

"The best you could manage? What the hell are we supposed to do with that?"

"It's not like ah didn't TRY to get a proper one. But it's not like you can just walk into Pets At Home and say 'What ho, kind sir, I'd like to purchase twelve of your finest pigs' is it?"

"So, you bought a guinea pig instead?"

"They only had one left."

"A fucking guinea pig, Chris. It's a meat potato! You've done some stupid, fat-headed shit in your time, but this is in a league all of its own."

"You know, it might work," said Benjamin. "And certainly, easier to drown than a full-sized boar.

"Don't you start sticking up for the dickhead too, Benjamin. It's bad enough when Jack does it. This is just one more fuck-up in a long line of massive fuck-ups."

"I'm perfectly serious," said Benjamin. "Assuming the ritual doesn't just make it explode or something. I mean, it would be better if we had somewhere to put it that was a little more intelligent; it would probably last longer. But if we're just going to drown the thing in the bath, we should be fine."

"So long as guinea pigs can't swim," Billie growled. "Fuck's sake. Fine! But just so you know, Chris, if that bloody thing explodes and I end up with a demon inside of me, the first thing I'm gonna do is feed your own balls to you."

"Aye, well we're outta time, so buckle up buttercups. Looks like sleeping beauty's back frae his nap, and ah'm fresh out of ket."

My eyes flickered open. We squinted at the light, turned my head and realised we were lying on my back in the middle of my living room floor. My arms and legs were pulled out into a star shape, and my wrists and ankles had been literally bolted to the floor. Heavy steel brackets had been screwed straight through the carpet into the wooden floor joists below, keeping us in place. They seemed pretty solid, but I'd seen my demonic passenger pull off some astonishing feats of strength, so I wasn't confident they'd hold us. Billie and Chris stood either side of us, and in front was a skinny man in his late forties, who I assumed was Benjamin. He had lank, unkempt hair, a goatee beard and wore open-toed sandals. *A fucking hippy.* Of course he was. All three looked terrified. Billie was clinging on to the arm of Chris's T-shirt, as though he'd be any help. Chris looked nervous too. He held a heavy wooden chair leg in his hands, but we could tell he didn't want to use it. Meanwhile, Benjamin looked like he was about to have a coronary. He brandished an iPad tablet computer in front of him as if it were some sort of shield.

"Guys," I croaked, "You don't know what this thing is capable of. The things it's done. The thing's it's made me do. It's not worth the risk. Just... set fire to the place and get out of here."

"That might work, you know," Benjamin muttered. "It's indirect."

"Fire spreads," snapped Billie. "It's too dangerous."

"Aye, just shut yer trap, ye fuckin' drama queen. We're gonna drag this bastard outta ye, drop him in Mr Nibbles over there, then drown the prick in your bath. Job done, eh?"

"Please, just trust us, Jack. Benjamin's been going over those pages you sent me, and he knows what to do."

The familiar cold sensation began to spread across my skull, burying into my psyche, taking over my body. "It's not worth it. Get out! Please! It's going to—"

"Jack?" said Billie, her voice trembling.

"Sorry, petal. Jack's not here right now," said the Nameless. "Would you like me to take a message?"

All three took a step backwards in fear.

"Well, I must hand it to you all," it continued with an almost jovial tone, "you've already survived far longer than I expected. That was a neat trick with the tranquilisers. Don't expect it to save you again."

Benjamin strode forward, his iPad held before him and began chanting in Latin. "*Circulus protectoris, te clauso. Nulla vi malevola, hic intrare licet. Virtute luminis, hanc sacram lineam firmo. Pax securitas intus maneant. Fiat lux, et finis malefictiorum. Sic itur ad astra."* Then, at the culmination, a circle of cold blue flame erupted from my carpet, sealing us within.

"You think that's going to stop me, you little beardy prick? I'm going to flay the flesh from your bones when I get out of here. And then I'm going to go pay your mother a visit. You remember Mother, Benjamin? Where does she think you've gotten to? Does she know why you left, or why you're too ashamed to return? She's all alone, Benjamin, and so very vulnerable. But don't worry, I'll take care of her. I'll keep her alive for a very long time, you have my word on that. I'll feed her slivers of your fucking flesh and then, when that eventually runs out, we'll start again with her own body, one slice at a time."

Benjamin shuddered violently, the colour draining from his face. He took an involuntary step backwards and looked like he was going to throw up. Billie put her hand on his shoulder lending him her strength and determination. "Don't give it the chance, Benjamin. You've got this."

Benjamin began a new chant in a different language. It was guttural and strangely familiar. The one Wells used, perhaps.

The Nameless snapped my head around, pinning Billie with our gaze and laughed cruelly. " Wilhelmina Richards. You poor little thing. So lost. So desperate for answers. Your dear Uncle Brian was a monster, Billie. Even when he was still human. Did you know that?"

Billie's eyes widened, and the demon laughed harder. "Oh, you thought he was just some kindly, dashing military man you remember from your childhood? Let me tell you, little Billie, your uncle was responsible for hundreds of deaths. Hundreds. And that was before his transformation. It's almost a shame you have to die in this disgusting hovel because part of me would have loved to watch you discover the full truth about him. Right before he tore your heart out."

I could feel the demon drinking deep from Billie and Benjamin. Relishing their anguish. Growing stronger as they faltered.

"Oi, gobshite," Chris snarled. " Ah'm gonna stamp on yer bollocks if ye don't shut yer hole. "

The demon laughed, "Oh, Christopher. How could I forget about you? You've been such a glorious failure. Do you know how happy she is with her new husband? How glad your son is to have a new Daddy? He only remembers your face in his nightmares. Those unfortunate alcoholic outbursts... Do you know, you've doomed him to follow in your footsteps? The sad thing is, he won't even know why. He'll hit his middle teens and just start drinking. It's how he'll cope. And as life becomes more complicated, he'll turn to drugs, just like his dear old dad."

Chris's face turned purple and he stormed forward to put the boot in. Billie screamed a warning, but he was beyond reason now. The pain and fear he kept buried in his heart had been exposed and that was unforgivable.

As he broke the circle of containment, the Nameless sent him flying backwards through the plasterboard wall to the kitchen, crashing into my cheap electric cooker.

It tried to move one of my arms, but the restraints still held us fast. I felt its momentary irritation and watched in horror as the bolts that secured my right arm began to undo themselves, spinning in squeaky circles. The bracket fell away with a metal clang in mere moments. Next came the left arm, then the demon physically tore the brackets off my feet. It cricked my neck, turned to face Billie and Benjamin and said, "That's better. Now, which one of you should I kill first?"

Billie and Benjamin backed away from the monster, eyes wide in absolute terror. The Nameless laughed, drinking it up like fine wine.

"Oh, don't feel too bad," it said in a conciliatory tone. "Your half-baked little scheme came worryingly close to actually working. Never mind, you can take some comfort in the fact that I've been at this game for thousands of years. In all that time, there are only a handful of times you apes have got even close to defeating me, so bravo! But I can't let this insult go unpunished."

With a flick of my fingers the iPad exploded like a grenade, leaving shards of glass and metal embedded in Benjamin's hands. Then the demon turned its attention to Billie.

"I've been thinking, Miss Richards, and of all the possible ways this can go, I think I'm going to get the biggest reaction - the most horror and despair - if I kill you first in front of your two friends."

Billie rose into the air, screaming in disbelief. Her limbs were forcibly straightened out into an X and I quailed inside. I knew what came next.

"I do have a fondness for this one," it said conversationally. Then, with another flick of its wrist, the bones in Billie's left forearm snapped.

Her shrieks tore at my eardrums, tore at my heart and, in the prison of my mind, I screamed with her.

All of my pain, my guilt and self-loathing came out in that silent howl, and the Nameless within drank it all down. The damned thing ejaculated, so intense was our feeling of despair. I'd given it everything it wanted in spades. Opened up my rotten soul and served it all up to the entity as lunch.

It closed my eyes, relishing this feeling. Bathing in it.

So distracted, in fact, that it failed to realise that Benjamin was still chanting quietly by the door to the kitchen. He strode forward now, holding his bleeding hand out before him, eyes blazing with fury and power.

"Udug.hul, urudug.se, gigim.ma!" he screamed at The Nameless, and he flicked the blood from his clenched fist right into my face.

The result was instantaneous.

Cold fire spread through my body, and the demon shrieked in agony and rage.

"You think this will stop me?" it screamed. "I'll come back and hunt you all down. I'll flay you all alive, and everyone you've ever loved!"

I felt it clinging on with those spidery claws, leaving deep scratches in my psyche, hot with infection, but it *was* dragged out of me, bit by bit. My body arched backwards as it began forcing its way up from my stomach, and I heard vertebrae crack. The thing started to congeal in my oesophagus returning to the boiling, writhing mass that tasted like burning tyres and rotting meat. My jaw cracked wide, blood trickled down my chin, and I thought I would choke to death on the thing.

Then it was out, this pulsating mass of corruption, and before we knew it, it had been sucked across the room, through the bars of the metal cage, and straight into the surprised-looking brown guinea pig that had been innocently munching on a piece of lettuce to that point.

The creature's eyes widened, then began to bulge, and for a moment, I imagined the rodent would simply split in half, unable to contain the Nameless. Then it was over, apart from a lingering stench in the air. A cold sweat washed across my body, my head spun, and I fell to my knees just as the vomit sprayed from my mouth. I puked until there was nothing left to come up, then wiped the yellow tendrils of bile from my lips and looked around the room.

Billie sat on the floor, cradling her broken arm, her face ash-white and her hair sticking to her forehead in sweaty clumps. Benjamin slumped to his knees, his blood-stained hands trembling.

Chris appeared in the doorway, looking shaken and bruised but largely unharmed from his encounter with my living room wall. I guessed he still had that stab vest on. "Is that it? Did we get tha bastard?"

Everyone turned their heads to the cage and regarded its occupant. The guinea pig's eyes were jet black, with a cold, silver pinprick of light flaring in their centres. Until then, it hadn't occurred to me that guinea pigs could have facial expressions, but this one did. It glared at us with unbridled malice. I was very glad Chris had bought a heavy-duty cage to contain it.

"My God, it worked!" said Benjamin. "We got it."

"Good enough fer me. Time for this wee cunt te have his bath."

"No, wait!" I managed to croak. "You heard it. It's been around for thousands of years. Even if we do manage to banish it, it'll come back sooner or later. We'd be looking over our shoulders for the rest of our bloody lives."

"So, what? Ye gonna keep it as a pet?"

Despite the pain and exhaustion I felt, that thought raised a little smile.

"You know what, that sounds like a great idea. Until Benny-boy comes up with a better solution, that's exactly what I'm gonna do. I hope Mr Nibbles here likes the taste of lettuce."

The guinea pig's expression changed from raw hatred to something like outrage as the Nameless pictured its future.

It's the little things, sometimes, that make all of the horrors of life bearable.

Chapter Sixteen

Benjamin spoke several incantations over the guinea pig cage and placed it within a circle of protection. Once we all felt a little more secure, he drove Billie and Chris to University College Hospital to get their injuries attended to. I declined the invitation to join them, though I did feel like I'd been through a threshing machine. I needed a bit of time to process what I'd just been through and to figure out what my next step would be. I still hadn't replied to Steph, so I sent a quick apology and asked if she was okay. There was no response, no indication that she'd seen the message, so I moved on to other thoughts. The demonic Mrs Wells was still out there, along with her pet Shart, and they could make my life very fucking difficult. I wondered if Benjamin could help there. If I understood it right, we'd have to find out her True Name first, though I had no idea how. There was something else nagging at me, but I couldn't quite think what.

Fuck it, I thought. *Shower first, then bed*. I limped into the bathroom, peeled my blood-soaked clothing off, and saw my chest in the mirror. Jesus! No wonder I ached so much. There were hundreds of intricate and arcane symbols carved into my skin in whirling patterns.

The wounds had been cleaned and dried, but they covered almost every part of my chest and stomach. Had the Nameless done this to me, or was it Wells? Goddamn. It could just as easily have been Benjamin and Billie while I was unconscious, but... why? What did it mean? I was still pondering this mystery later as I fell into bed, but I was no closer to an answer when sleep claimed me.

I don't know how long I was out for. I don't remember dreaming, which was a mercy after all I'd witnessed. I probably would have slept for days if left to my own devices but, unfortunately, that was not to be.

I woke to the sound of my front door being rammed open. "Armed police!" a voice shouted, far louder than necessary. As my eyes adjusted to the bright light, I found my gaze drawn to the muzzle of a semi-automatic rifle.

Ah, yes. Of course.

***

I looked around the interview room and decided that the Tottenham Police Station was in even more need of refurbishment than the Wembley station I'd been stuck in after Marcus and Zoe took their dive. The avocado paintwork was peeling off the walls in places, and salt deposits had oozed from the bricks over time to form white blooms across the walls. They reminded me of fungus I'd once seen sprouting from the decomposing body of a murder victim. The ancient steel-legged desk and laminated wood fire door were artefacts from a different age. The only vaguely modern item in the room was the Digital Interview Management System, just like the one they'd used in Wembley. I guessed the Metropolitan Police had bought a job-lot of the things.

God knows where they found the money. Back in my day they still used twin cassette recorders.

Of course, the other difference between my interview today and the one I'd given last week was that this time, I was under caution. The handcuffs chafed something rotten.

They'd allowed me to put some clothes on, thankfully, though I didn't look my best. When you are gazing down the barrel of several Heckler and Koch MP5s, you tend to grab the first items of clothing that come to hand – and grab them very slowly indeed. From the nervous expressions of the arresting officers, it seemed that sudden movements would be a very bad idea.

So, I'd spent several hours sitting in a cell, wearing a pair of sweatpants with some rather nasty spaghetti stains down the legs, and a t-shirt that smelled as if someone had died in it. Not ideal. And that was before my chest wounds started bleeding through the fabric.

It was standard procedure to make you sweat while officers went through your property, bagging everything up as evidence. I didn't mind the quiet time in the cells, though; it gave me time to think.

The Authorised Firearms Officers had told me I was under arrest for murder. Given the aggressive incursion, I could only assume that I'd been spotted leaving Big Eddie's warehouse and identified, which meant there would be CCTV footage. To the best of my knowledge, the Nameless hadn't killed anyone else. The combination of likely CCTV footage and witness statements would be bad enough, but, when you added in the dripping, gore-soaked pile of forensic evidence in my flat, I was pretty much screwed. They had me bang to rights from an evidential perspective. That gave me two options: I could clam up, responding to everything with 'no comment', or I could try to argue the case for self-defence.

I'd been treated badly enough by the police – in uniform and beyond – that I genuinely toyed with the idea of making them work for it. It was relatively easy to keep your mouth shut when the alternative was having your arse pounded by the full weight of the law. Trouble was, the evidence was pretty damning, and there was a lot of it.

The self-defence plea was difficult, but it did have some things going for it. I had, after all, been beaten and abducted by a gang of known villains, then taken to an abandoned warehouse for a proper old-school gangland execution. The problem here was this: if I went down that route, the 'why?' would very quickly be replaced with 'how?' And 'how' was not something I could answer very easily. If I started to talk about being possessed, they'd stick me in the nuthouse quick as shit. Again, not ideal. However, given my past career as a policeman, it was a lot less likely to get me killed than throwing me into the general populace of Wormwood Scrubs.

Oh, boy.

By the time they finally escorted me to the interview room for my second period of waiting and sweating it out, I'd already run through my admittedly limited options and decided on my course of action.

And then DI Julie Adams walked into the room.

Bollocks.

Julie sat opposite me at the table, a heavyset, grey-haired man beside her. The blood vessels in the man's bulbous nose were beginning to show, a sure sign of career-copper alcoholism. One look at his rumpled suit and the fact he'd missed several spots of stubble while shaving told me all I needed to know about his domestic situation. Detective Sergeant at best, divorced or separated. Pisshead. He could have been *me*, the poor bastard.

Julie leaned across, started the recording, and began the official spiel. "I am Detective Inspector Julie Adams, and this is Detective

Sergeant William Holloway. The date is Tuesday, 11th March 2025, and the time is 10:00 a.m. We are in the interview room at Tottenham Police Station. This interview is being audibly recorded. The purpose of this interview is to ask you questions regarding the murders of several men in Haringey on the 10th of March 2025. Please state your full name and date of birth for the record."

I rolled my eyes and obliged. "Jack Carlton, the 22nd of November 1989."

Julie continued her script without looking up. "You do not have to say anything, but it may harm your defence if you do not mention, when questioned, something which you later rely on in court. Anything you do say may be given in evidence. Do you understand?"

"Yes," I sighed. "I understand."

"This interview relates to the deaths of six men in an industrial unit on Markfield Road on 10th March 2025. We will now begin asking you questions about this matter. If at any point you need a break or do not understand something, please let us know."

I leaned back on the chair, looked from Julie to DS Holloway and then asked them where the duty solicitor was.

Julie cleared her throat and made a show of looking at some papers. Holloway chipped in to say, "Mr Timus is currently caught in traffic. He'll be joining us presently."

I smiled at her, ignoring the man once more and said, "I think I'd better wait then, don't you?"

If I was going to stand a chance, I needed every card I could get on my side. Julie ploughed on regardless. I couldn't blame her. It was a tactic that actually worked once in a while.

"Can you tell us what you were doing at the industrial estate on Markfield Road yesterday afternoon?"

"No comment."

"What is the nature of your relationship with Mr Edward Halliwell of Finsbury Park, London."

"No comment."

"What was the nature of your relationship with the deceased schoolgirl, Chloë Davidson?"

That one shocked me and, while Julie's face remained impassive, I could see in her eyes that she'd seen it. "No comment," I said, trying to keep my voice even.

"What were you doing with Chloë Davidson on Windmill Road, Hampton Hill, at the time of her death on Saturday the 8th of March 2025?"

"No comment."

"Did Chloë Davidson run out in front of that bus while trying to escape from you?"

"No comment."

"Are you responsible for the disappearance of your ex-wife, Sarah Carlton and your daughter, Stephanie Carlton?"

I went ice cold at this, trying to process what she'd just said.

"Have you done something to your ex-wife and daughter, Jack? Are they all right?" Julie said, leaning forward. "Can you tell us where they are, Jack?"

My composure was gone. I managed to keep my voice low, but my tone was urgent. "When did this happen? Why am I only hearing about this now?"

Julie leaned into the microphone. "To be clear, are you telling me that you do not know where they are?"

"Of course, I don't know where they are. I didn't know they were missing until you told me just now. Christ! Steph tried to call me yesterday morning, but I was on my way to—" I shook my head. "That fucker, Hartington, and his demon bitch client. They must have them. Listen, Julie – I know things look bad, and I'll tell you everything you need to know, but you need to get some units down to Chemosh Property Management Services. Margaret Wells, the CEO, has a secret elevator down to some abandoned subway tunnels. I'll bet you anything that's where they took them."

Julie shook her head, and I saw some genuine sadness in her eyes. "Hartington? Do you mean Stuart Hartington?"

"Who the fuck else would I mean?"

She sighed and rubbed her forehead. "The man whom your ex-wife is currently involved with. The man you blame for wrecking your career... That Stuart Hartington?"

"Jesus, did everybody on the planet know except me?"

"Listen, Jack, you're clearly not well at the moment. We want to help you, but we need to help *them* as well. Just... tell me where they are and whether or not they're okay."

I slammed my fists onto the desk. "I just fucking told you, Julie. I swear to God! *Listen.* Wells has some sort of demon in her. It's all connected to the King's College massacre. And she can... she can make people do things. Whatever she wants them to do. And Hartington, he's up to his neck in it. I know it sounds crazy, but I'm telling you the truth. You've got to let me go! I have to save her!"

Julie opened her mouth to reply – something dry and pitying, I'm sure – but the door to the interview room opened, and Mrs Wells waltzed in, calm as you please, flanked by two large, and very much armed men.

"Who the hell are you, and what are you doing here?" barked Julie. She started getting to her feet, then her mind registered the semi-automatic pistols.

"Sit down!" Mrs Wells said sternly, and Julie obeyed. Wells turned her glare on me. "Mr Carlton, you are proving to be rather problematic. You should have been dead by now, but I suppose that can be remedied easily enough." She turned her black eyes onto DS Holloway and said, "Sergeant, would you be so kind as to delete all copies of this interview?"

Holloway got to his feet, pressed a couple of buttons on the DIMS and said, "It's done," in a flat voice.

"Good," said Mrs Wells. "Now, please sit down and stop breathing." She turned to Julie, fixing her with her empty stare and leered. "Now, if you would be so kind as to remove any record of Mr Carlton's arrest. Oh, and any evidence of us having been in this station, please."

"What?" Julie demanded. "Don't be ridiculous! I don't know who the hell you think you are, but you aren't going to get away with this."

Mrs Wells's brow furrowed, bemused by this resistance. She turned her gaze to me instead and released a sharp sigh. "Very well. Mr Carlton, please strangle Detective Inspector Adams, then follow me."

I felt the familiar cold probing sensation as Mrs Wells tried to exert her influence and then, just as quickly, felt those tendrils withdraw. Her eyes widened in shock. I think perhaps mine did, too.

"Performance problems can be common in middle age," I said, unable to keep the grin from my face. "I hear there are pills you can take for that. Now, why don't you tell me what you've done with my daughter, you piece of shit?"

"Hmm, interesting," Wells murmured to herself, glance pinging from me to Julie and back again. "Bring him," she said to the muscle-bound thugs. "Her, too." Then she glanced over to Holloway, whose face had turned purple. "Detective Sergeant, you may breathe again." Holloway sucked air into his lungs with a huge gasp. "There, that's better, isn't it? Once you are satisfied that no evidence of our visit remains, please burn this station to the ground – with yourself in it."

Holloway nodded and left the room while Julie and I were dragged to our feet and shoved along the corridor at gunpoint.

"Jack," Julie gasped, "what the hell is going on?"

"I tried to tell you, Jules. Demon bitch; mind control; secret lair. I swear to God, sometimes I think you don't listen to a word I say."

One of the hired goons jabbed her in the back with his pistol, and we started walking.

"Well, pardon me for not immediately buying into your bullshit," she growled. "In my defence, your stories haven't always proven to be accurate in the past. 'Sarah's just a friend.' Remember that one? 'She's nothing for you to be worried about.' Hm?"

Ouch. Fair enough.

As we walked through the station, we passed at least four dead police officers who lay spread out in the corridors, eyes wide open in terror, the tell-tale blue tint of cyanosis dulling their lips and the tips of their fingers. It didn't take a genius to work out what had happened to them. The lack of smoke damage to the lungs would come out in the autopsy, no doubt, but the coroner would have a hell of a time explaining how these healthy young men had asphyxiated *before* the fire broke out. The assumption would probably be some sort of gas leak, which went on to trigger the fire. Media outlets would report on the tragedy, it would be written off as a terrible accident, and not one person would be looking at Margaret Wells. God! How many of her competitors – or even people who had mildly inconvenienced her – had died of apparently natural causes over the years? It boggled the mind. Murder was easy when you could kill with a word and leave no evidence.

We were ushered out through the front door and into the rear of a black SUV with darkened windows. The gun-toting slabs of muscle slid in either side of us. I felt the barrel of the pistol jab up beneath my ribs and, from the yelp that escaped Julie's lips, I could only assume she got the same treatment.

The vehicle pulled away from Tottenham Police Station as the first licks of flame illuminated the downstairs windows.

The journey across the capital would have taken an hour at the best of times, but with the unseasonable snowfall and the backlog from rush hour traffic, it took almost twice that. So, yeah. Two hours crammed into the back of a car with a 9mm pistol sticking into my ribs. Fun. The city's roads were torturous at the best of times, even without the snow. The traffic was all stop-start, with angry motorists expressing their feelings through the liberal hammering of their horns. As much as I loathed the underground, I was reminded why I didn't even bother owning a car in London. The fact that I couldn't afford to run one was beside the point.

After a few miles, Julie turned to the man beside her and said, "Look, I don't care what orders you think you're following. I'm a Detective Inspector in the Metropolitan Police Service. If you let myself and Mr Carlton out of this car, right now, I promise that it will go in your favour in court."

The man looked at her, then laughed. "You hear that?" he said to the other man. "If we let her go, she'll go easy on us. Ain't that a relief?"

"Yeah. I heard. She doesn't even make the top ten of all the people I'm worried about upsetting right now." Mr Muscle dug his pistol further into my side, presumably as a warning against trying something, and leaned across the seat. "I'm going to say this once, Detective Inspector. My colleagues and I have been instructed to deliver you *alive* to a specific place. There is no qualification as to whether you are conscious or not. Maimed or not. Are you getting the picture? Such details have been left to our discretion. So, I strongly recommend you sit back, enjoy the journey and keep your fucking mouth shut for the duration. Otherwise, my colleagues and I may decide to take a more... scenic route."

I felt Julie's body stiffen beside me, and she sat back in the seat, eyes fixed on the road. I took her hand in mine and gave it a gentle squeeze. It had been something we'd done long ago, when we were together. A bit of human contact, just to let each other know that we weren't alone. That we understood each other. She didn't turn her head, but she gave my hand a small squeeze in return.

Eventually, the Mercedes turned off the main roads and into a small blind alley with a single metal roller door at the far end. As the SUV approached, the door began to rise. The vehicle drove through and, as the rollers fell again, the car's headlights flicked on.

The vehicle descended a long concrete ramp, deep into the earth, for what seemed a good two minutes. Eventually, the ramp levelled off and we continued into the darkness. At times, the spaces were open, with concrete floors and thick support pillars, as if we were traversing an abandoned car park. Other times, the passageway was tight – barely wide enough for the chunky vehicle to make it between the narrow red-brick walls without scratching its paint job. Water flowed down the walls in these places, staining the bricks with algae and salt deposits. It became impossible to keep track of the direction or distance travelled, though I'd made every effort. At one point, we went down another ramp, deeper into these mysterious, abandoned spaces. Once, I thought I saw the flashing lights of a tube train off in the distance as it sped past an access point; another time, I thought I saw a pale face peering out at us from the darkness, but it swiftly vanished into the Stygian blackness. My best guess was that we'd been travelling beneath the city for at least half an hour before we arrived at our destination – a wide-open space with three identical SUVs already parked beside a pair of heavy steel-reinforced doors. Mr Muscle climbed out, tapped the window with the side of his pistol and waved me out.

I didn't think he'd kill us – the Wells thing clearly wanted us alive for a reason – but I knew he'd quite cheerfully put a round in my elbow if I gave him any shit. There was a world of difference between these professionals and the barely trained gorillas Big Eddie Halliwell used as enforcers. The way they moved gave it away. There was an economy to everything they did. Their movements achieved everything they wanted their bodies to do in the fastest, most efficient way possible. They didn't speak unless it was necessary; they didn't put fear into someone or hurt them unless told to, or if they perceived it as the most efficient way to achieve their goals. If that were the case, they would do what was needed without a second's hesitation or regret. I'd have been scared shitless of these men if I weren't already far more scared of the woman they worked for.

We were ushered through the doorway into the semi-circular white tiled corridor beyond. Whilst I couldn't be sure this was the same abandoned underground complex I'd been in the previous day, it seemed more than likely. I could only assume that the circuitous route had been born of a desire to keep our arrival far from prying eyes. Whilst the receptionist of Chemosh Property Management Services may or may not have been complicit in the goings-on, having a man in spaghetti-stained sweatpants and a bloodstained t-shirt escorted to the secret elevator at gunpoint didn't really fit their corporate brand image.

Julie and I were marched through identical tunnels until we arrived at a section with several heavy steel doors in the walls. Mr Muscle pulled open the first door and motioned for us both to enter. The room beyond was dark, but the stench of decay hit us like a punch to the face. We hesitated at the threshold, gagging at the stench.

"Wait, please..." Julie said, but her guard shoved her into the room with sufficient force to drive her to her knees. I shrugged and stepped inside under my own steam. I was under no illusions as to my ability to either fight our way out of the situation or talk our captors into letting us go. And honestly, my various injuries were screaming at me. I had no desire to add to the chorus of agonised nerve endings. As I crossed the threshold, the door clanged shut behind us, leaving us in darkness. Who knew how long it would be before we'd see the light of day again?

"You two behave yourselves," said Mr Muscle from the other side of the door. They conversed briefly then I heard both men's footsteps echo down the tunnel as they walked away in different directions, each to their next duty.

There was no illumination except the cracks of light around the doorframe, so I joined Julie and waited until my eyes adjusted to the darkness. We were in a large, empty room – a concrete cube roughly twenty feet square. No other doors. The stench emanated from a corpse in the far corner. It was hard to tell by sight, but it smelled as if it had been there for quite some time. He'd once been a large man, but the flesh had tightened across his bones, and most of his body mass had long since liquified, spreading out to leave stains of corruption beneath him. I couldn't see any obvious signs of trauma on the body with my cursory look. I checked his pockets and found a petrol lighter that sparked to life instantly. Nothing else was on him, not even a packet of cigarettes to accompany the lighter. I'd not had a smoke in two days now, and my nerves jangled at the thought of a nicotine rush. As if I wasn't on edge enough.

Julie had managed to pull herself together, and she came over to join me by the corpse.

"Who do you think he was?" she asked, her voice trembling.

"Just some poor bastard that pissed Wells off by the looks of it. That suit was expensive once. They just threw the poor fucker in here and forgot about him."

Julie shuddered at the thought. I didn't have the heart to tell her that our fate would likely be settled long before we died of thirst.

"Okay, Jack," she said. "No more bullshit. You need to tell me everything. Now. Every last sodding detail."

It was good to see her detective training beginning to reassert itself. Gather the facts. Don't prejudge the evidence. Don't try to form a narrative – not yet. "Okay," I said, "but fair warning, this is going to sound insane. I've been caught up in this for a while and I still struggle to believe half of it, despite everything that's happened."

"I saw what she did at the Tottenham nick," she said. "I know there's something very wrong at the heart of all this, but I need to know it. So spill."

"Sure," I said, taking a seat on the cold concrete as far away from our fragrant cellmate as I could. "Why not? I guess we've got time…"

I told it all in as much detail as I could remember, starting with Wells and the King's College gig. There were spots where I could have fudged things, made myself look better – or at least not quite as bad – but she knew me too well. Besides, she deserved the truth. Julie listened intently, only speaking to prompt clarification or to shut down any speculation about causes or intentions. I stuck to the facts and, hearing myself relay it to her in this way, my brain began to synchronise with her thought processes. It was like the old days. We weren't two people trapped in a dungeon with a corpse; we were two trained detectives going over the evidence. Laying it all down to get a clear idea of the whole. To start looking for patterns and gaps.

When I finished, she was silent for a moment. Then she began to check things off with her fingers.

"So, there are a few things I still don't understand. Firstly, why did she make Marcus and Chloë Davidson take their own lives?"

"She was tying up loose ends. Getting rid of the witnesses, so there'd be no one to challenge her version of events. She needed King's College to go away, and she wanted to clear her daughter's name."

"Okay, I get that, though Marcus wasn't the only person on the scene. Hm. We might need to review the evidence, see if it's been tampered with at all. The other question is this – *how* did she do it? From what you said, she was always present in the room to give verbal commands when she took control. But she wasn't in Marcus's flat, and she wasn't around when Chloë killed herself. So, how did she do it?"

I'd been asking myself the same question for the last few hours. "If you're asking how magic works, I haven't got a clue," I replied, "but if you're asking how she *directed* it, my best guess is the fucking raven. It keeps popping up. I think she uses it to keep an eye on things remotely, and when necessary, to take control. It's the only thing that makes sense to me."

I looked her dead in the eye as I said this, daring her to mock me. She swallowed hard and shook her head.

"None of this makes sense, Jack. The whole thing is nuts. I don't have the faintest idea as to how we'd even begin to build a case around this. They'd laugh me out of the room if I brought even half of this to the CPS. There's not a shred of physical evidence, and nothing to tie her to any of it. And even if there was, even if we could show them a fucking spell book, you know what they do with anything they can't sell to a jury."

I sighed. "Yup. Bury it. Can't go wasting taxpayers' money on woo woo bollocks."

"I mean, it makes sense," she said. "You remember how mad everyone went back when we were doing basic training? The panic over that fake YouTube video? Half the country swore werewolves were about to burst through their front doors."

"Fair enough," I said, rubbing my chin. "But given the shit we're in right now... I dunno, I'm starting to think my friend Billie's right about an awful lot more than I ever gave her credit for. God fucking dammit!"

"So, what's the plan?"

"Well, we're going to escape from this cell, rescue my daughter – and my ex, I suppose – find Robyn, and then I'm going to kill that demon bitch. Oh, and kick Hartington's balls into his throat. After that... I don't know. Pub? I figure I owe you a drink or two."

"Great plan," she said. "But you can keep your drinks. Any thoughts as to how we get out of this cell?"

"Not a fucking clue."

We started laughing then. It was ludicrous, horrible, but we couldn't stop ourselves. It was all so hopeless and desperate. There wasn't a damned thing we could do about the door, the demon in Wells, or any of it. I half wished we could stay here, have the dignity of being forgotten like the corpse in the corner, but we'd have no such luck. If I knew Wells, she had something particularly nasty in mind for us. All we could do was wait.

So we waited.

And waited.

And—

The cell door flew open, and my guts coiled. This was it. I got to my feet and tightened my hands into fists, squinting into the light. I'd rather go down fighting than face whatever horror Mrs Wells had in store for us. As I charged at our captors, a booming voice rang out.

"Alright there, pal? Either of ye cunts order an Uber?"

Chapter Seventeen

I grabbed Chris in a bear hug and said, "Mate, I could fucking kiss you!"

His eyes mirrored the relief in mine, but Chris was… well, Chris. He shoved me away playfully and said, "Yeah, I can feel ye gettin' hard, too, but ah've told you before, pal – I dinnae swing that way."

Julie and I hurried out of the cell to find Billie and Benjamin in the corridor, looking nervous and dishevelled but no worse than when I'd last seen them. Billie's arm was in a cast now, and she held it to her chest as if that might protect it from further damage.

"What happened to you?" I said. "How the hell did you find us?"

"I go by Sherlock Barnes these days, didn't ya hear?" said Chris.

"Twat!" Billie muttered. "Ignore him. They were waiting for us when we got back to your flat." Her voice seemed to be slurring slightly.

"Aye," said Chris. "Sneaky bastards waited until we were all inside, then stuck us with needles. Oh, your flat's fucked, by the way. Even more than usual, I mean."

An ice finger ran down my spine. "Oh, God. Did they...? Is it still there?"

"Yer demonic guinea pig? Aye, it's right where we left it, divvnae worry. Fucker was starin' daggers at us, mind."

That was some small relief, at least.

"So, they brought you here, did they?" Julie said, suspicion in her voice. "How did you get away?"

Chris side-eyed her and laughed. "The daft twats shot us up with ketamine. Knocked these two on their arses, of course, but ah've had plenty o' practise wi' ket. It barely gave me a head-tickle. Ah just played possum until the right opportunity presented itself to, shall ah say, extricate ourselves from the situation."

"Extricate?"

"Aye. Ah waited until the big bastard was dragging me inte the cell, then grabbed the taser off his belt and stuck it in his bollocks."

Yeah. That'd do it.

"So, you've got his taser?"

Chris's face spread into a wide grin. "Oh, ah've got a wee bit more than that. Check this shit out."

Chris tugged an extendable riot baton from behind his back with one hand, then produced a 9mm pistol with his other.

"Oh mate, are you sure I can't give you a kiss?"

"Only if ye don't mind me shoving that baton up your arse. Anyway, don't get too excited. Ah've not even gotten to the really good shit yet..."

He tucked them away again, then showed us the taser, a canister of CS gas, and what I could only assume was a fucking hand grenade.

"Jesus," I said, suddenly terrified. Chris Barnes packing high explosives... Like I didn't have enough nightmare fuel. "Why don't you just let me have those, eh, mate? Before you blow your nuts off."

"Get te fuck. Ye can have the pistol, though; ah wouldn't know how te use that if mah life depended on it."

I shook my head. When Chris got like this, there was no point arguing. And we really didn't have the time to waste. "Okay, let's divide up what we have. Jules, take the baton. Billie, take the taser and give the gas grenade to Benjamin."

Julie stepped forward. "I should take the firearm. Just possessing one of those is a mandatory five-year stretch."

I shook my head. "No way, Jules. Full respect, but you're a serving police officer; you're bound by certain rules – like warning people before you fire. If I get Wells in my sights, I'm sure as fuck not going to give her a chance to use her mojo; I'm going to put a round between her eyes. You can arrest me after if you like." I tried to give her a reassuring smile and said, "Besides, just think of all the paperwork if you have to use the thing."

Her exasperation was all too familiar, but she conceded the point with a sigh. "Fine. But if you use that for anything other than self-defence, I'll throw away the key. Now, shall we get the hell out of here so I can call for backup?"

I looked up and down the corridor, noting a couple of closed doors. "Chris, did you see Steph and Sarah? Or Robyn?"

"Nah. The far door there is where they were keepin' us. The other one's some sort of generator room."

"Okay, the rest of you, get out of here. Try to work your way back to those SUVs if you can. With any luck, they'll have left the keys in the ignition. I'm going to go find my daughter."

"Bollocks te that," said the truculent Scotsman.

"Chris is right," said Billie. "If they catch even one of us, we could be used as leverage. We stand a better chance if we stay together."

I looked at each person in turn. We were all scared, but there was determination on every face.

"Alright. We know the cars are parked that way," I said, motioning to the left corridor. "We'll check down this way. Stick together, and don't make a sound. These guys are professionals, and they'll wipe the floor with us in a straight-up fight. We just need to find our people and get the hell out of here. Sound like a plan?"

Everyone nodded their assent, and we moved off as a group down the right-hand corridor. I just hoped I wasn't about to get everyone killed.

The place was eerily quiet. The screams and cries I'd heard on my previous visit were now absent. We came across several machine rooms, storerooms and the like, but found no sign of any other captives. Every time one of the reinforced steel doors creaked open, I had to fight the rising tide of fear that I'd find a more recent corpse behind it, one that was all too familiar. Twice, we heard footsteps echoing through the complex, and each time we managed to duck into one of the side rooms, huddling in the darkness until the footsteps receded. The place was a maze, and I began re-evaluating my earlier thoughts of this being some sort of abandoned tube station. It was too labyrinthine for that. More likely some form of old, Second World War governmental shelter, no doubt purchased for an extortionate amount by Chemosh Property Management.

Ahead of us, the corridor branched out in three different directions. To the left and right were more of the same tunnels, but the space opened up ahead into what seemed to be a larger chamber with a domed ceiling. There were faint voices coming from there. I motioned for everyone to stay where they were for now, and I crept forward.

As I came to the entrance, I realised this was the room where Wells had dragged the Nameless out of Alice and poured it into me. I was on a mezzanine level, though, a floor above the black altar. My eyes were caught by two figures standing at the base of the wall opposite. It was Steph and her mother, flanked by a pair of mercenaries. Both seemed unharmed, although I noticed that Sarah's glasses were missing. At least a dozen more hired guns were standing around in the chamber below, while others carried wooden crates into the room. Orchestrating it all was Margaret Wells – or the creature wearing her skin. I spotted her when she started screaming obscenities at one of the mercenaries. The poor bastard almost dropped the crate he was carrying, and that was enough for Darth Wells. She held her hand out and the man fell to his knees, clutching at his throat. Moments later, he lay still.

"You there!" Wells shouted at one of the guards. "Get rid of this fool, then help the others with the artefacts."

I glanced back to Steph and Sarah. Mother and daughter glared at their captor with glacial expressions. The resemblance between the two of them was uncanny. Demonic powers or not, I didn't fancy Wells's chances if they got themselves free.

My options for rescue were extremely limited. I doubted whether Steph and Sarah were here for the good of their health. The demon bitch queen had something big in mind, I could tell. Some nasty arse ritual that needed people. And it seemed this was a lot more complex than the one she'd performed on me.

I needed to act. *Now.*

I hurried back to the group. "Okay, Robyn's still MIA, but I've found Steph and Sarah. The bad news is they're being guarded by at least a dozen armed mercenaries and Wells is in the room, being her usual charming self. So, here's the plan..."

Plan. Plan. I needed a fucking plan.

"I'm just gonna straight up shoot that monster between the eyes. She's the biggest threat by far. Benjamin, once I've done that, I need you to chuck that CS gas canister in there. You don't have to be particularly accurate, just get it in amongst the guards. That should cause enough confusion for me and Julie to free Steph and Sarah without getting shot. Then, when we make it back up here, Chris, I'll need you to lob your grenade down there behind us. Yeah?"

"Yes!" Chris was practically glowing with anticipation.

"What then?" asked Billie.

"Then we run like fuckery. Any more questions?"

Julie raised an eyebrow. "Did you just pull that out of your arse?" I nodded. She snorted. "I'm almost impressed. We'll probably get cut in half by automatic rifle fire before we make it halfway across that room, but given what we have to work with, it's probably our best shot. Small tweak, though, if I may? Chris shouldn't use the grenade in here. See those steel pipes on the walls? Look at the stickers on the side. They're carrying fuel oil. We don't want to burn the place down with us still inside."

I nodded in agreement, although poor Chris looked crestfallen. "Good call. Okay, everyone. It's shock and awe time."

They were big words, but I didn't feel them. My heart hammered in my chest, and I had to calm my breathing for a few seconds. I'd never killed anyone before. Not *me*. Big Eddie and his goons were all undone by the Nameless, and those acts had sickened me. In addition, I knew what Wells was going through. She'd done terrible things for many years and would do worse if she wasn't stopped, but I couldn't help picturing the woman she'd once been – the weak voice screaming for freedom in the back of her brain. I didn't know how this all began: whether she was taken by force or if she'd invited the damned thing inside, but there was a person in there somewhere. A human being.

I wiped the sweat from my eyes, gripped the pistol with both hands to stop them from shaking, and lined the shot up. Dead in the middle of Mrs Wells's forehead. The main body mass would be easier to hit, but we needed a kill shot. One and done. She couldn't be allowed to use her power.

I took a deep breath, then let it out slowly. But my finger was frozen.

It's got to be easier in the heat of the moment, in a fight, when you're defending yourself, or caught in a mindless rage. The military spends a long time training their recruits to switch off the part of their brain that sees the enemy as people. They just need you to aim the weapon, squeeze the trigger, find the next target. The problem was, I'd never had that training. I kept imagining mother and daughter before the demons came. It made me think of Sarah and Steph. It made me hesitate.

"Jack," said Julie.

I tried to ignore her words. *Come on! Aim and squeeze. You've got this.*

"Jack!" Julie said again. Louder this time. Too loud.

I spun around in anger, to see Mr Muscle and his gym buddies standing behind us, weapons raised.

"Hey, Jack," the mercenary said. "Good to see you. I was wondering where you'd gotten to. Best drop your weapon, eh? Right. Fucking. Now."

I considered firing anyway, but the submachine gun would turn me into dog meat before I'd raised my arm. It would have been a quick ending, sure. A better ending than whatever Wells had in store for us. But that was the coward's way out. It'd leave everyone else to her tender mercies, and I wasn't that much of an arsehole. Besides, I had a back-up plan. She'd tried to make me strangle Julie before and it hadn't worked. Why? I had a couple of theories: perhaps it was some residue of the Nameless spoiling her connection or maybe it was my close connection to Julie in the past. In the end, it didn't matter. The point was this – she didn't have the same level of control over me that she'd had over that poor bastard Holloway. If she made the mistake of letting me get close, gloating at my capture like some fucking Bond villain, I could punch her in the throat and collapse her windpipe. Not an instant death, but it'd fuck up her voice commands long enough to finish her off.

My adrenaline spiked at the thought, but I kept my movements slow to disguise my intent. I dropped the Glock on the floor and kicked it over to Mr Muscle, who picked it up and waved us back to the crossroads.

"I hope you're going to find us better accommodation this time." I winked over at Julie, who looked aghast. "The last room you gave us wasn't exactly up to scratch. I mean, not only hadn't it been properly cleaned after the last occupant, but you hadn't even bothered to clean up the corpse of the last occupant."

"Shut the fuck up and keep moving," he growled, clearly not appreciating my attempts at humour.

"Don't say I didn't warn you when my Tripadvisor review goes up. Secret Underground Demonic Sex-Dungeon – cold and uncomfortable. No Wi-Fi. Rotting man in the corner. One star. I mean, does this place even have a bar?"

The mercenary jabbed me in the spine with the barrel of his gun. There would be a bruise in the morning, assuming I lived long enough to complain about it.

Within a few minutes, the corridor circled downwards and back on itself, bringing us to the same level as the main ritual chamber. It seemed we weren't returning to our nice, cosy cells after all.

Wells looked up from one of the wooden crates and smiled at Mr Muscle. "Ah, Vincent. I see you've located the rest of our guests."

"Yeah," he said. "They were up on the mezzanine. That one had a Glock aimed at you."

"Then it's a good job you arrived when you did. Has the weak link in your team been taken care of?"

"Yes. Not sure how the fat one got the drop on Carl, but it won't happen again. We'll dump his body with the others offshore once we're all done here."

"Excellent. You never fail to please me, Vincent. However, your recruitment process needs to be a little more rigorous in the future. There have been a couple of disappointments with your current team."

Vince nodded curtly. "I'll vet the next intake myself. There won't be any problems from now on."

She turned her attention to us next, her smile twisting into a snarl. "You have proven to be extremely irritating. If we had more time, I would have enjoyed teaching each and every one of you the error of your ways. Unfortunately, I have other concerns of greater import this evening, so I shall just have to be satisfied with your deaths." She nodded past us and gave her order: "Put them with the other sacrifices. Oh, and if any of them so much as moves, shoot them in the kneecaps – starting with the girl."

We were walked across the room, past the unholy altar and its thousand screaming faces. As I got close, Steph broke away from her mother and threw her arms around my neck. "I knew you'd come! I knew you'd come!"

Vince dragged her away from me and pointed his weapon at her knees. "Sorry, kid, but you heard the boss."

"Jesus, no," I cried, and leaped between Vince and my daughter. "She's just scared. Please! I won't give you any more trouble."

Vince looked at his employer, and she rolled her eyes as if to say she really didn't give a damn either way. Vince lowered his weapon, and I thanked him over and over.

"Next time, I won't hesitate," he said. "No noise. No talking. And no fucking movement until you're told. Got it?"

We got it. We stood there in silence as the crates were unpacked and the artefacts positioned carefully around the chamber. There were ornate candlesticks, carved with images that hurt my eyes, tapestries depicting the most appalling acts of cruelty, a long, heavy trough carved from black stone, with hundreds of screaming faces depicted in bas-relief on its surface. It was like the altar, but the faces were alive, moving, screaming silently within the stone. This was placed in front of the seven of us, and I couldn't help wondering if the writhing host had knelt before this same trough. Finally, Wells produced her long, engraved dagger with those chromatic patterns swirling across its surface, and a chalice carved from the same black stone as the trough. The dagger and cup were placed on the stone altar, then the mercenaries cleared all the packing detritus away.

I had a very bad feeling about this.

The lights in the chamber went out and, as they did so, each of the five black candles burst into flame as one, painting the chamber in a flickering orange light. Wells began chanting once more in that strange, guttural language.

"Bring forth the ascendents!" she cried, and three hooded figures strode through the doorway at the far end of the room. They positioned themselves around Wells in an equilateral triangle, their pride evident in their postures.

"Witness the ascension of the three, as was foretold," Wells intoned. Strangely, the guttural chanting continued in the background. Echoes? A recording? I looked around, but the mercenaries were all stony faced and silent.

"For the first ascendent, we offer my loyal servant, Stuart Hartington, to you, my lord Asmodeus."

The tallest figure swept back his hood to reveal the Shart's eminently punchable face. There was something in his eyes I'd never seen before, though. He looked crazed, ecstatic with a fervour bordering on the religious. A few more puzzle pieces fell into place.

"For the second ascendent, we offer my first-born daughter, Robyn Louise Whittaker, to you, my lord Belial."

The hood swept back, revealing Robyn's head.

Motherfucker.

I'd been played every step of the way. She'd kept me drunk, I realised. Wormed her way into our group then reported right back to Hartington and her mother. They'd known our every move before we'd made it. I was an idiot, and that stupidity seemed likely to be about to cost us all our lives. I was surprised at how much the betrayal stung.

Her hair was different, abandoning the grungy look from when I first met her or the more professional styling when we broke – as I thought – into Hartington's office. This time, it was slicked back with so much product that it probably could have doubled up as a crash helmet. She had way more makeup on than the other times I'd seen her. Complete gothic overkill that would, improbably, still have looked good on her if not for the cruel sneer plastered across her face. She met my eyes for a second and the sneer curled into a smirk.

"Robbin' fuckin Cunt!" growled Chris from beside me. I had to agree with his sentiments.

"For the final ascendent, I offer my youngest daughter, Alice Wells, to you, my lord Azazel."

Alice, of course. Her ascendancy. She wore her hair and makeup in the same manner as her older sister, and now I saw the two of them together – alongside their mother – the family resemblance seemed obvious. The same facial shape, dark eyes, dark hair, and strong jawline.

Idiot, idiot, idiot. It was staring you in the face all along!

Hartington looked like he was about to come in his pants. This was obviously something he'd been working towards for a very long time. Robyn looked arrogant; a privileged woman who, it seemed, was about to receive her birthright – joined with a demon lord in a symbiotic relationship that would grant her power and influence beyond her wildest dreams. Something about Alice's expression bothered me, though. She looked excited, sure, but there was something sly in her expression, too. She looked like she could barely contain a furtive snigger.

I felt something, then. A nagging thought, just on the edge of consciousness. Something was wrong here. Something beyond the obvious demonic ritual and sacrifice. I couldn't piece it together, but there was more than one betrayal happening here.

Powerful hands forced us to our knees before the trough and Mother Wells strode up to us, the swirling knife held before her.

"One shall open the gateway; two shall bring the lord to this world."

I tried to push back against the huge hands grasping my shoulders, but I couldn't move. Steph began to cry next to me, while Sarah screamed a torrent of abuse at Hartington. Chris tried to slam his head into the man holding him fast, but the angle was all wrong. Another mercenary joined the first to hold him in place.

Wells pulled the dagger hard and fast across Benjamin's throat, cutting deep, and Billie screamed in horrified denial. Blood jetted from the wound in a spray and the mercenary shoved him down into the trough to collect the fluid.

Benjamin's eyes locked with mine, a look of terror and disbelief on his face. The jet of blood lessened, then slowed to a trickle.

The mercenary released his shoulders and Benjamin's corpse slumped to the ground while his blood swirled, steaming in the trough. Billie screamed, and when I saw Benjamin's face appear on the inside of the stone trough, I felt like screaming as well.

"One shall open the gateway, two shall bring forth the Lord," Mrs Wells repeated and brought the blade up to Steph's throat.

In circumstances like this, your mind can go to some very strange places. Most of my focus was on that black blade, swinging toward my daughter's throat, in the slow motion of adrenal horror, but my subconscious – nagging at me this whole time – chose that moment to howl its warning and my eyes flicked across to Alice. She was laughing at my pain, drinking it in. And her eyes were jet black.

If you kill one of the Nameless, it inhabits your body.

That was what Benjamin had told us. You invite it in. *Oh, shit.*

Anastasia Grier-Snelling. Cassandra Eulalia Foss. Aldous Jerome. Jarod Virgil Darby... and Alice Wells.

Five possessed teenagers. One still alive.

Alice Wells hadn't just had one Nameless demon inside of her. She'd had five of the bastards.

One was trapped in the body of a guinea pig in my flat, but that meant there were still four of the fuckers here. Biding their time until the right moment. This moment, now. When the gateway to Hell had been opened.

Chapter Eighteen

Things went from godawful to worse almost immediately. Alice raised her right hand and her mother flew backwards, dropping the black blade, which skittered across the floor. It was tantalisingly close to where I knelt; I just couldn't risk grabbing it yet. Not with so many weapons pointing in my approximate direction.

Alice's voice filled the room, but it wasn't *just* her voice. Four distinct personalities were at work, each chanting the same thing from Alice's mouth.

"Exorcizo te, Chemosh, obsolescens daemon, per vim tenebris et potentiam abyssum," they called. *"Recede ab hac aula et servis tuis. In nomini daemonium potentiae, te expello. Revertere ad tenebras tuas et relinquas hanc terram. Per vires obscuras et voluntatem maleficarum, exeo te, Chemosh!"*

The effect was instantaneous. Her mother screamed, her voice warping into a twisted bass tone that resounded oddly from the octagonal chamber walls. The mercenaries closest to the three Ascendants looked shocked. This was most definitely not part of the plan. I felt the meaty hands leave my shoulders and I spun around to see what was happening.

Margaret Wells was on her knees, hands clawing at her throat which seemed to have swollen to twice its usual size. The skin began to split and bleed, her jaw cracked audibly, and blood ran down her chin in rivulets as the black, monstrous demon lord, Chemosh, was dragged from his host.

I'd thought it was bad enough when the Nameless had been pulled out of Alice and poured into me, but that oozing, leprous cloud of flesh and smoke was like a kitten compared to this thing. The creature was primarily composed of a single, red-rimmed eyeball, with a feathery crest of rippling flesh fluttering around it, displaying smaller eyeballs like a peacock. It had four huge, leathery wings edged with vicious claws, while thick tentacles writhed and thrashed from the main body. Each of these ended with a vicious, needle-fanged mouth. Human faces cried and screamed within its flesh. Every part of it that wasn't an eyeball seemed to contain the anguished faces of some damned soul. And the fucking thing was only about ten feet away from us.

Each of the mouths began screaming. A cacophony of outrage and fury. Flesh started peeling away from the entity, igniting as the layers were stripped from its body by the banishment spell of the Nameless. Black, malodorous ichor sprayed from the open sores that broke out across the surface of the demon lord like bubbles, only to burst into green fire as it came into contact with the air. The demon tried to move – to escape or go on the offensive, it was impossible to say, because Alice had held up both hands, sweat pouring from her forehead, and Chemosh found itself frozen in place, howling in pain and rage as its corporeal form dissolved. Within seconds, the only evidence it had been there was the stench of burned flesh and a pile of ash.

For a moment, everything was silent. Then Alice turned her attention to her mother, who found herself raised by invisible hands and floated over to the stone altar.

Alice made two fists and then pushed them out to the sides. Margaret Wells's body was simply torn in half with an awful, wet ripping sound and the cracking of bones. Blood and entrails splashed out from the still-floating corpse, despoiling the altar. Then, with a flick of Alice's wrist, the two halves of Mrs Wells were tossed aside like a discarded toy.

The mercenaries really didn't know what to do. The chain of command had been severed in a particularly graphic and violent manner, the likes of which I doubted any of them had witnessed before. And with the evisceration of their employer, the likelihood of any of them collecting their payment became almost non-existent. As did their chances of survival.

Robyn fell to the floor and screamed, "What have you done, you stupid fucking bitch?" failing to register the fact that Alice was not in charge here. That Alice had not been here in any meaningful way since King's College.

With her arms still outstretched, Alice levitated three feet off the floor and glided across to the steaming heap of entrails that used to be her mother. She stroked the bloody mass gently, then stuffed both hands into the pile and emerged moments later with Mrs Wells's heart in her hands. She smeared the blood across her face, then took a large bite out of the organ.

Hartington did what he usually did. He took in the devastation he'd helped to cause and began slowly edging away from the two sisters, eyeing up his escape. Several of the mercenaries decided that they'd had enough, raised their submachine guns and emptied their clips into

Alice Wells's back. Her body twitched in mid-air as the hollow point rounds slammed into her and, incredibly, she began laughing.

"Stop firing, you fucking idiots," Vince screamed and began sprinting across the chamber, desperate to stop the men before they made things worse. But it was too late. Far too late.

As the MP5s fell silent, Alice's body fell, face down and broken on top of the altar, splashing gore out from beneath her.

Then the body began to spasm and twitch of its own accord.

Black, vaporous tendrils began to rise from the bullet holes, tentative at first, probing the air. The wounds began to stretch, and Alice Wells's back tore open, exposing the white, blood-streaked bones of her spinal column as, one by one, the Nameless entities emerged. The billowing black and yellow forms coalesced into semi-solid masses of eyeballs and tentacles. Nightmare squids that swam almost languidly into the air and began circling the room.

Any restraint the mercenaries had held on to vanished then and there. Thunder filled the room as round after round ripped holes in the demonic entities, only for the wounds to heal over almost as quickly. One of the Nameless made a beeline for the hapless merc that first lost his nerve, crossing the distance so quickly that my eyes had trouble registering the movement. Its tentacles wrapped around the man's head, and it forced its way down his gullet.

Only one mercenary, more disciplined than his colleagues or perhaps more terrified, remained behind us, his aim wavering nervously between the supernatural entities and the prisoners at his feet. I began weighing up my chances of reaching the blade and taking the man out before he blew holes in me with his submachine gun. It was easy, but the thought he might get a few rounds off and hit Steph was almost paralysing. If we stayed here though, death was assured. I tried to regulate my breathing before I made my move.

As it happens, Billie had been thinking along the same lines, and she moved first.

She'd been cradling her broken arm so carefully I'd presumed she was in immense pain. But she was smarter than any of us. When the taser appeared in her hand and she slammed into the merc's testicles, I realised just how much I'd underestimated her. She must have crammed the weapon inside her cast as we were captured, and none of the mercs had thought to check it.

I grabbed the knife up from the floor and hissed, "Move! Now!"

No one needed to be told twice. We scurried around the perimeter of the ritual chamber, keeping our heads low while bullets blew ceramic tiles into dust around us.

The other three Nameless seemed to have found their hosts, each forcing their way inside the hapless mercs who had opened fire on Alice.

The remaining men didn't stand a chance. The possessed mercs punched holes clear through their Kevlar body armour and out of their backs. One man rose up into the air and his limbs were torn off like petals from a flower. His tormentor discovered that 'he loves me not', and discarded the screaming remains.

Billie's tasered merc struggled to his feet, looking for us. He spotted us across the room, but before he could take aim, one of his possessed colleagues bounded towards him, black eyes glinting with hunger. The merc panicked and, wailing in horror, emptied an entire magazine into his erstwhile friend. The bullets blew a fist-sized chunk of his head clear off, but before the corpse could even hit the ground, the Nameless had spewed from the body and into the killer's mouth.

It was a slaughterhouse. The Nameless couldn't be killed. Not by direct confrontation, anyway. More than half of the men in the room had already been gruesomely murdered, and it would continue until only the Nameless remained.

Several surviving mercs came to the same conclusion. Some backed away, laying down suppressing fire while the others simply turned and fled.

We followed their example and sprinted up the stairs to the mezzanine level. Billie made it up first, followed by Chris, then Steph. I covered their rear. I'd got about halfway up when I heard a familiar scream from behind. I looked back and saw one of the Nameless lifting Sarah off the floor by her throat.

"I'll peel the skin from your daughter's face while you watch," it hissed gleefully.

Sarah pulled a pistol from a holster on the mercenary's belt, spat "Fuck you!" into its face and shot it to shit.

I wanted to cry out a warning, but it was far too late. The dying mercenary grabbed the back of my ex-wife's head and pulled her forward into a bloody kiss. I watched in horror as first the mercenary's throat, then Sarah's neck expanded to make way for the parasitic entity. The merc's corpse dropped to the ground, then Sarah turned to me, eyes jet black and gleaming.

She wiped the blood from her mouth and said, "Jack, we should discuss your late maintenance payments. And then you can tell me what you did with my brother."

I backed away, unable to take my eyes off her, as she stalked towards me, cat-like.

A metal object sailed over my head into the chamber and began spewing clouds of yellow gas, hiding the creature from view. Strong hands grabbed me from behind and Chris bellowed, "Move, ye twat!"

"Where's Mum?" Steph called, her voice thick with fear.

"I... I'm sorry, Steph," I said, shaking my head. "She's gone."

"No! You're wrong!" she cried, stumbling back down the stairs, trying to barge past me. "She can't be..."

"Steph, she saved us. She shot one of them, but she didn't realise what would happen. They don't die. It got inside her. It took her over."

Steph's jaw clenched. "But she's not dead, right? She's still in there somewhere? We need to save her. Find a way to get it out again."

"Love, I wish we could, but if we stay here much longer, we're all gonna die. We need to get out of here. Now."

Steph screamed defiance and battered her fists against me, but I couldn't let her past. Julie helped, bless her. She put her hands on her shoulders and pulled her into a hug.

"Stephanie, your dad's right. We can't do anything for her right now, but we *can* come back later with some proper backup. Find a way to help your mother then. But honey, we have to survive this first. That means being strong. Can you do that? Can you be strong for your mother?"

Tears rolled down Steph's cheeks. For a moment, I thought she was going to fight, but sense prevailed. She screamed in frustration, but she was strong. We turned together and fled down the corridor, leaving the sounds of death and destruction behind us.

I tried to remember the way we'd come, but all the tunnels looked the same. Had we even climbed back up the same stairs or were we on the other side now?

"Christ, I don't know where we are. Billie? Chris? Jules? Any idea?"

None of them knew.

"Shit," said Julie. "We should have marked the walls or something."

"No point in worrying about it now. I guess we need to keep an eye out for any stairs or ramps going up—"

Julie held a finger to her lips. She'd heard something. I listened, but all I could hear was sporadic gunfire and a few final screams. I stuck my head down the right-hand passage and was almost deafened by the sound of an explosion that echoed through the ceramic-tiled tunnel. Tendrils of smoke crept along the ceiling, passing over the fluorescent lighting like wraiths.

"Okay, looks like we're going the other way," I said, staggered by the noise. Even to my own ears, I sounded a little crazed. Shrill with forced positivity that was hopelessly out of place in this environment. Not that anyone seemed to notice. From their expressions, each of them was holding onto their nerve and their sanity by the smallest margin.

Steph's expression betrayed no emotion whatsoever. She'd completely disassociated from everything that was happening now. Trauma didn't begin to cover what she must have been going through.

Billie didn't seem to be faring much better. Her cheeks were stained with tears, but her eyes were dead, her movements mechanical. Shock, I guessed. For a woman who had spent most of her adult life looking for evidence of the supernatural, it didn't seem to have occurred to her what it would mean to actually find it.

Chris was getting through things in his usual way. When booze and piss-taking fail, use anger to power on through. He was a coiled spring – shoulders tense, his hands clenched into white-knuckled fists, his top lip a snarl. I knew from experience how useful rage mode could be, but it was draining after a while and made a man prone to stupid decisions. Not that Chris needed to be tense or angry to do something stupid.

Only Julie seemed to be holding it together. She took the lead position and hustled us along the corridor, signalling us to stop and be silent whenever she detected danger ahead of us. She was every inch the professional and the leader. I'd seen glimpses of the person she would become back when we'd been together, but it was magnificent to see those traces had developed. God, what a fool I'd been.

I moved beside Billie and asked, "How are you holding up?"

"Oh, I'm fucking great, Jack." She shook her head, then said, "Sorry, I just keep thinking about Benjamin. I mean, I didn't really know the guy very well, but he came down here to help anyway. And now he's dead." She barked a small, bitter laugh. "I suppose at least it was quick. He might have gotten off easier than the rest of us."

I thought about Benjamin's screaming face appearing in that stone trough and shuddered. In a rare moment of common sense, I decided to keep that particular horror to myself. There was no reason to burden anyone else with that knowledge.

"Listen, Billie," I said, eager to get my mind away from Benjamin's tormented face, "I owe you an apology. I owe you a shitload of apologies."

She shook her head. "Don't worry about it. God knows we have plenty of other things to be worried about."

"No, I can't let it go. Whenever you've talked anything... out of the ordinary, anything monstrous, I've been an absolute arsehole. I've been rude, I've taken the piss out of you. Been dismissive. You deserved better from me. You were right, and I'm sorry."

"Fucking hell!" she said. "An apology from Jack Carlton. That's going in my diary. The world really *is* coming to an end."

"I mean it. I'm sorry, and I'll do whatever it takes to make it up to you."

"Well, if you get me out of this place in one piece, we'll call it quits. That work for you?"

I smiled tightly. "That works. Oh, and nice move with the taser," I said off-handedly. An attempt to mask my nerves. "If you'd not done that, we'd all be dead already."

"I doubt that somehow. I saw that knife near your hand and knew you were thinking the same thing. I was just better placed to get at his nuts."

I was about to say something else when Julie raised her hand and shifted her feet into a fighting stance.

"What's hap—" Chris began, but Julie hissed at him, and he fell silent.

"Someone's coming. Fast. Be ready!"

A wave of tension rippled through the group as we each heard the footsteps, distant at first but getting closer. We looked around, desperate to find someplace to hide. Some hidden alcoves or storage rooms that had gone unnoticed until now – but this section of the complex contained nothing but smooth ceramic tiles, neatly laid across the walls and ceilings. There was nowhere to go.

"Kick the shit out of it if you get a chance," I murmured. "Demon or not, there's a person underneath it all. If we can knock them unconscious, we have a chance to get away. But don't fucking kill it. If you do, you'll just become its next holiday home. Got it?"

The footsteps pounded closer and closer, faster if anything, and I could feel the fear and anticipation building until the source of the noise came into view.

Not a mercenary, not one of the Nameless, just Stuart fucking Hartington, scumbag extraordinaire, pale with terror and sweating like a bastard. He was almost upon us before he even registered our presence.

"Oh, thank God," he exclaimed, his face a mask of relief. "Stephanie, I'm so happy to see you're okay. You have to believe me; I was just biding my time before I made my move."

Steph grabbed the taser from Billie's hands, strode towards Hartington and kicked him hard between the legs. His eyes bulged, his face turned beetroot, and the weasely fuck dropped with enough force that I heard his kneecaps impact on the concrete.

"Tell me again, you piece of fucking shit," she snarled. "Tell me how glad you are to see me alive!" Then she slammed the taser into the side of his neck and held it there.

Hartington twitched and spasmed, and a dark patch began to spread across the crotch of his Armani suit. I can't lie, it was incredibly satisfying. I watched his eyes roll back in his head, and then he collapsed entirely.

Julie stepped forward and took the taser from her hands with gentle but insistent force. "That's enough, Steph."

She tried to grab the weapon back, but Julie held her off.

"It's not enough. This is his fault! All of it!"

"I know, love. But if you'd carried on any longer, you'd have killed him. I don't think you want that on your conscience, do you?"

Steph lunged for the taser again. "I could live with it. He *should* be dead! For what he did to me. For what he did to my dad, and—" Her voice broke into a sob. "Especially for what he did to my mum."

Hartington scrabbled for purchase, trying to stand, only to slip in his own urine. "I didn't know what she was going to do, Stephanie, I swear!"

"LIAR!" she screamed. "You were happy to sacrifice us both, but for what? For what?! You deserve to die!" Hartington flinched but he had no answer. There was nothing he could say that would make this right.

"I understand, Steph. Believe me, I know," Julie crooned. "But we can't let him get off that easy." She turned to face Hartington, and in a coldly official tone said, "Stuart Hartington, I'm arresting you for kidnapping, conspiracy to commit murder and for being an accessory to multiple murders. You do not have to say anything, but it may harm your defence if you do not mention when questioned something which you later rely on in court. Anything you do say may be given in evidence."

"You're kidding," the lawyer said. "What a joke! There are actual demons back there, looking for us all, and you think this is a good time to play with your handcuffs? How about we focus on getting out of here alive first, eh? Then we can see what the CPS say about your 'charges'."

There was no point trying to argue the case, I just kicked Hartington in the face as hard as I could. His head snapped back, and when he finally staggered to his feet, I felt nothing but satisfaction. Blood streamed from his shattered mouth, running down his chin, while chunks of blood-stained enamel decorated the floor. "He's right, the charges would never stick. The arsehole's made of Teflon. Let him take his chances with whatever the hell those things are."

Having made the arrest, I assumed Julie would object to this, but she seemed to be seriously considering it. As the rest of us began heading off, he got to his knees and sputtered, "Wait. Please! Don't leave me here with them."

Nobody looked at him, though he began sobbing. Only Julie hung back, responsibilities weighing on her. She always was better than me.

"Wait," Hartington screamed as we were about to turn the corner and leave him to his fate. "I know the way out. We can take the elevator."

I stopped, turned around and looked at my worst enemy. He pulled a lanyard from around his neck and waved it at me. "I've got the key card and the access codes."

Shit.

Chapter Nineteen

Hartington led the way, since he was familiar with the facility's layout. Julie kept close. She didn't have handcuffs with her, but she was damned if she was going to give him a chance to escape. She'd appropriated the taser from Billie and held it ready, should it be necessary. Billie and Steph came next, with Chris and I bringing up the rear. Progress seemed slower than before, despite Hartington's assurances that he knew exactly where he was going. I kept scanning the corridor behind us for signs of pursuit. The complex was almost silent save for our footsteps and the distant hum of machinery. No more screams or gunshots came from the branching corridors, no further explosions. I could only conclude that the remaining mercenaries had either escaped or been killed. There was always a chance that the Nameless, having finished off the last of the mercs, had departed to wreak havoc on the surface, but I didn't believe that. Not really. We were unfinished business, and that meant all four of the monsters were likely scouring the corridors and storage rooms right now. Searching for us.

But something was nagging at me. Alice betrayed her mother – or rather the Nameless betrayed Chemosh. Why? What did they want, and why did they wait until the gate was opened? The possibilities were enough to turn my legs to rubber. Even if we got out of here alive, this wasn't over. Not by a long shot. The urge to find a dark corner and hide was becoming almost overwhelming, but we had to keep moving.

Not least of all because something was on fire down here – most likely some electrical circuits or fuel pipes hit by automatic weapons fire. Whatever it was, the smoke was getting thicker, and there was a distinct petrochemical tang to its smell, as if things weren't bad enough.

Julie raised her hand, indicating that we needed to stop. I moved up the line to see what was going on.

It was one of the mercenaries. Or rather, what was left of him. The top half of his head was practically embedded in the wall, hit with sufficient force that he remained partially standing, though he was clearly dead. The man's mouth hung open in an expression of surprise. Everything above it had been pounded into a red sludge of brain, bone and skin.

Julie began searching the man's body delicately, seeking any armaments or useful items. Most of his weapons and equipment were gone, discarded in panic or used against the monsters. His Glock was still in hand, though, with three rounds left in the magazine. He had an extendable baton in a nylon sheath strapped to his belt but nothing else.

Julie handed the taser back to Billie, took the pistol herself. She offered me the baton, but I refused. I still had the knife. Steph should have it, I said. Steph gave a half-smile when the extendable metal pole clicked out. Two feet of carbon steel with a solid metal sphere on the end. You could give one heck of a whack with one of those. She took a half step towards Hartington, eager to try out her new toy, but the grown-ups in the room stopped her. She gave me a beseeching look, but it wasn't gonna wash. In the end she contented herself with menacing the man, letting the baton slap into her left hand while she glared daggers.

"Shouldn't I have a weapon of some kind, seeing as I'm out in front?" Hartington mumbled. The shattered teeth did little for his elocution, but his pain was doing wonders for my mood.

"No, Mr Hartington, we are not giving you a weapon. Unorthodox as this situation is, you'd do well to remember that you're in custody. Now, how much further is this elevator?"

"Not far," he said.

"Good. Shall we get a move on then? I'm rather keen to get you in a nice cosy cell and make a start on my paperwork."

Hartington's shoulders sagged, but he didn't have anything else to say. Perhaps the whole 'right to remain silent' thing was finally clicking with him, or maybe his mouth just hurt too much.

Shame.

We turned the corner and had gone only a short distance when we heard her, the thing that had once been Robyn.

"Jaaa-aack! Where are you, lover?"

"Ah still cannae believe ye shagged that bint," Chris groused.

"Fucking move," hissed Julie, and we began running along the passageway, all attempts at stealth forgotten. I'd gone about fifteen feet, level with another set of steel doors when my body froze. It wasn't fear, and it wasn't possession; no cold tendrils spread across my skull. I simply stopped, held in place by an invisible force. My limbs locked tight, and my bones began to ache. Then my body was lifted from the ground, turning slowly to face the monster.

"Go," I gasped, and something tightened around my throat. "Get the hell out of here. I'll keep the bitch busy."

"Daaaad!" Steph screamed, throwing herself at me, but Julie and Billie grabbed her, dragging her back out of danger.

I heard Steph's cries fading as my friends fled, and I wished them every bit of luck. I felt a strange mixture of elation, loneliness, and absolute terror. I was glad that Steph wouldn't see this, glad we'd had a chance to reconcile, but that was tempered with the hollow realisation that I was going to die now, alone, full of pain, at the hands of something unspeakably evil.

It was fair to say Robyn had seen better days. The Nameless had almost torn her lower jaw off as it forced its way inside her. It hung now at an odd angle, with bright red blood staining her chin. Her head flopped to the right, poorly supported by a neck that had taken massive damage from gunfire, and her face was bleeding from dozens of shrapnel wounds. Her right ear was missing completely, and her right arm was badly burned from the explosion, the skin carbonised in places, with an oozing redness showing through the cracks. It must have been agony for the woman held inside, but it wasn't affecting the creature controlling her flesh one little bit. It moved sinuously towards me, accentuating the swing of its hips with mocking sensuality.

"What's the matter, Jack? Don't you want to fuck me anymore?" it purred. "So shallow..."

"Yeah, that ship sailed when I realised Robyn had been playing me all along. If anything, you're actually less repellent than she is."

"Why, Jack," it said, "I'm flattered. Maybe I'll give you one last go as I kill you. I can't promise it will be as fun as before. I mean, you'll be dead when I put you inside me. But it's the thought that counts."

I knew that every second I kept this thing talking was another second closer to the exit for Steph and the others.

"Believe me," I said, "it's probably on par. Robyn wasn't much good in bed. And her breath fucking stank."

"Oh, that's a good one, Jack," it laughed. "Believe me, she's raging in here. She's got quite a high opinion of herself, hasn't she? She's calling you some things that are even making *me* blush. I have to say, I'm quite impressed at the level of petty vindictiveness she's showing. It's a shame this body will be dead soon. It could have been the beginning of a beautiful partnership."

"Yeah, I can see how a soulless monster like her and a demon like you would work well together. It still wouldn't address the general lack of personal hygiene thing, though. Surely, if other people can smell her, she can smell herself, right?"

Robyn's body tried to smile, but the broken jaw rendered it more a lopsided grimace. "I know what you're up to, Jack. And while I respect the fact you're buying time for your friends, it won't help. Even if they manage to get out of here, we'll hunt them down, one by one. You're buying them hours at best. Aaaaaanyway," it said, "enough of the foreplay. I think it's time we got down to business, don't you?"

I felt my throat constrict, and my body rotated until I faced the floor. Breathing became harder. My arms and legs were pulled out, stretched into that familiar X shape, and my bones began to groan with the pressure. I clamped my jaw closed, determined not to give it the satisfaction of hearing my pain. I lasted maybe ten seconds and then the shrieks began.

Robyn closed her eyes, savouring my pain, lost in orgasmic delight.

Then one of the steel doors opened, and I heard another voice.

"Oi! Robbin' Cunt. Remember me?"

The demon's eyes snapped open, and it turned its head sharply to see the intruder, as six feet and eighteen stones of furious Scottish bastard rammed into her.

I fell to the ground, the pressure suddenly gone. I tried to scramble to my feet, desperate to help, but it was too late.

The Nameless had recovered from the surprise of his initial attack and now had Chris firmly in its grip. Robyn's arms tightened around him, and I heard bones snap in his arms, in his chest. Blood coughed out from between his lips.

"You should know something, Chris," the thing whispered. "Robyn despised you. She's been looking forward to this."

"Aye?" Chris wheezed. "Well, there's something ye both should be aware of, too."

Robyn's body gave that same lopsided smile, and she said, "Oh? Do tell."

Chris laughed. "Ye should both know that this grenade's been up my fucking arsehole."

Robyn's eyes widened as understanding dawned, but by then, it was far too late. I'd assumed that Vince had taken the hand grenade from Chris when he'd searched us, but it seemed that, like Billie, he'd managed to stash the weapon, albeit in a very different place. Robyn's eyes widened as the metal pin dropped onto the concrete floor with a small, barely perceptible tinkle. And then the grenade, irrevocably trapped between Chris and Robyn, exploded.

The shockwave threw me back into the tunnel, and my ears rang with a high-pitched whine. The world spun, and I struggled to work out which way was up. The air was thick with the smell of gunpowder and blood. Smoke swirled above me. I leant against the wall and tried to get to my feet, but my legs wouldn't support my weight. Then I felt hands slide beneath my armpits, and I was half-dragged to my feet by Steph and Julie. Julie was screaming something in my face, but I couldn't hear anything except the tinnitus whine ringing in my ears. I gently pushed her away and staggered toward where Chris and Robyn lay.

The explosive had blown a hole through his chest. Chris's ribcage was splayed out, revealing nothing but charred meat and bone fragments within. His eyes were wide open, mouth curled in a defiant snarl. My friend. It was all too much. I gently closed his eyes with my fingers, then removed the black dagger from my belt and checked on Robyn.

The corpse was hardly recognisable. Chris had been taller than her, so the blast had hit higher up. Most of her face was gone. Only one burned and bloodied eyeball remained in anything like a recognisable state. A few sinews remained to keep her head attached to what remained of her body, and her chest cavity had been torn asunder. She was very much dead, and, since her killer had joined her in death, the Nameless demon had presumably suffered the same fate.

Billie stood beside me, tears streaming down her face. She said some words over the bodies, things I wished I could hear. Then she spat on Robyn's corpse, kissed Chris on the forehead, and walked away with dignity.

With all the death and horror I'd seen, some part of me had felt detached from it all. Most of the casualties had been strangers. Images on screens, criminals or mercenaries. Not so with Marcus and Zoe, but they hadn't been part of my life for a decade or more. Their deaths had shaken me, sure, but the loss of Chris – his sacrifice – shook me to the core. I'd been in denial about just how much danger we were in, about my part in dragging the people I loved into the line of fire. And now my best friend lay dead on the ground in front of me. He didn't deserve that. And I didn't deserve his sacrifice.

I wanted to scream, to cry and lash out at the evil bastards that had done all this. I wanted to burn this fucking place to ashes, with everyone and everything inside it. I sobbed until my chest ached, until my throat clogged with grief and fury, but nothing could change what had happened. Nothing would ever be right again.

I felt a soft hand slip into mine and looked down to see Steph gazing up at me, eyes red with tears. I could see fear there and the crippling loss that threatened to overwhelm her.

Fractious as their relationship had been, she'd just lost her mother and thought she'd lost me, too. I couldn't imagine how she was holding it together.

"Dad," she said, her voice burbling in my ears like I was underwater. "Dad, I'm sorry about your friend."

I gave Chris one final look and then turned to my daughter and squeezed her hands. She threw her arms around me and squeezed until my ribs felt like they'd crack. I didn't care. I pushed the pain aside and held my little girl close for the first time in forever.

Julie tapped me on the shoulder. "Jack, we have to go. We need to get out of here before the rest of them find us. Hartington says the elevator's close. Are you okay to move?"

I nodded, released Steph, and we began making our way back through the corridors.

Finally, I began to recognise some of the places that we passed. Generator rooms I'd spotted the first time I'd been brought here. Sleeping quarters lined with rows of bunk beds, dressed in white hospital-cornered sheets and thick brown blankets. We all began to move faster as freedom beckoned, or at least as fast as our injuries allowed. I was struggling to keep up. Every step was agony, and I was painfully aware that I was slowing everyone down. Billie and Steph were helping me along, while Julie stayed up front with Hartington.

"Jack," Julie hissed as she glanced over her shoulder and saw the three of us lagging behind. "Move your fucking arse! We're almost there."

She'd only taken her eyes off Hartington for a second, but that was all the weasel needed. The sound of metal scraping and rattling across concrete made me look up, and Julie spun around, cursing. The Shart had pulled a metal scissor gate across the corridor between him and us, clicking it into place with a flourish.

Julie slammed into the gate and tried to pull it open, but it wouldn't budge.

"Hartington," she snarled. "Open the damn gate. Right now."

He tried to give us an apologetic grin but was hampered by the damage I'd done to his teeth.

"I'm sorry, Detective Inspector," he mumbled, "but I don't see what's in it for me. If you escape, I'll have some difficult questions to answer to the Crown Prosecution Service. It's just so much easier if you all die here."

"Hartington, you shit," I howled, slamming my fist into the metal struts of the gate. "I'll kill you for this!"

The scumbag laughed at that. "Really, Jack? How?"

I pulled out the knife, screaming obscenities, but they curdled in my throat as the elevator door behind him slid open. Something twisted and horrific emerged from the space within. An arm first – covered in blood and bent at an unnatural angle. It shot out from the elevator ceiling and planted a big, bloody handprint on the pristine white tiles. It was followed by a foot, then another arm. The motion was tentative at first, but as my ex-wife emerged like some giant blood-soaked spider, I saw the cunning in her eyes. The hunter's glee.

I began backing away from the gate, with Julie following my lead. Billie gasped and turned Steph around before she could see what her mother had become. She was barely human anymore. The bones in her body seemed to have reconfigured somehow into a new form. Something insectile. I wondered if this was closer to the natural form of the Nameless, wherever they came from. The children at King's College had moved like this, I recalled. Sarah's forearms and shins were far longer than they should have been – almost twice the length, it seemed. Her hands and bare feet were splayed, each finger and toe curling into vicious talons.

I continued to back away, but I was unable to take my eyes from the scene. Sarah released her grip on the ceiling and dropped down behind her former lover, almost soundlessly.

Hartington realised something was wrong, of course, but turned too slowly to defend himself. As the creature leapt and his screams began, we fled the scene. Part of me wished I could have stayed to see the Shart meet his fate, but I knew I'd be next if I had. The man's howls echoed through the corridors and in my mind for quite some time.

The smoke was getting thicker and darker, filled with the smell of burning plastics and cooking meat. Billie began to cough badly, and Julie went to check on her. They spoke briefly, then Julie tore some material from her blouse and gave it to her to breathe through.

"We need to get out of here, fast," she said. "We'll suffocate in this smoke if we don't find an exit."

"If we can get back to that ritual chamber, we might be able to find another way out. Maybe we can get to those SUVs?"

She nodded, but the expression on her face told me how much hope she really held. Sarah might be occupied with Hartington, but two other monsters still roamed the complex.

We'd not gone much farther when the ground shook beneath us, gently at first, then a secondary explosion hard enough to throw us to the floor. A blast of hot air blew through the corridors. Then the lights went out.

It took a moment for the emergency lighting to flicker into life, casting everything in green and black hues.

"What the hell was that?" asked Billie.

"I don't know. Maybe one of those fires reached a gas line or something."

"Great," she replied. "Do you think things can get any worse?"

"Oh," came a voice from round the corner, crackling like car tyres on a gravel driveway. "Things can always get worse."

I looked up in horror to find the creature that used to be Vince, the mercenary commander, striding toward us.

Julie was the first to her feet. She brought up her pistol, but Vince's arm slashed out, disarming her, while the other pushed forward, palm out, to slam her into the wall. Ceramic tiles cracked under the impact.

Billie threw herself between Vince and Steph, but the creature swatted her aside like a fly and Billie landed in a motionless heap.

"Hello, pretty," it growled, reaching towards Steph with a hand that was barely human anymore.

Something inside me snapped and I threw myself at the monster, shoving Steph aside in the process. The pain didn't matter anymore. Nothing did but protecting my daughter. I charged straight into the arms of a nightmare. Vince's mouth was filled with shattered stubs of teeth and half of the skin on his lower face had been peeled back, accentuating the effect. I got the impression that he'd done this to himself. He laughed as I reached him and said, "Oh yes, this will be much better, Jack. Free me from this flesh. I'll wear your face while I butcher your friends. It'll be glorious! And don't worry, I'll make sure you feel it all."

I didn't care. I knew what was coming, and as far as I could tell, there was nothing we could do to stop it. I was beyond hope and reason. I screamed, "Steph! Run!" and then brought the black dagger up beneath his chin with all my strength.

The blade punched through his flesh, ground against bone and came to rest in his brain. The mercenary was laughing as he died, and the black tentacles of the Nameless started forcing their way out. His skull split in half as the demonic squid burst free, and it began wrapping its tentacles around the back of my head, ready to pour itself down my gullet. Two of them pushed my jaw open, and the mass began pulsing down my throat, only to tense and recoil.

An unholy shriek pierced the air and the Nameless began to disintegrate, black pseudopods burned white hot and fluttered to the floor as ash, and within seconds it was gone.

"Dad..." Steph said from down the corridor, her voice thick with fear. "Are you still... you?"

I searched my mind for those tell-tale cold tendrils but found nothing. No sign of it at all.

"Yeah," I said. "It's me. But I don't know how."

"Fucking hell," said Billie. "It worked!"

"What worked?" I asked, heading up to join them.

"Benjamin found something in those scanned pages; a protective charm, he called it. He wasn't super confident about the translation, but he carved it into you while you were out in case the whole guinea pig thing went wrong."

"So – wait a minute. We'll get back to my little carve up later – you're saying they can't get inside me anymore? You're saying I can kill them for real?"

She grinned. "So it would seem."

"Well, then," I said. "That changes things just a little bit."

Chapter Twenty

We hurried along as quickly as we could manage, but it didn't seem anywhere near fast enough. The smoke flooding the corridors was black now, and we had to bend almost double to breathe. The tunnels seemed to be filling up faster, as if whatever was burning had accelerated. We didn't have much time left.

The tunnels were no longer the pristine, white-tiled corridors we'd left behind. Evidence of the mercenaries' last stand was all around us. Bullet holes riddling the walls. Sharp tile fragments covering the floor, crunching beneath our feet. And the blood. *So much blood.* The emergency lighting made it all look black, but there was no doubting what was sprayed up the walls, pooled on the floors, and in some cases spread in long drag marks. Chillingly, the light also left Julie, Billie, and Steph's irises looking like dark, empty pools. The effect was far too close to the jet black, silver-glint eyes of the Nameless, and I found myself growing paranoid.

"Dad," said Steph. "Where are they?"

"Where's who?"

"Everyone else. The bodies. Look around. There's been a massive fight here. Everything's covered in blood, but there aren't any dead people. It's like…"

"Like they collected all the corpses?"

She nodded. There had to be a reason for that. They thrived on chaos. They were hardly likely to take time out to clean their mess up – not without a very good reason. I didn't want to freak everyone out by speculating about food or rituals, so I kept my mouth shut.

"Maybe it was the rest of the mercs taking care of their wounded," Billie chipped in.

Steph didn't look convinced, and I couldn't say I blamed her. However, she let the matter drop and fell in behind me, gripping her riot baton tightly. Billie came next. She didn't look well. Sweat beaded on her forehead, and her breathing was laboured. Rasping. As if on cue, she began coughing again almost uncontrollably. I came back to her, worried, but she waved me away. "It's my asthma. This smoke's making it flare up. I'll be fine. Just need to get back to some fresh air."

I nodded. Pistol gripped in my right hand, black dagger in my left, I pushed on as quickly as possible.

It didn't take long to find our way back to the ritual chamber. From this direction I could now recall the route to where the SUVs were parked. The only problem was that we'd need to cross the entrance of the ritual chamber to get there. And, from the anguished moans and screams from within, it was pretty clear that the space was not as empty as we'd hoped.

The opening that led to the chamber was about four meters across, and I could see from the abandoned packing crates and blood smears in the corridor beyond it that most of the fighters had tried to go in that direction. I volunteered to check our escape route while the others hung back, ready to run if needs be. I dropped into a crawl and poked my head around the opening at floor level.

I regretted that decision almost immediately.

The two remaining Nameless had been busy. In the centre of the chamber, on top of the stone altar, was an atrocity: a sculpture made from the corpses of the dead as well as the mutilated, screaming bodies of those still living, although it boggled my mind how any of them could still be conscious or even alive, given the state they were in. Their bodies were fused together. Warped, twisted and melted into a shape that didn't seem to conform to the laws of geometry. The angles seemed wrong, somehow. As if they weren't made up of the usual three hundred and sixty degrees as everything else, but as if they had gone beyond those dimensions and back out the other side. I couldn't even look at it without a sharp pain slicing through the front of my skull. And there was a high-pitched buzzing sound, barely audible above the cries and screams of the mercenaries welded into the abomination. I thought it was the after-effects of the explosion at first, but that had been more of a whine. This was powerful enough to make my fillings vibrate.

Sarah and the other Nameless were busying themselves on their little craft project. Limbs were torn from corpses and secured in place with strips of flesh and sinew that hissed as they came into contact with the horrific tableau, fusing the new additions into the whole. Sarah bent down and peeled another foot-long strip of flesh from a pile of screaming wet meat that I realised was all that remained of Stuart Hartington, and applied it to the face of a still-living mercenary.

They looked for all the world like children experimenting with plaster of Paris. The mercenary howled in agony as the wet flesh burned into his face, pulling his head tight against the seething, writhing pillar of muscle, sinew and skin.

I wrenched my head back, unable to watch more. The three women looked at me expectantly.

"Okay," I whispered. "I'm not going to lie. It's bad in there. Really bad. They're building something. I don't know what it's for, and I don't *want* to know. The important thing is that they're occupied. So, let's keep it low, fast and quiet. Get across that gap; it should be plain sailing from then on. We just follow that path straight down to where the cars are parked. If we're lucky, one of them will still have its keys in the ignition. If not, we just follow the tyre tracks. Okay?"

Julie, Billie and Steph nodded their assent and crept closer to the entrance. I crouched again and watched the Nameless at work, building their monument to pain and suffering. When I judged they were each angled away enough, I gestured *Go! Go! Go!*

Julie scurried across the opening without so much as glancing into the chamber. She took me at my word and made it across in two seconds flat, ducking behind one of the empty packing crates.

"You next," I mouthed to Steph.

"I don't know if I can, Dad," she said in a low voice, close to tears. "I'm scared."

I took a breath, then murmured, "I know, love. I'm scared as well. But that's the only way out. Just wait until I give you the all-clear then run to Jules. Don't stop for anything, and *don't* look inside that chamber. It's just two seconds. You can do it."

She didn't look convinced but nodded anyway. Sarah returned from her creation to peel more pieces from the Shart, and my heart almost stopped. From this distance, it seemed she was looking straight at me. However, she didn't seem to register my presence. I held in a nervy chuckle when I suddenly realised that the Nameless inside was having to deal with Sarah's physical restrictions. Her distance vision was terrible. She couldn't even drive without corrective glasses. They may be able to push the human body to perform superhuman feats of strength, but that ability didn't extend to her myopia. She bent over and whispered something to her former lover that made him scream even louder, then she turned her attention back to the sculpture.

Go! Go! Go!

She was as good as her word. Steph kept her eyes on the floor and sprinted lightly across the gap. On the other side, Julie gathered her up into her arms and hugged the girl tight. After a moment, they both crouched behind the packing crate.

"OK, Billie. You're next," I mouthed.

But she shook her head. "No, you should go, Jack. I'll be okay."

"Fuck that. We're on the home stretch."

"Jack... I..."

"No more talking. Get ready and go when I tell you."

Both demons were occupied with securing the unfortunate merc to the monstrous pillar of flesh. Each strip of Hartington's skin seemed to weld more of the man into place, and as it did so, the mass began to pull him in of its own accord. Only half of his body was visible now. The rest of him was already absorbed into the screaming, writhing tissue. As the monstrous sculpture sucked the man's body into it, his clothing and weapons were extruded – spat out onto a pile of other discarded items from the previous victims.

Go! Go! Go! I gestured again, and Billie started to move.

She'd made it three-quarters of the way across when her lungs betrayed her, and she began coughing violently.

She reached Julie, but not before the heads of the Nameless snapped around to spot her movement. With an unholy screech, they scampered across the ritual chamber towards us and the entrance.

In panic, I motioned for the women to get out of there. Julie tugged at Steph and the two of them fled the advancing monsters, but Billie had all but collapsed to the ground.

I remained prone, took careful aim with the pistol and shot at the possessed mercenary.

The pistol barked, but I missed his speeding form. The round sparked off a series of metal pipes on the far side of the room.

Fuck!

I had two rounds left and no time. I steadied my shaking hand, held my breath and squeezed them off.

These ones connected. The first hit the Nameless merc square in the stomach, causing him to stumble, and the second blew the back of his skull off. The corpse took another two steps forward before it slumped to the ground, black blood leaking across the concrete floor.

I saw Sarah grin at this as she stalked towards Billie. The amorphous, black mass spewed from the gaping head wound, streaked across the room towards me, and I felt a moment of doubt. Were Benjamin's carvings a one-off deal or a permanent thing? And had my use of the black ritual knife played a bigger part than I'd realised? The tentacles slapped round my head, my mouth was wrenched open and then – blessedly – I felt the searing white heat against my skin again as the creature screamed out of existence.

Sarah's eyes widened as she witnessed this, but she acted immediately. An invisible wave of force dashed the gun from my hand, while another lifted me from the ground. Billie finally managed to stop coughing. She stood raggedly, defiantly, but the demon lashed out with a vicious backhand and sent her flying.

"I see you still have some tricks up your sleeve," Sarah rasped. "Once I've added your friend to the artefact, you'll be next. Then I'll go find our daughter. It's always nice to have a little angel at the top, don't you think?"

I felt myself pulled into the ritual chamber. Sarah grabbed Billie by the throat and dragged her along with us, then she threw her to the floor in front of the living totem.

"Let's put you over here first, Jack, where you can't cause any more trouble," she said, and I flew back against the wall of the ritual chamber, held taut and immobile several feet above the ground.

Now I was closer, I could see the scale of the monstrous artefact. It was over six feet across at its base and extended almost all the way to the ceiling. Around half of the faces within were screaming in pain and fear, begging for death. Half-submerged hands reached from the blood-soaked mass, clawing for purchase, desperately trying to find some escape. To my everlasting horror, I saw Chris in there, one face among many. His chin was buried, his jaw unable to move. Inarticulate groans of pain and regret seeped from his lips, and my heart clenched at his anguish.

"It's quite the craft project you've made there," I gasped. "I didn't realise you were so creative."

The twisted monstrosity wearing my ex-wife's face smirked. "Still making jokes, Jack?"

She lifted Billie to her feet and stroked her face with the side of her thumb.

"Well, if you can't laugh, you'll cry," I replied, mind racing. I might not be able to move, but I wasn't about to give up. Not yet. "So, come on then. Is it actually *for* something, or are you just decorating? It's almost as naff as that IKEA crap you used to buy."

She chuckled at my poor attempt but indulged my curiosity.

"Think of it as a doorstop. The gateway Chemosh opened would have closed long since. Our artefact keeps it open. Soon, I will bring forth my brethren – multitudes of Nameless – and together, we shall murder this world. Then we will earn our reward."

"Reward? What reward? And who would be giving it to you?"

Sarah turned to face me fully and my blood ran cold. "Enough talking, Jack," she said. She shoved Billie's left arm into the pulsating, screaming mass of blood-soaked flesh.

Billie's eyes snapped wide open, and she howled in pain and despair. She tried to pull away, but Sarah held her in place, tore off another strip of Hartington's flesh and slapped it against her like a sticking plaster. I could hear the sizzle, smell the burning skin, and watched in horror as Billie's hand was subsumed into the thing.

Sarah closed her eyes and started touching herself, a look of almost orgasmic pleasure on her face. "Oh, I can feel your pain from here, Jack. Your anguish is sublime. *Feel* that guilt; it is all your fault, after all. Let it wash over you. It's already too late for silly Billie but rejoice! The suffering of her soul will help to keep this gateway open forever."

Billie screamed and tried to pull away, but it had her now; her arm sank into the mass until it was almost up to her elbow. The protective cast split and fell into the pile of shredded clothes and military equipment at the base of the artefact.

"Don't worry, though, Jack. You'll be joining her in a moment."

"You know what?" called a voice from the far side of the room. "You always did like the sound of your own voice a bit too fucking much."

I looked up and saw Julie standing in the doorway with a submachine gun in her hands. She let out a short burst of fire that raked across Sarah's legs, blowing holes in her thighs and shattering her kneecaps.

Sarah screamed in rage and collapsed. Julie's attack had split her focus, and I found myself dropped to the floor.

"Jules, remember – don't fucking kill her!" I shouted. I stumbled towards the sickening sculpture with urgent purpose.

"Don't worry," she snarled. "I won't kill the bitch. She'll just wish I had."

Sarah scrambled up, using the artefact for purchase, but another burst of automatic fire tore her right hand into bloody ribbons.

"Billie," I yelled and tried to drag her from the screaming sculpture.

"No," she cried. "It's too late! My arm... it's... it's part of it now. I can feel them here, in my mind. All of them."

The artefact seemed to shudder in a motion that was all too reminiscent of swallowing, and Billie's arm was sucked deeper inside.

"I'm sorry, Jack. It's just too late."

"I'm so sorry, Billie," I said. "For everything." Then I pulled out the ritual blade and drove it into her arm.

Blood sprayed from the wound, and Billie shrieked. I wanted to throw up, but I couldn't stop sawing, not even for a second. Skin, muscles and tendons all parted under the oily black blade. It was like deboning a chicken, only these bones had to break if I was to get her out. It wasn't going to be pretty. She couldn't look at the mess I was making, couldn't bear the pain, and yet her body refused to let her fall unconscious. That only happened when I kicked through her radius and ulna, tugging her clear of the thing. The artefact slurped the last parts of her forearm inside, and she fell to the floor, dead to the world, her arm pumping blood like no tomorrow.

Nearby lay Sarah. Julie had advanced, step by step, shooting through hands and feet, taking forearms and calves, removing her means to move or use her powerful gestures. It was a cruelty the creature inside her had earned. I wasn't so sure about Sarah, but she wasn't my priority right then.

I whipped my belt off and tightened it around Billie's stump. It slowed the bleeding, but not much. I needed a proper tourniquet as soon as possible. As I began to drag her away, I felt the remains of a hand loosely grasp my ankle. I looked down to see Sarah – or what was left of her – leering up at me.

"Where do you think you're going, Jack?" she spat through a mouth full of blood.

"I'm taking my friends, and we're getting out of here. You, though... Sorry, Sarah, but you're going straight to Hell."

I pulled out the petrol lighter I'd found on the rotten corpse a million years ago and gave it a waggle. A momentary confusion crossed the demon's face, then it registered what I'd already smelled. By chance, my stray round earlier had found a fuel pipe which, for the last few minutes, had been spraying petrochemicals across the floor, soaking the piles of discarded clothing, the mercenaries' weapons, and it had pooled around the base of the screaming artefact.

I struck the wheel against the flint, lit the flame and dropped it into the pool of kerosene.

The effect was instantaneous. Blue flames washed across the chamber, engulfing Sarah and the monstrous living pillar. The artefact screamed, dozens of voices howling in agony as their flesh melted under the intense heat. I half carried, half dragged Billie away from the conflagration consuming the ritual chamber and its hellish residents.

Julie met me halfway and helped me carry Billie down the corridors. We'd gone maybe twenty yards when the discarded munitions went off. The force of the explosion threw us from our feet, and the fire began boiling across the ceiling. I couldn't see where I was going. Couldn't breathe. Couldn't see Julie anymore.

Then a loud horn rang out, and twin headlights broke through the smoke. I struggled to my feet, threw Billie over my shoulders and somehow managed to carry her through the smoke and flames to the black SUV. Julie helped lay Billie down in the back seat while I tried to open the driver's door.

"Get in the other side, Dad," Steph snarled.

"But you're fourteen years old," I said. "You can't drive."

"You don't know half the things I can do. Fucking ground me afterwards if you need to, but you can hardly stand up, let alone drive. Get in! I know what I'm doing."

There was no arguing with her, and Julie was too busy seeing to Billie's arm to back me up. Making a proper tourniquet, I guessed. I lurched around to the passenger side, clambered in and had barely got my seatbelt on when Steph gunned the engine, spinning us away from the nightmare complex and into the darkness beyond.

Chapter Twenty One

Three months later...

"So? What do you think?"

I did my best to force a smile, but I was writhing in misery. "It's great," I said without much conviction.

Billie frowned. "Jack, can you at least try to show some interest? It's not like I'm dragging you around a thousand shoe shops."

We were sitting in the Royal National Orthopaedic Hospital and had been for the last two hours. The chairs were uncomfortable, and the antiseptic stink reinforced my generalised hatred of hospitals. But the main reason for my discomfort was the reason for our visit. For the last hour, a nurse had been tinkering with Billie's prosthetic arm. The guilt I felt was almost crushing. Every time I saw her, my mind flashed back to the ritual chamber, replaying the events, exaggerating the savagery of my act and the screams of pain she'd let loose. It haunted me, and I couldn't understand – couldn't believe – how pragmatic she'd been about it since our escape.

"I'm sorry," I said, leaning forward on the hard plastic chair to appear more engaged. "It's very... Robocop."

"Robocop? Seriously?"

"The remake, I mean. Not the chunky one from the eighties."

"Yeah, stop talking now, Jack. We don't mention the remake, remember?"

I did remember. The three of us had watched it around Chris's flat a few years ago on a streaming service account he was 'borrowing' from a neighbour. During the film, we smoked enough weed to suffocate a donkey, drank so much gin that, even now, the thought of the stuff made me bilious, and ripped the piss out of every script, acting and directorial choice. Then, for balance, we put a gram of white powder up our noses and watched the original on repeat until the sun came up.

"It's okay, you know," she said.

"The remake? Fuck off, it's shit. We were all in agreement."

"It's okay to miss him. I know I do. I mean... he was a drunk, misogynistic, homophobic, drug-addicted arsehole..."

"Yeah," I said and managed half a smile. "But he was *our* arsehole."

The nurse finished her tinkering and asked Billie to run through some basic movements, testing for comfort, fit and all that. There was some chafing still, she said, pointing to a couple of places on her elbow. The nurse got back to it.

"I missed you at the wake," Billie said. "We all did."

"I'm pretty sure Jean barred me for life."

"Oh, you know she didn't mean that. Christ, she used to bar you for life every other week. She's got a soft spot for you. You got away with murder in The Dolphin."

I choked up at that, picturing Chris flying back into the bar and over the top. Imagining the damage I'd have caused if he hadn't been wearing the Kevlar. I wiped tears from my eyes and looked away, throat taut.

Empathic to the end, she placed her hand on mine. "You can't keep blaming yourself for what you did when that thing was in control."

"I know. And I'm trying. I wanted to go to the wake, I really did, but... I just— I couldn't face it. He'd still be alive if it hadn't been for me."

The nurse coughed, indicating she was done. Billie ran through the movements again, smiled, and gave the nurse a mechanical thumbs up. She went to check on her next patient, leaving us in privacy.

Billie caught me in a serious gaze. "Honestly, none of it was your fault. That shit was set in motion months before you were dragged into it. You came through, Jack. You saved everyone. And if Chris hadn't saved you, the whole world would be fucked, so don't you dare minimise his sacrifice. He might have been a dickhead, but he was brave and loyal as well. He was your friend for a reason, and he died a hero."

I sighed heavily, shakily, but I nodded at this.

"I suppose it was a better end than him getting kicked to death by a jealous boyfriend or choking on his own puke."

Billie smiled. Probably the first genuine smile I'd seen from her since it all happened. "Damn right. It was fucking epic. Just like he was." She wiped the tears from her eyes. "Now look what you've done, you dick. You've made me cry! I'm gonna have to drag my arse across London looking like a fucking panda."

We laughed a little, but it soon sputtered into an awkward silence.

"So..." she said eventually, as bright and brittle as glass, "now I've played therapist, you can return the favour. The arm. Be honest, what do you think?"

I looked at it properly, weighing my thoughts. It was a sleek black and chrome affair, strapped to her shoulder and running along her bicep. "It's very cyberpunk," I said. "But it works. Could do with neon lights on it, though. A USB charging point, perhaps? A coffee machine?"

Billie looked at it thoughtfully, turning the mechanical arm over. And then she raised the middle finger, right in my face.

"Yeah." I laughed. "You'd never know the difference."

Billie laughed at that, then kissed me on the cheek.

"You sure I can't persuade you to come down The Dolphin later? Have a couple of drinks for old time's sake?"

"Nah, I'm trying to stay off the stuff. It's... better that way. For Steph as much as anything, but my liver's pretty grateful."

"A new leaf? I'm impressed."

"Twelve weeks and counting. I've even started going to AA sessions in the local church hall. So yeah, it's best I stay away from the pub for now." Billie smiled, but I could see the disappointment in her eyes. "I'd love to catch up properly, though, if you can bear me sober. Something to eat, maybe?"

"Are you cooking?" she asked, all cagey. "I don't much fancy shitting myself to death."

"Don't worry, I'll get us a takeout. Hell, I'll even wash the dishes first."

Her smile lit up the room. "Then it's a date!"

***

The evening rush hour was just easing as I left the sweaty hell of the tube station. It was mid-June now, and temperatures were well above the seasonal average. I was not built to cope with such things. It was hard to believe that I'd been trudging through three feet of snow just a few short weeks ago. None of Billie's conspiracy theory friends had been able to confirm or refute whether there was any direct connection between the blizzards and the demonic incursion, but things began to normalise the following day. I didn't think that was just a coincidence. The sweltering, uncomfortable heat we felt now seemed like nature trying to balance things out.

On reflection, I think I preferred the snow.

I still felt a momentary disorientation coming 'home' to a new part of the city, though I'd spent nearly a decade living here in my old life. Steph had insisted on moving back to the family home, and since she technically owned it, the solicitor had been happy for us to take up residence. Probate was dragging on because, in the absence of a body, Sarah had yet to be formally declared dead. They assured us the decision would be made soon, but solicitors experience time very differently to the rest of humanity. One thing was clear, though: my flat was *not* a suitable place for a teenage girl to grow up in. It was a shithole, and the area was as rough as a badger's arse. I kept it on as my office for now, but I'd started looking around for something a little more... appealing to clients. It was time to grow up, and grow the business, too, if I could.

"Mr Carlton, do you have a moment?"

I spun around to find Julie leaning against a lamppost, a mischievous grin on her face.

"Jesus, Jules. You made me jump."

"I know," she said innocently.

"How did you know I'd be here?" I asked warily. Was I under surveillance or something? I imagined Julie being recruited into some super-secret agency after her brush with the supernatural and... Yeah, okay. Billie was starting to rub off on me.

"Oh, Billie called me. She said you were being a maudlin twat at the fitting, so I thought I'd drop by. Catch you on the way home."

"Maudlin twat?"

She shrugged. "Her words, not mine. To be honest, her voice sounded a bit raw as well. How's she doing?"

I sighed. "She puts a face on. And I think part of her enjoys the whole 'cyborg' thing. But it's affected her badly. It's affected us all."

"Yeah, well, after all we've seen I'm surprised none of us have been sectioned yet. Trauma like that, it doesn't just fade."

She looked at me just a little too long for comfort, like she was weighing me up.

"Look..." I cleared my throat. "It's lovely to see you but I don't quite buy it. You didn't come here for a social visit. What's really on your mind?"

The shadow of doubt passed from her face, and she smiled tightly.

"It's not bad news. Serious Crimes are having a field day with the stuff they brought out of the Chemosh offices. Seems like they had their fingers in a lot of juicy pies: gun running, people trafficking, drugs. You name it, Wells and her cronies were involved in some way. And Hartington's been helping her for a while now, it seems. Lots to unravel, if you take my meaning. This is one gift horse they're happy to take without a full dental exam."

"So, they bought it? The story?"

"Let's just say that they are not currently pursuing any leads in connection with the fire at the Tottenham police station, nor regarding the deaths of several local criminals. The fire beneath Chemosh has been rightfully attributed to a fuel leak. You're in the clear, Jack. In fact, I've been asked to thank you for the tip-off from the Chief Super himself."

"He must have hated that," I said.

"Oh, he was sucking pickled arseholes when he said it, but he's not stupid. The big chair will be coming up next year, and busting a massive Organised Crime Group right in the middle of the city puts him in a very good position for it."

"The right arse for the job? That's about right. People like him always seem to come out of the shit smelling like roses."

"Well, you came out of it pretty well, yourself. 'Discredited private investigator blows open King's College Massacre case; brings down international arms dealer; reveals deep corruption in previously respectable firm of solicitors in the process.' Quite the turnaround from where you were a few months back."

I nodded. "You're not wrong. But honestly, I'd be hard pushed to say it was worth it. Too many people got hurt. Marcus and Zoe. Billie. Chris. Chloë. God knows what it's done to Steph. She puts a brave face on, but I don't know, Jules. I feel like I'm just waiting for the other shoe to drop."

"I know what you mean. Look, tell you what, I'll send over details of some trauma therapists we work with. I've seen them work wonders."

We'd reached the end of the street. "Sounds good," I said. "Do you want to come in for a cuppa? Steph would love to see you?"

She shook her head. "Another time, perhaps. I've still got a mountain of paperwork to get through."

"Still?"

"Always," she replied with a wink. "Listen, I've got to go. Take care of yourself, okay? And Steph, of course."

"Always," I said, and watched her walk away.

I pushed open the front door of my house, or rather, Steph's house. The family home was one of the things I'd lost in the divorce, and even after being back here for a few weeks, I felt like a trespasser every time I stepped through the front door.

I was surprised that Steph had wanted to return here, if I was honest. There were too many memories in the place. Her mother's presence was imprinted in every square inch of the house, from the expensive Laura Ashley wallpaper to the Scandinavian furniture. Everything had been picked according to Sarah's taste. The property hadn't been touched in years. Ever since they moved in with Hartington, Steph said.

Dustsheets had been put over the furniture, the curtains had been closed and that had been that. According to Steph, her mum had been sitting on the place. There was no mortgage, and apparently, the council tax payments were more than offset by the annual rise in its value. Knowing Sarah, she would have wanted to keep hold of the place in case things didn't work out with Hartington. My ex-wife had been many things, but stupid was not one of them. I almost tripped over a discarded school bag in the hallway, then followed the trail of coat and shoes to the kitchen. I found my daughter by the refrigerator, door open, her head inside.

"Good day at school?"

She grunted and shrugged her shoulders without turning around. One of the other things that she'd been adamant about was that she was moved back to her old school, but oddly enough, her enthusiasm had faded as day-to-day normality reasserted itself.

"Why is there nothing to eat?" she groaned and slammed the fridge door. I opened it again to check and saw no shortage.

"No food at all, or nothing deep-fried?" I asked, receiving a chilling glare in return. She was her mother's daughter in so many ways. I grabbed a pack of sliced ham and a block of cheese from the fridge and went looking for the bread.

"Well, I'm having a sandwich. Want one?" I asked.

"Eww! God, no. You make the worst sandwiches in the world."

A loud crash came from the utility room and my heart lurched.

I dashed from the kitchen to find Ozzy looking into the guinea pig cage intently, his eyes like saucers and backside wiggling.

"Get the hell out of here!" I yelled, all but chasing the cat out of the room. The guinea pig glared at me from the depths of its cage, pure malice etched across its features.

"Steph, for Christ's sake. I've told you not to leave the utility room door open. The cat nearly got the bloody guinea pig again."

She shrugged. "I don't know why you don't just kill the thing if it's so dangerous to have around."

It was a fair point, and I'd honestly thought about taking a hammer to the rodent more times than I could count. The thing was, the Nameless contained within the small furry animal had been inside my head. It knew me in ways I probably didn't even know myself, and it had expressly threatened to target me and my family the next time it made its way back to Earth. I knew that a guinea pig's lifespan wasn't exactly measured in decades, but for now I reasoned that I'd be happier knowing exactly where the bastard thing was, at least until Billie's contacts could find a more permanent way to contain it. And, if I was completely honest with myself, it felt like justice for the evil fucker. It didn't have access to its powers while stuck in this form. Maybe it was something to do with the brain of the small mammal not having the correct wiring, or there just wasn't enough grey matter to summon the energy, but for now, it seemed powerless. And furious.

"I'm keeping it here so it can't do any more damage," I said. "But unless you want it getting into the damn cat, keep the bloody door closed, okay?" I closed the utility room door with more force than was strictly necessary and turned around to find Steph halfway through getting changed in the kitchen. Her school uniform had been dropped on the floor, and she was wriggling her way into a mini skirt and Lycra top that would have made a seasoned vice cop blush.

"Don't leave your crap all over the floor like that," I said. "What are you even doing – don't you have homework or something to do?"

"I'll do it later," she huffed. "I'm going out."

"Why later? It'll take you two seconds to pick your clothes up."

"Can't talk right now; my boyfriend's outside and he can't park because of the double yellow lines. See you later!" She practically skipped out of the front door—

"And don't slam the door!"

—slamming the door behind her.

I picked up her clothes and shoved them into the washing basket, cursing under my breath. Then my brain caught up.

Boyfriend?
With a car?
Shit!

Epilogue

Doctor Annabelle Phillips was exhausted. She'd been on the wards for eighteen hours straight and, just as she'd been about to escape, she'd been caught by one of the consultants to help out on the rounds. What she needed was to go home and lie in a hot bath for an hour, wash the ward stink off and fall asleep with a glass of wine. Unfortunately, norovirus had flattened four nurses and three junior doctors in the last week. No, four; Kevin had called in poorly that morning, which was why she'd done a double shift in the first place. The fact Kevin had a new girlfriend was almost certainly a coincidence, but if it turned out he'd pulled a sickie for a shag-a-thon, she'd make him pay big time. She had access to all kinds of nasty equipment. However, right now she had no evidence, and the consultant's tone brooked no argument. *Pompous arsehole.* He could have checked on his fucking patients himself, but he had a previous appointment.

On the golf course with the other bloody consultants, probably.

It was enough to make you spit.

She checked the schedule and groaned. The first patient she needed to see was one she usually avoided wherever possible. Not that the woman had ever done or said anything unpleasant. She couldn't; she'd been in a coma since they brought her in three months ago. She was just... so hard to look at.

One of the nurses, Mary, met her outside the private rooms.

"What the hell are you still doing here, Belle? I thought you were off an hour ago."

"Oh, you know. I love the place so much I decided to stay. It's part of my saintly duty. Sleep and food, they're just selfish pleasures, you know."

"Did Mr Hanning rope you in again?"

"Yeah. Sod caught me before I made it to the elevator."

Sally shook her head and pursed her lips. "That man is a lazy shit, pardon my French. It wouldn't kill him to do his own rounds once in a while. You've been here, what? Twelve hours now?"

"Eighteen, but don't worry. I plan to get around this lot in record time, head home and sleep for the next three days."

"You have three days off? Cow! I was feeling sorry for you, but now you're just showing off."

"I had a few days in lieu. They said I had to take them before the end of the month, or I'd lose them. Don't worry, you know what'll happen: someone else will come down with the shits, and they'll have me back in by tomorrow lunchtime."

Mary laughed bitterly at that. "No doubt. Shall we crack on, then? See how sleeping beauty is today?"

Annabelle felt her stomach flutter, but she pushed it down like a professional and entered the room.

Jane Doe was barely visible beneath the bandages and tubes.

Mary shook her head and sighed. "I know life is precious and all that, but when you see people in a state like this, you have to wonder what they have to look forward to. It might have been kinder to just let them die."

Annabelle didn't say anything, but Mary's thoughts mirrored her own – more than she cared to admit. The woman had third-degree burns across her entire body. There wasn't a single patch of skin that hadn't been torched. She'd lost her right hand, and her legs had been amputated. No, that word was too surgical. Destroyed. Whatever had happened to the woman had been done brutally. Most of the injuries were the result of gunfire, apparently. The police were keen to speak to her, of course, should she ever regain consciousness, but that was deemed highly unlikely. Honestly, Annabelle hoped she passed away peacefully in the coma. If she ever did wake up, she'd be in unspeakable agony for the rest of her life. The fact that she was still breathing was something of a miracle. Cruel, but a miracle, nevertheless.

Annabelle checked the levels of the woman's drips and said, "Mary, can you get another amoxycillin from stores, please? This one is going to need changing."

The nurse nodded, then stepped out of the room, leaving Annabelle alone with the charred woman.

"You poor mare," she said. "Don't wake up. Never wake up."

The monitor beside the woman began beeping, and Annabelle checked the machine. If the woman died, she decided, she wouldn't try to resuscitate her. It was the only kindness she could offer.

The woman's heart rate was increasing rapidly now, from forty beats per minute to over one hundred and fifty.

This is it, then, Annabelle thought. *Cardiac arrest.*

Then the woman's left hand shot out, grabbing Annabelle's wrist in a vice-like grip. Her eyes snapped open, but they were almost entirely black, glinting with a strange silver light.

The woman's mouth opened wide, and she began to scream.

Anna recoiled, tried to pull away, but she was trapped. The grip tightened, and pain – agony – shot up her arm. She flailed, trying to get away, trying to press the alarm, but the woman pulled her close, shrieking in her face.

Annabelle came to an abrupt decision.

And wrapped her fist around the burned woman's oxygen pipe.

ABOUT THE AUTHOR

Graeme Reynolds was born in England in 1971. Over the years, he has been an electronic engineer in the Royal Air Force, worked with special needs children, and been a teenage mutant ninja turtle (don't ask).

He started writing in 2008, and over thirty short stories were published in various ezines and anthologies before his first novel, High Moor, was published in 2011. He has now written five novels.

When he is not breaking computers for money, he hides in the South West of England and dreams up new ways to upset people with delicate stomachs

You can find him on Facebook – graeme.reynolds2@facebook.com

THANK YOU FOR READING

Thank you for taking the time to read this book. We sincerely hope you enjoyed the story and appreciate letting us try to entertain you. We realise that your time is valuable, and without the continuing support of people such as yourself, we would not be able to do what we do. As a thank you, we would like to offer you a free ebook from our range in return for you signing up for our mailing list. We will never share your details with anyone and will only contact you to let you know about new releases.

You can sign up on our website

http://www.horrifictales.co.uk

If you enjoyed this book, please consider leaving a short review from wherever you bought it or anywhere else that you, as a reader, visit to learn about new books. One of the most important parts about how well a book sells is how many positive reviews it has, so if you can spare a little more of your valuable time to share the experience with others, even if it's just a line or two, then we would really appreciate it.

Thanks, and see you next time!

THE HORRIFIC TALES PUBLISHING TEAM

ALSO BY GRAEME REYNOLDS

HIGH MOOR

"Makes The Howling look like Twilight!" – Amazon Reviewer

John Simpson returns to his hometown, haunted by a werewolf attack he survived 20 years ago. As a new wave of killings begins, John must confront his past and an impossible dilemma: How can he stop a werewolf when he becomes one every full moon?

Blending '80s nostalgia with modern horror, "High Moor" pits man against beast in a heart-pounding tale of survival, where the hunter and hunted are one and the same.

ALSO BY GRAEME REYNOLDS

HIGH MOOR II
MOONSTRUCK

The people of High Moor are united in horror at the latest tragedy to befall their small town. As dawn breaks, the town is left to count the cost and mourn its dead, while breathing a collective sigh of relief. John Simpson, the apparent perpetrator of the horrific murders, is in police custody. The nightmare is over.

Isn't it?

Detective Inspector Phil Fletcher and his partner, Constable Olivia Garner, have started to uncover some unsettling evidence during their investigations of John Simpson's past – evidence that supports his impossible claims: that he is a werewolf, and will transform on the next full moon to kill again.

However a new threat is now lurking in the shadows. A mysterious group have arrived in High Moor, determined to keep the existence of werewolves hidden.

And they will do anything to protect their secret. Anything at all.

ALSO BY GRAEME REYNOLDS

HIGHMOOR III BLOODMOON

The war has begun...

As the humans make their move against the werewolf threat in their midst, and civil war threatens to break the pack apart, John and Marie struggle to free the only person who can unite the werewolf factions against their common enemy: Marie's brother, Michael.

However, their efforts may be for nothing. As tensions mount, the Moonborn prepare to combat the human aggression with an assault of their own. An attack that could spell doom for both man and werewolf alike.

ALSO BY GRAEME REYNOLDS

DARK AND
LONELY WATER

When Samantha Ashlyn is forced to return to her home town to write an article on a series of drownings, she initially resists, finding disturbing similarities to her childhood experiences. However, once she starts looking into the assignment, she finds that things are not what they seem. An ancient evil is rising again, aided by what appears to be a centuries-old conspiracy to keep it hidden. With the help of a disgraced police diver, Sam races to stop the nightmare before more lives are lost. Not realising that her investigation has put herself and those she loves in terrible danger.

ALSO FROM HORRIFIC TALES PUBLISHING

High Moor by Graeme Reynolds
High Moor 2: Moonstruck by Graeme Reynolds
High Moor 3: Blood Moon by Graeme Reynolds
Of A Feather by Ken Goldman
Angel Manor by Chantal Noordeloos
Doll Manor by Chantal Noordeloos
Bottled Abyss by Benjamin Kane Ethridge
Wasteland Gods by Jonathan Woodrow
Dead Shift by John Llewellyn Probert
The Grieving Stones by Gary McMahon
The Rot by Paul Kane
Deadside Revolution by Terry Grimwood
High Cross by Paul Melhuish
Rage of Cthulhu by Gary Fry
The House of Frozen Screams by Thana Niveau
Leaders of the Pack: A Werewolf Anthology
And Cannot Come Again by Simon Bestwick
A Song for the End by Kit Power
Wild Hunters by Stuart R Brogan
When the Cicadas Stop Singing by Zachary Ashford
http://www.horrifictales.co.uk

Milton Keynes UK
Ingram Content Group UK Ltd.
UKHW040844131024
449481UK00004B/174

NIGHT BLEEDS INTO DAWN

GRAEME REYNOLDS

Published by Horrific Tales Publishing 2024

http://www.horrifictales.co.uk

Copyright © 2024 Graeme Reynolds

The moral right of Graeme Reynolds to be identified as the author of this work has been asserted in accordance with the Copyright, Designs and Patents Act of 1988.

All rights reserved. No part of this publication may be reproduced or transmitted in any form or by any means, electronic or mechanical, including photocopy, recording or any information storage and retrieval system, without permission in writing from the publisher.

A CIP catalogue record for this book is available from the British Library.

Paperback ISBN: 978-1-910283-41-7

Hardback ISBN: 978-1-910283-42-4

Ebook AISN: B0D7ZXGWVJ

This book is a work of fiction. Names, characters, businesses, organisations, places, and events are either the product of the author's imagination or used fictitiously. Any resemblance to actual persons, living or dead, events, or locales is entirely coincidental.